FACE DOWN
BENEATH THE ELEANOR CROSS

By

Kathy Lynn Emerson

DELPHI BOOKS

ISBN 13: 978-0-9765185-9-4
ISBN 10: 0-9765185-9-7

Published in 2009 by arrangement with Delphi Books, www.DelphiBooks.us.

The text of this Large Print edition is unabridged. Other aspects of the book may vary from the original edition.

Set in 16 pt Plantin by Steve Brooker at Just Your Type.

Printed in the United States on permanent paper.

Library of Congress Cataloging-in-Publication Data

Emerson, Kathy Lynn.
 Face down beneath the Eleanor Cross / by Kathy Lynn
Emerson. — Large print ed.
     p. cm.
 ISBN-13: 978-0-9765185-9-4 (trade pbk. : alk. paper)
 ISBN-10: 0-9765185-9-7 (trade pbk. : alk. paper)
 1. Appleton, Susanna, Lady (Fictitious character)—Fiction.
 2. Herbalists—Fiction. 3. Murder—Investigation—Fiction.
 4. London (England)—Social conditions—16th century—Fiction.
 5. Large type books. I. Title.
 PS3555.M414F294 2009
 813'.54—dc22
                                        2009016747

Also by Kathy Lynn Emerson

The Face Down Mystery Series

Face Down Under the Wych Elm
Face Down Before Rebel Hooves
Face Down Across the Western Sea
Face Down Below the Banqueting House
Face Down Beside St. Anne's Well

The Diana Spaulding Mysteries

Deadlier than the Pen
Fatal as a Fallen Woman
No Mortal Reason
Lethal Legend

Large Print Titles

Face Down in the Marrow-Bone Pie
Face Down Upon an Herbal
Face Down Among the Winchester Geese
Face Down Beneath the Eleanor Cross

**This Large Print Book carries the
Seal of Approval of N.A.V.H.**

Chapter 1

Westminster
January 3, 1565

"Back again, eh? 'E's gone on without ye. In a powerful hurry, 'e were, too."

Susanna Appleton broke off her survey of the tavern known as the Black Jack to stare at its proprietor. Until a moment ago, she'd never set foot in the place, but there might be some use in letting his misconception stand, especially if the mysterious "'e" turned out to be the man she sought. "How long ago did he leave?"

The tavernkeeper was shorter than she, a small, wiry man in a canvas apron. When he took a step closer, Susanna smelled garlic and stale, spilled wine, a pungent and unpleasant combination when trepidation had already made her queasy. A pockmarked face and brown teeth did nothing to alleviate her first, negative impression.

"Come and sit with old Ned, sweeting," he invited, leering at her, "and I'll tell you everything I know. But let's see what's under the 'ood this time."

Before she could stop him, he flipped the heavy wool away from her face, narrowing his eyes to get a better look. As he leaned in, the stench of his breath nearly made her gag.

Repulsed, Susanna backed away. Beneath her cloak, she fumbled for the small sharp knife suspended from the belt at her waist. She could expect no help from customers who frequented a place such as this, and for once she did not think it likely she'd be able to talk herself out of trouble.

The Black Jack Tavern was as disreputable as the lowest tippling house. A smoky fire burned in the chimney corner, spreading its murky light over four rickety trestle tables in a windowless, low-ceilinged room. Around them, occupying rough-hewn benches and stools, with not a chair in sight, were more than a dozen patrons, men who appeared down on their luck and potentially dangerous. A few of them were eating, but most ignored offerings of cheese and meat pies in favor of beverages served in black jacks, wooden cans treated with pitch on the inside.

To Susanna's relief, a call for more beer distracted Ned. The moment he turned away, she fled, escaping into the narrow street outside.

Frigid air lanced through her like a thousand ice-tipped arrows. Hugging herself beneath her warm wool cloak, Susanna left the slight shelter of the building's overhang and started walking. Her heart was racing, but she no longer had any immediate fear for her safety.

When she reached the corner, she glanced back at the tavern. Its sign, showing a crudely painted black jack, creaked as a chilly gust of air set it swinging. A second pole bore a picture of leaves, proclaiming that wine, as well as beer and ale, could be found within.

Shivering and stamping her booted feet to keep warm, Susanna considered what to do next. She'd arrived almost an hour late, delayed by this uncommon cold weather. The Thames was frozen solid. She'd planned to hire a boat to take her across. Instead, she'd been obliged to walk, or rather to slip and slide, until she reached the opposite shore.

For whom had the tavernkeeper mistaken her? One cloaked and hooded woman looked much like another, she supposed, especially in a poorly lit room. But why would Robert have been with someone else when he was expecting her?

Her lips twisted into a mockery of a smile as Susanna silently answered her own question. With Robert, there always seemed to be another woman.

Their marriage had been arranged as soon as Susanna turned fourteen and solemnized when she was eighteen. Robert, then twenty-seven, had expected to acquire a quiet, obedient spouse, one content to remain in the background, to stay in the country while he was at the royal court. For the most part, at least in the early years, she had obliged him.

A door opened a few feet from where Susanna stood. Giving her a suspicious look, a shopkeeper hung out a lantern containing a candle. A hook had been set into the doorframe for that purpose.

The action served as a pointed reminder of the foolishness of remaining where she was when the sun was about to set. She'd come alone, as Robert's coded message had instructed. Now she was acutely aware that she was in a strange neighborhood without the protection of servant, friend, or husband.

Susanna was tall for a woman, and sturdily built. Along with a sharp mind and an inquisitive nature, both characteristics had been inherited from her father. Neither, however, made her any match for footpads or cutpurses. The fact that she had on her person a pouch containing the gold coins Robert had requested she bring with her rendered her even more conscious of her vulnerability.

Where was he?

Why had he not waited for her, especially if he was in need of money? Susanna was torn between relief and disappointment and beset by the same anxiety that had settled over her five days earlier, when she'd first opened the letter and realized it had come from Robert, a man most people supposed to be dead.

Leaving the environs of the Black Jack, she began to walk toward Charing, in the north part of Westminster. She'd suspected all along that Robert had not drowned eighteen months earlier. Seeming to do so had provided too neat a solution to his problems at the time. And to her own.

Susanna had allowed others to persuade her to declare him dead and go on with her life. She'd had no real choice, and it had scarce been a hardship, not when the result was complete control over all Robert had owned. She was honest enough with herself to admit she enjoyed the freedom her false widowhood entailed. In her opinion, the advantages of the married state were much overrated.

During the previous year and a half, while waiting for some word of or from her "dead" spouse, Susanna had come to the conclusion that Robert must have planned well, secreting funds sufficient to spirit him safely out of England. She'd begun to think she'd never see him again. On the other hand, she had not been unduly surprised to receive what amounted to a demand that she secretly come to him and bring with her a considerable sum in gold.

Despite the acrimonious nature of their relationship, she and Robert knew each other well. He'd have had no doubt she'd obey. Her sense of honor compelled her to comply with his wishes, no matter how much she resented doing so.

She had made certain vows when they wed. Robert might hold them in little regard, but Susanna had always been a woman of her word. As long as her husband lived, she was bound by her obligations to him. For that reason, she had come to Westminster in secret, and she had not betrayed Robert's whereabouts to his enemies.

This would be their last meeting, she'd decided on the long, cold journey from her home in rural

Kent. They would clear the air between them. She'd remind him that he had a most pressing reason not to be seen by anyone who might recognize him. Then she would explain that the money she'd brought, invested wisely, should be sufficient to allow him to live comfortably for the rest of his life. If he followed her advice, he'd have no need to contact her again.

At Charing, where King Street met the Strand and both noisy thoroughfares were crowded enough to make Susanna feel safe, she paused in front of a bookseller's shop and contemplated her next move. The buildings directly across from her comprised the Royal Mews. In spite of the name, which implied the presence of falcons and other hunting birds, this mews housed the queen's horses. Robert had been wont to leave his own mount there when he was in attendance on Queen Elizabeth. On such occasions, when he could not secure a bed in the palace or impose upon the hospitality of friends with lodgings in the vicinity, it had also been his custom to take a room in a nearby inn called the Swan.

She would spend the night there, Susanna decided. It was possible that Robert, following her logic, would look for her at that inn. If he did not, then in the morning she would return to Leigh Abbey. She had, she assured herself, obeyed every instruction in the coded letter. After a dozen years of betrayals, her sense of obligation was worn thin. Any true affection for

Robert Appleton had long since withered and died.

Susanna had just turned toward the Swan when she heard a commotion erupt behind her. Shouts and laughter drew her attention to the ornate Eleanor Cross at the center of the intersection.

Like similar memorials in Cheapside and thirteen other locations throughout England, this Eleanor Cross had been erected by King Edward I to mark one of the stopping places of his beloved queen's funeral cortege. A tower of Caen stone, decorated with sculptured scenes from the life of Christ, and with Eleanor of Castile's image and arms, rose above a flight of stone stairs.

In the last rays of the setting sun, Susanna saw a man, apparently much the worse for drink, struggle to climb them. His slow progress was marked by considerable weaving and stumbling. To the delight of the jeering, hooting crowd that quickly gathered to watch him, he suddenly clutched at his throat and tottered, his footing precarious on the icy surface of the top step.

Beset by an uneasy premonition, Susanna joined the throng moving toward the cross. She was too far away to do more than gasp when the man seemed to lose control of his legs. Before anyone could aid him, he tumbled headfirst down the stairs, losing his bonnet on the way and striking his unprotected skull several times before his limp form came to rest at the base of the monument.

A sudden hush fell over the spectators. The man lay still, sprawled face down at the foot of the stairs. Bright blood stained the back of a bald head. That, together with the unnatural angles of his limbs, made it likely he was beyond human help.

All the same, Susanna stepped closer. She was a skilled herbalist. A healer. If any spark of life remained, she felt obliged to do what she could to ease the fellow's pain and suffering.

Another would-be Samaritan reached the body ahead of her, turning it over only to recoil in revulsion.

At first, in the rapidly fading twilight, Susanna did not recognize the dead man. She did not know anyone who was both completely bald and clean shaven.

Then someone brought a lantern forward. Silhouetted by its light was a familiar profile of brow and nose and chin.

Susanna heard a choked sound and realized with a dull sense of surprise that she had made it. She squeezed her eyes tightly shut, struggling to exert some measure of control over her rapidly fluctuating emotions.

The dead man was her husband, Sir Robert Appleton.

Chapter 2

Leigh Abbey, Kent

"She did not go to Penshurst Place," said Jennet.

"Where is she, then?" Mark Jaffrey, Lady Appleton's steward, gave his wife an exasperated look and was answered by one of equal annoyance. Jennet had once been Lady Appleton's tiring maid. More recently, she had become Leigh Abbey's housekeeper.

"I do not know, but she left behind a capcase she should have taken, the one containing skin creams for Lady Sidney." Jennet had thought it odd that their mistress should suddenly decide to spend Twelfth Night in the company of a girlhood acquaintance she'd not seen in years, and even more peculiar that she had not taken any of the Leigh Abbey maidservants with her.

"An oversight," Mark concluded.

"So I thought, too, when I found it a few hours after her departure. I sent Fulke off in pursuit. He has just returned with the news that she never arrived, nor was she expected."

"Then you misunderstood her destination."

A snort of derision conveyed what Jennet thought of that explanation. "She made a point of telling me she hoped she could help Lady Sidney, since the poor woman is so much disfigured with smallpox scars that even her own husband cannot bear to look upon her face."

Beneath deepening lines of concern, Mark's pale eyes narrowed. "If she lied to you, 'twas doubtless to keep you from meddling. Let it be, Jennet. Lady Appleton always knows what she's about."

They had been speaking in whispers, but their altercation had attracted the attention of everyone in the hall. Leaving a game of leapfrog, a small, serious-faced girl edged close, grabbing with sticky fingers at a convenient section of Jennet's skirt. Bunching the fabric in one fist, she clung and lifted beseeching blue eyes. "Mama, do not be angry at Papa."

Jennet sighed but made no effort to detach the child's grip. "I am not angry with him, Kate."

The three-year-old looked doubtful.

Mark fought a grin at Jennet's dilemma. She could hardly confess to a child that both her irritation and her concern were directed toward their mistress, the absent Lady Appleton.

Resigned to a delay before she could reveal what else she had discovered, Jennet led young Catherine back to the other Jaffrey children. Four-year old Susan, named in honor of Lady Appleton but called by the shorter ekename, was attempting to throttle two-year old Robert. That child had been a handful from the day he was born. Jennet prayed daily that he would not grow up to resemble his namesake.

Like her mistress, Jennet had never believed Sir Robert was dead. More's the pity, she'd always thought.

Lady Appleton wore widow's weeds and had erected a suitable monument in Leigh Abbey's chapel, but she'd confided in Jennet that she did not think Sir Robert had drowned in the choppy waters of the Solent. She'd also warned that Sir Robert might turn up again one day. The book and letter Jennet had just found in Lady Appleton's study seemed to prove she'd been right.

Jennet chewed on her lower lip and watched for another chance to speak with Mark alone. If Sir Robert decided to come back from the dead, trouble was sure to follow.

Chapter 3

Forcing her eyes open, Susanna looked at the body again, confirming the unpalatable truth. It was Robert. Then she squared her shoulders. She could fall apart later. Right now she needed to keep her wits about her.

On unsteady legs, she covered the remaining distance to the Eleanor Cross. Bending close, aided by the light of the same lantern that had revealed his identity, she took note of the slight blue tinge to Robert's skin and saw that he had recently been sick to his stomach. Forcing her personal feelings into abeyance, she knelt to touch the side of his neck, searching in vain for any flutter of life. There was none. Clearly, he had fallen to his death.

But what had caused him to fall?

Robert's skin felt clammy beneath Susanna's fingertips. Years of training had made her sensitive to certain signs. Oblivious to her surroundings, she quickly examined his arms and legs, noting that both hands were tightly clenched.

Her heart began to beat more rapidly. It was unlikely she could be mistaken. She had studied such signs for years. Not drunkenness, but dizziness and nausea, symptoms of the early stages of poisoning, had caused him to lose his balance.

Robert's first death, the one by drowning, had taken place eighteen months earlier. Three months later, in order to hide the circumstances under which he'd taken a small boat out onto the waters of the Solent and disappeared, official word had been issued that he'd succumbed to the plague while on a secret mission in France. The second death, Susanna thought, her expression bleak. As much a fabrication as the first.

Her gaze returned to the injuries the stone steps had inflicted. This latest demise was undeniably fatal and seemed likely to remain so. If one of those cracks to his shaven head had not killed him, the same deadly work would soon have been accomplished by poison.

Robert had been spared considerable agony. She could not help but be grateful for that small mercy. But who had poisoned him? And why?

Belatedly, Susanna became aware of an excited buzz coming from the others who had witnessed Robert's death. Whispered words just too faint for her to make out were punctuated by louder speculation.

"Taken in a planet," one man declared, using the popular term for a seizure of any sort.

"Nay. 'E were cup-shotten," someone else argued. Drunk.

And then, softer, just as Susanna heard the sound of rapid footfalls, a woman's voice said, "May be 'e were poisoned."

A pair of butter-soft leather boots came into

her line of vision. "Appleton?" Astonishment laced a voice that seemed familiar to her.

Susanna lifted her head. The earl of Leicester stood before her, staring down at the corpse. For a moment she could not think why he would be in Charing. Then she realized his presence made perfect sense.

Queen Elizabeth's most favored courtier, only recently elevated to his new title, was also Master of the Queen's Horse. No doubt he'd been in the Royal Mews and come out to investigate when he heard the exclamations of the crowd.

"Has someone sent for the coroner?" Leicester demanded, never shifting his gaze away from the body. Two liveried servants carrying torches had come up behind him and now waited for his instructions.

"Aye, my lord," came a prompt reply from one of the milling spectators. "The Coroner of the Royal Household."

This, too, made sense to Susanna. The man who held that title was responsible for investigating any death within the verge, the area encompassed by a twelve-mile radius around the queen's place of residence, and Queen Elizabeth, at present, was at nearby Whitehall.

Satisfied with the answer he'd gotten, Leicester shifted his gaze to the woman who knelt by the body. His dark brown eyes fixed on her face, but his gaze contained none of the warmth Susanna remembered from bygone days. Indeed, it took him a few moments to recognize her, even though they'd once known each other well.

As a girl, after her father's death, Susanna had been his father's ward. At times they had lived under the same roof.

Robert had also been part of that household.

"How can this be?" From the astonishment that laced the words, Susanna knew Leicester had been told his old friend died in France and that, until now, he'd had no reason to disbelieve the story.

"He was murdered, Robin." Saying it aloud brought the reality of her husband's gruesome death home to her. Stunned and shaken, she felt the tight grip she'd so far managed to keep on her emotions begin to slip.

"Pushed?" Leicester's question was uttered in a sharp voice that jerked Susanna back from the abyss.

At once, she understood the reason for his alarm. Not all that long ago, his wife had died in a fall down a flight of stairs. There had been many who'd wondered if he'd had a hand in it.

"No. Oh, Robin, no. Robert was poisoned."

The instant the word was out, Susanna realized she must be more overwrought than she'd supposed. So much for keeping a clear head. Muddled thinking had just led her into making a grievous error.

Several people in the milling crowd had overheard her ill-considered statement. Within seconds, astonished murmurs had become lively debate. Susanna scarce heard a word of it. Her attention was fixed on the man who now held her fate in his hands.

Leicester's dark eyes had turned sharp, cold, and calculating. Although he offered a hand to help her rise, it was obvious he was contemplating all he knew about her, Robert, and their marriage.

In the old days, Lord Robin had been far more Robert's friend than Susanna's. As young men, they'd shared adventures, in love and in war, and spent a great deal of time together at various royal courts.

Leicester knew well what Robert Appleton had thought of his wife. And he was aware that Lady Appleton possessed an expertise with poisonous herbs unsurpassed in England. She had even written a book on the subject.

That fact alone made her conduct suspicious. Susanna could not blame Leicester for thinking the obvious. As the "widow" of a wealthy knight, she had a most compelling reason for wanting him to remain dead. "I like this not," Leicester said in low tones. Susanna was unsure if he referred to Robert's death, her involvement, or the fact that he was now embroiled in a situation he'd have preferred to avoid.

Susanna got awkwardly to her feet. Only one person could untangle the web of lies surrounding Robert's several deaths. He might also be the sole individual to whom Leicester would listen.

"Send for Sir Walter Pendennis, Robin. He can explain."

Telling the whole story might create its own difficulties, but Pendennis, thanks to his successes as an intelligence gatherer for the queen, wielded considerable influence at court. He had also, like Robert, been a friend in Leicester's youth.

The earl stroked the drooping ends of his mustache, considering her suggestion. Susanna had no trouble guessing his thoughts. That Robert had been poisoned made Leicester believe she must be involved. The simplest solution would be to order her placed under arrest and have her charged with her husband's murder.

"Escort Lady Appleton to my house," Leicester ordered his servants. "She will remain my guest until this matter is settled."

Guest? The word was preferable to *prisoner*, but it still had an ominous ring.

Shock had made her stupid, Susanna thought as one of the earl's men took a firm, unyielding grip on her arm. As soon as she'd recognized the body sprawled face down beneath the Eleanor Cross, she should have fled. Had she not had ample proof over the years that when it came to catching criminals, most officials chose the easiest route? They did not concern themselves overmuch with innocence or guilt, not as long as they had someone to blame.

Leicester's two liveried retainers hustled her along the Strand, giving her no choice but to accompany them. They did not have far to go. They turned in at a familiar gatehouse just east of Charing.

Startled, Susanna balked at entering. "Why have you brought me here? This is the Spanish Embassy."

"It was. Now Durham House is leased to the earl of Leicester."

She had vivid memories of this place. Twice before she had been here, and both visits had thrown her life into turmoil. Her recollection of the last time, shortly before Robert's disappearance, tormented Susanna as she was escorted through an inner courtyard and into the high, stately house.

She'd had no idea then what Robert was involved in, though the signs would have been obvious if she'd had the wit to look for them. She'd thought he might be a murderer, she reflected, feeling her lips twist at the irony.

She remembered how angry she'd been with her husband that day. After they'd left the Spanish ambassador's residence to ride back to their temporary lodgings in London, she'd blurted out a secret she'd planned to keep from him until a more appropriate moment—that he was the father of a bastard child. The unfortunate timing and hurtful manner of her revelation had ended forever any hope that they might resume an amicable marital relationship.

"This way," one of the guards said, breaking in on her unhappy reverie.

Squaring her shoulders, Susanna marched up several flights of stairs. She knew where they were taking her now, to one of the little turret rooms that looked out over the Thames. Located at the back of the house, it was very private. She was unsure whether this boded well or ill.

"My lord's study," one of his retainers announced, opening the door.

She preceded him into the room, well lit by candles in wall sconces, and scanned it curiously. Her gaze was drawn to a small table holding an ebony chessboard. The pieces, set up ready for a new game, were made of crystal and precious stones inlaid with silver and garnished with Leicester's crest of the bear and the ragged staff.

Susanna removed her heavy wool cloak and draped it over the back of one of the chairs drawn up to the chessboard. A fire blazed in the hearth. The heat felt good after the temperature outside, but instead of stepping close to warm her hands, she moved to the window to stare through the frost-covered panes at a landscape encased in the darkness of a late afternoon in winter.

Lights shone on the opposite shore, at Bankside in Southwark. Both torches and lanterns pinpointed figures walking on the frozen surface of the Thames. Free. As she was not. Alive. As Robert was no longer.

Silently, she grieved, as much for the loss of what might have been as for the man himself. In the beginning, their marriage had been filled with hope for the future. She'd believed she could trust her own husband not to betray her, that his vows meant as much to him as hers did to her. How innocent she'd been! A deep sadness engulfed her at the waste.

But she felt anger, too, the dull, throbbing sort that lasted far longer than any mere flash of temper. Robert had died before his time. All life was precious. Ending his was a far greater crime than any Robert himself had committed.

"Will you take refreshment?" one of Leicester's servants asked.

His words were kindly meant, but they had a devastating effect.

"No," she whispered, and sat abruptly, feeling her legs lose their strength and her face its color.

Robert must have passed the time while he waited for her by eating. No doubt he'd purchased a set meal at that tavern—a hot meat dish, bread, cheese, and ale.

He'd gotten more than he'd paid for. Because she had been late for their appointment, someone else had been given an opportunity to speak with him, sit with him . . . add a fatal dose of some poisonous substance to his last meal.

Chapter 4

Nearly two hours passed before Jennet could show Mark what she had discovered. At first, he did not see the significance of *The First Blast of the Trumpet against the Monstrous Regiment of Women.*

"A book. What of it? Such items are scarce unusual in this house." At Leigh Abbey, almost everyone could read and write. Lady Appleton's father, old Sir Amyas Leigh, had believed that even servants, even female servants, should be literate.

"This particular book is the one she was wont to use when she and Sir Robert wrote to each other in code." Mark's slowness tried her patience, but Jennet attempted to stay calm long enough to explain. "She'd have no reason to read Master Knox's insulting opinions on womankind except to use his text to translate this." She seized up the letter she'd found and waved it in her husband's face.

Mark took the paper from her and unfolded it. He gazed without comprehension at a list of numbers neatly arranged in three columns. "What is this, then?"

"How am I to know?" Snatching the missive back, she flung it onto the table next to the book. "I only know that Lady Appleton told me once that she and Sir Robert used this book, which only the two of them knew to do, in order to keep secret the content of messages between them. He wanted to use her herbal as the key. She thought it a great jest to insist upon Master Knox's treatise."

Lady Appleton had also spoken with disdain of the entire practice of using codes and ciphers, seeing little need for such extreme measures. She'd complied only at Sir Robert's insistence. Because of his work as an intelligence gatherer for the queen, he'd feared his letters might be intercepted by some enemy.

Jennet thumped a fist down on the capcase Fulke had brought back again from Penshurst Place. "I know her, Mark. I am as much companion to her as servant. She left this evidence here to be found, if and when we had reason to worry about her safety."

Jennet doubted Lady Appleton had expected her to come upon it so soon, but she was certain her conclusion was sound. She chewed thoughtfully on her lower lip. Only one question remained—what was she meant to do once she made her discovery?

"She had this message from Sir Robert and went to meet him," Jennet reasoned aloud. "And do not tell me he is dead, for 'twas never proven."

"I know he is not dead."

"What? How?"

Raking agitated fingers through a shock of mole-colored hair, Mark sighed. "He was here some weeks after he was supposed to have died in France. I saw him from a distance, but there was no mistaking him."

"Did he meet with Lady Appleton?"

The rims of Mark's large ears reddened. "Lady Appleton had company that day. Sir Robert must have recognized her guest, for he crept away again without coming nearer to the house than the far apple orchard."

"Sir Walter."

"Aye. Sir Walter."

Sir Walter Pendennis believed Sir Robert had drowned, but in order to protect Lady Appleton's interests, he had given out that plague was the cause of her husband's death, striking him down while he was abroad on the queen's business. Ever since, Sir Walter had been a frequent visitor at Leigh Abbey. It was no secret that he had tender feelings toward its mistress. He'd have little tolerance for a "dead" husband's reappearance on the scene.

"Why did you not tell me?" Jennet demanded of her own husband. "Why did you keep Sir Robert's return a secret?"

"What need to upset you? Or Lady Appleton? And it is not as if either of you had any doubt he was still among the living."

"A paltry excuse."

"If you are right about this letter," Mark asked, ignoring her grumbling, "where would she meet Sir Robert?"

"London?" That destination made sense to Jennet. A man could more easily hide among so many people. In the country, especially here in

Kent, Sir Robert's chances of being recognized were much greater. It amazed her to hear he'd dared come so close even once.

"The journey to Penshurst Place requires two days," Mark said, also thinking aloud. "The same length of time as a trip to London."

Jennet nodded. Even on a fast horse, riding a messenger's long hours, Fulke had taken three to complete the trip to Penshurst and back.

"She's not likely to have reached London before late today, this being winter."

"Aye." Jennet sighed. "I should have suspected she was plotting something when she chose two green lads to escort her and left Fulke behind."

Mark's expression grew solemn. "Fulke would have recognized Sir Robert, no matter how well he disguised himself."

"We must go after her at first light. You and I. Fulke. And Lionel." After Mark, they were the Leigh Abbey servants she most trusted.

"'Twill mean hard riding in bitter cold," he warned.

She'd have to travel perched on a pillion behind Mark. Jennet's backside began to ache just thinking of the torment to come, but she set her jaw. "She needs us. I feel it in my bones."

"And how do we find her once we reach London? She might be anywhere."

"We will go to Sir Walter's lodgings in Blackfriars. He will tell us what to do next."

He might even be able to read the coded letter.

28

Chapter 5

Sir Walter Pendennis reached Durham House only moments after the earl of Leicester arrived there. Leicester had brought with him the Coroner of the Royal Household, two constables, and a rough-looking fellow the coroner identified as Ned Higgins, keeper of the Black Jack Tavern.

"There has been a mistake," Walter protested, drawing Leicester aside for a private word. The earl's message had been brief, just a few sentences to inform him that Lady Appleton was being detained in connection with the murder of her husband.

"Aye, a mistake you made some time ago." Leicester looked annoyed. "You told me Appleton died in France." In a few succinct phrases, he conveyed what had happened less than an hour earlier at Charing Cross, adding that Sir Robert had shaved off all his hair and his beard and that he'd carried no papers to identify him.

For one brief moment, Walter was tempted to claim that Appleton had been in disguise as part of some recent mission for the queen. Then common sense prevailed. Anticipating that Susanna's husband might one day turn up again, alive, Walter had given considerable thought to plausible explanations for his apparent death. He had to keep in mind that he did not know where Appleton had been or what he had been doing and that lies had a way of coming back to haunt one.

"My information came from a reliable source," he told Leicester, "but I never had the opportunity to examine the body. Because it was a death from the plague, the remains were not shipped home for burial. To stay the spread of infection, they were interred at once in foreign soil. Appleton's passport and other papers were found on the corpse. I had no reason to suppose it was not him."

"Cases of mistaken identity are not uncommon during an epidemic," Leicester conceded. He gave Walter a hard look. "A word of advice, Pendennis. Under the circumstances, it may not be wise for you to take a personal interest in Lady Appleton's well-being."

"She did not kill her husband." Walter might have said more, but with matters already so far progressed, he chose instead to step back and wait until the formalities were complete. When he had heard all the evidence, he would decide what was best to do.

A few minutes later, eight men crowded into the turret room where Susanna had been confined. She rose to face her accusers, a tall woman all in widow's black except for the white linen cap beneath her French hood and small wrist and neck ruffs. Above the snowy cambric folds of the latter, her countenance was pale but she showed no other outward sign of distress.

Walter tried to catch her eye to signal that all would be well. Susanna did not notice his attempt at reassurance. Her gaze went at once to the tavernkeeper and remained fixed upon his face.

"Is this the woman?" the coroner asked.

"Aye," Higgins said.

"She twice came into your establishment?"

"Aye."

"And on the first occasion, only a short time before she returned alone, was she in the company of the man who soon after lay dead beneath the Eleanor Cross?"

"Aye. She were friendly with 'im, too." He leered and winked. "Give 'im a kiss, she did, like she'd not seen 'im in years. Or may'ap 'ad plans for the night to come."

Susanna's face, already ashen, paled still more.

"You have looked at the body and are certain of your identification?"

"Aye, sir. That I am. The man, 'e come in first and ordered a set meal. Then the woman, she joined 'im."

"How long did she stay?" the coroner asked.

Higgins scratched his shaggy head. "'alf an 'our. No more."

"And then?" the coroner prompted.

Walter continued to watch Susanna, marveling at her composure but concerned when she made no attempt to deny the tavernkeeper's claims. *Had* she poisoned Robert? Knowing her as he did, he thought it doubtful, but God knew Robert had given her sufficient provocation over the years.

With continued questioning, the rest of the story came out. A man and woman had talked in low tones for the span of half an hour, then left separately. Sir Robert Appleton had departed in a considerable hurry. Higgins had not noticed if Appleton was ill.

"I thought 'e were wanting to catch up with 'er," he volunteered, gesturing toward Susanna, "but not a quarter of an 'our later, she come back alone."

"Thank you, my good fellow," the coroner said, and sent him on his way. Then, telling the constables to wait outside until he called them, he ignored Susanna to address Walter and the earl. "The evidence speaks for itself. Lady Appleton had opportunity to poison her husband."

"Higgins could be lying," Walter objected.

"Why should he?" Leicester asked. "What profit in admitting a man was poisoned while in his tavern?"

"He did not volunteer the information," said the coroner.

"Then how did you find him? Why go to the Black Jack at all?" Walter knew the place. It was not in sight of Charing Cross.

"A bystander told one of the constables that he'd seen the dead man and the lady together a short time earlier. He'd left the Black Jack to drink at the Bull Head Tavern."

"And where is he, then? This bystander."

"Gone. In all the confusion, the constable lost track of him." The coroner seemed unconcerned by this lapse. "We have Higgins's testimony, and that is sufficient. I fear there is no help for it, Sir Walter. After the inquest, I will be obliged to order Lady Appleton's arrest."

Walter swore softly. "Leicester—"

"I can do nothing." By his abrupt tone and stony countenance, he believed Susanna was guilty.

Bowing to the inevitable, Walter swallowed further protests. "Will you permit me a few moments alone with Lady Appleton?"

"A quarter of an hour. No more."

Only after the two men had left the room did Walter cross to Susanna and gather her into his arms. He felt her start of surprise, for he had never embraced her before, but after a moment she accepted the gesture as one of comfort and allowed herself to cling to him for support.

"I did not kill him." Those words, the first she had spoken since Walter's arrival at Durham House, were muffled against the velvet of his doublet.

"Can you imagine I do not know that?" He hugged her more tightly, resting his chin on the top of the ebony-hued silk of her bonnet. Then, reluctantly, he released her. "We do not have much time. Tell me what did happen."

"Robert sent for me. I was to meet him at the Black Jack. I was to wear a plain, black cloak with a hood and keep my face hidden."

With a sweep of one hand, she indicated an enveloping garment thrown over a nearby chair. The movement produced a distinctive clinking noise. She had coins concealed on her person, quite a lot of them by the sound of it.

"He said I must come alone and bring money."

Walter's anger at Appleton had no outlet, not when the man was already dead. "Bad enough to demand a woman travel unescorted, but to require her to carry a heavy purse, attracting thieves by the very sound . . . " Words failed him.

Susanna sighed. "My behavior seems passing foolish to me now, but at the time I believed I was doing the only thing I could."

Her words reminded him of his priorities. They had little time, and there was much he needed to learn from her. "How did he send word to you? A letter?"

"Yes."

"You're certain it was his handwriting?"

"I'm certain he used the code the two of us devised years ago when he was attached to the Scots court."

The Knox cipher, no doubt. He supposed Susanna believed its secret to be known only to herself and Robert. "What happened when you talked to him?"

"I did not talk to him. I arrived too late. He had already left. I stayed only long enough to make sure he was gone."

"Then why did Higgins—?"

"Whoever he saw with Robert earlier was also wearing a dark cloak and was careful to keep her face hidden." She paused, frowning. "A woman, that much is certain, since she kissed him. But for that, I'd think it could have been a man. The interior of the Black Jack was dark and murky."

"Why is Higgins so certain you and that woman are one and the same?"

"I fear I encouraged him to think it, hoping to learn something from him." She sent a small, rueful smile his way. "Higgins got a good look at my face before I left."

Walter took her hand, chafing her fingers when he felt how icy they were. "We need to find proof you were not there in the tavern with Robert. How did you get to Westminster? Where are your servants?"

"I left them behind at the Crown Inn."

"The Crowne without Aldgate?" He could not keep the surprise out of his voice. Robert had sometimes used that place for assignations.

Susanna shot him a questioning look. "In Rochester. It is the inn at which I customarily break my journey from Leigh Abbey to London. Do not look so worried, my dear." Her smile was genuine now, and very gentle. "I did not ride the rest of the way on my own. I joined a party of travelers, strangers, leaving their company only when we reached Bankside. I do not know their names or destinations, nor did I tell them mine."

So her servants could not vouch for her whereabouts. Those fellow travelers would be next to impossible to locate. "Your horse?"

She hesitated. "I left her at the Sign of the Smock."

Worse and worse. Walter had been appalled, even knowing her reasons, when he'd discovered, months after the fact, that Susanna had paid several visits to one of Southwark's most notorious brothels. If it became known she still had acquaintances there, the revelation would only do more harm to her good name.

"I do not want to cause trouble for anyone there," she told him.

"You will not. There is no sense in asking anyone at the Sign of the Smock for help. No one will believe them, not even if they can swear you were still in Southwark at the exact moment Robert met that other cloaked and hooded figure." Another question distracted him from the complications Susanna had created by stopping where she had. "Why did you go to Charing after you left the Black Jack?"

"I hoped to secure a room for the night at the Swan. It was pure chance that put me in the vicinity of the Eleanor Cross when Robert died."

"Unhappy chance. But for your presence, the body might have gone unrecognized."

"Leicester was nearby, in the Royal Mews."

"Yes. Leicester. More bad luck."

"How will you explain, Walter? Questions will be asked about the earlier report of Robert's death."

36

He almost laughed. Trust Susanna to worry about other people first. "'Tis obvious he did not die in France as I claimed, but I have already persuaded Leicester that 'twas a simple case of mistaken identification."

Another faint smile flickered across her features. "What happens next? Do you know?"

"When I was at Cambridge, I studied civil law, and I have had some few dealings since with crime and criminals. The procedure is straightforward enough. Based on what he thinks he knows, the coroner at his inquest will produce a formal charge and the order to take you into custody."

"Where will I be held?" She could not hide her dismay at the thought of being imprisoned, but Walter was well enough acquainted with Susanna to be certain she'd prefer the truth to pretty lies.

"Newgate."

A sharply indrawn breath was the only indication of her anxiety.

"You have money to pay for comforts. Your stay there should not be too onerous."

"How long must I remain imprisoned?"

"At the least, a day or two. Within three, the law requires that you be brought before a justice and examined."

"And if I am bound over for trial?"

"Longer."

"Then I must send a letter to Leigh Abbey."

Walter watched, full of admiration, as she squared her shoulders and visibly gathered her courage. Then she raided Leicester's writing table for ink, parchment, and a quill. He could only suppose, from her appearance of calm, that even now she did not fully comprehend her situation.

He, on the other hand, was all too aware of what awaited her. Because Susanna seemed to have means, opportunity, and motive to kill her husband, a bill of indictment was certain to be drawn up against her. A pity the murder had taken place just outside London, he thought. There were no twice-yearly assize courts here, but rather quarter sessions, and the next term was almost upon them.

Unless Walter could find some way to prove her innocent, Susanna Appleton could be tried within a matter of days. If she was found guilty of murdering her husband, she would be sentenced to death and executed.

He would have to take swift, decisive action or risk losing the woman he loved.

Chapter 6

A practical approach was best, Susanna told herself. It would do no good to weep and wail and lament the hand fate had dealt her. She needed her wits about her if she was to survive this.

Once her letter was written, she entrusted it to Walter Pendennis, then broached again the subject of her coming incarceration. "Have I hope of being let to bail?" she asked. "Will the justices accept sureties from my friends?"

That was the usual way to get out of gaol. The threat of having to forfeit large sums of money if a released prisoner escaped encouraged acquaintances to keep a close eye on him or her to guarantee an appearance in court on the appointed day.

One look at Walter's morose expression warned Susanna she would not like his answer. "It is customary to deny mainprise when the crime is murder."

"Murder," she repeated, shaking her head in disbelief. She found it hard to credit that she should be accused of such a heinous crime.

Then she remembered something, and for a moment her composure was shaken. It became difficult to breathe, impossible to swallow.

The charge would not be murder. The head of the household was akin to a head of state. A wife accused of killing her husband, or a servant who killed his or her master, was charged with petty treason.

The torment Susanna saw in Walter's eyes reflected her own increasing sense of horror. She swallowed convulsively.

It should not matter, she told herself. Any felony carried the death penalty, and death was equally final, no matter how it came about. But while mere murderers were hanged, a quick thing if the hangman were skilled, women found guilty of poisoning their husbands were condemned to be burnt at the stake.

"I will find a way to secure your release." Walter once more seized her hands in his.

Susanna longed to believe him. She clung to his promise all the way from Durham House to Newgate, but once she was behind the massive grey stone walls of the prison, a sense of hopelessness engulfed her. She kept terror at bay not by any strength of will but because of the sheer number of more immediate concerns.

Irons were prominently displayed in the keeper's room to which she was taken first—fetters, shackles meant for the ankles, iron collars to go about one's neck. All were designed to be chained to a ring in the floor or a staple in the wall.

"You must pay an admission fee," the keeper told her, "and another fee for exemption from ironing."

At her hesitation, he fingered a particularly nasty set of leg irons while a crafty expression flashed in his eyes. "Widows' alms," he said, identifying them. Or was the word arms? Either way, Susanna could not miss his meaning. The prospect of being restrained, being helpless, pushed larger fears out of her mind.

"How much?" Her hand fisted around the pouch concealed in the placket of her skirt, in part to reassure herself it was there, but also in a vain attempt to still her trembling fingers.

Walter had assured her no one would take her money from her by force, but she had never felt more vulnerable. The keeper was a big man, his muscles heavily corded, his biceps bulging. And he had dozens of men at his command. If he chose to behave dishonorably . . .

He looked her up and down, assessing her worth. "Five pounds," he announced.

By feel, she extracted five gold sovereigns and handed them over.

A gap-toothed smile was her reward. Still grinning, the keeper locked the coins away in a strongbox, then indicated she should follow him. He led her smartly along a corridor, up one set of stairs and down another. Within moments she was completely lost. She knew Newgate stretched as far along Old Bailey Street as the gardens beside the new Sessions House, and that the north end formed an arch over the street, but she had the uneasy sense that, instead of traveling laterally, they had descended deep into the bowels of the earth.

They stopped before a thick wooden door. "Within lies the Limboes," the keeper informed her, indicating that she should peer through a barred opening. "The common dungeon."

Inside, she saw a large dark room lit by a single candle. She drew back with more speed than grace when the smell of human waste and unwashed bodies assaulted her.

"Horrible," she whispered.

"That is where most accused felons spend their days and nights until they come to trial."

Susanna swallowed hard and silently blessed Walter for the last few words of advice he had managed to give her before she was taken away from Durham House. She need not suffer any indignities, he'd assured her. Newgate had separate accommodations for women and, on something called "the master's side," offered private rooms for those who could afford them.

"Female felons are not kept in there," she said in a firm voice.

The keeper seemed amused by her show of spirit. "Aye. We have other dungeons for women."

"On the common side," Susanna said, hoping she sounded more haughty than frightened. With one hand, she jiggled her purse, allowing the keeper to hear the siren song of coins rubbing together.

Grinning, he rattled off his schedule of fees. The rental of a special apartment was only one of the charges she was expected to pay. She'd have to spend extra for a bed, mattress, sheets, and blankets. Further disbursements would provide her with firewood, water, food, and ale. In return for an uncomfortably large portion of the money she had brought to London for Robert, Susanna was installed in a furnished turret room in the area the keeper called "the castle."

"A cellarman," he told her, "one of the prisoners, will visit you within the hour. He has candles and other luxuries for sale."

"Paper, quills, and ink?" she asked.

The keeper seemed surprised that she would want such things, but nodded. Then he left her alone in her new quarters.

The next hour was one of the longest Susanna had ever spent. It was impossible not to dwell on the bleakness of her prospects, impossible not to be afraid.

But when the cellarman had come and gone, she told herself sternly that she now had everything she could wish for except her freedom. In gaol or out, she must do more than sit idly by and let her fate be decided by others.

"No more doubts," she vowed. "No more wasting time in fear for the future." Resolute, she lit several candles, dipped her quill into the inkpot, and began to make lists.

Chapter 7

The noise of the revelers in the inn below made Jennet's head ache. How could they celebrate Twelfth Night when Lady Appleton languished in some dank prison cell? When Sir Robert lay dead? When Jennet's entire world had been shattered?

Mark placed his hand over hers, silently offering his love, his understanding. Husband and wife, they lay atop a sinfully comfortable mattress in one of the best of the thirty beds available at the Saracen's Head on the north side of Snow Hill without Newgate. But Jennet could not rest easy. The accommodations had been bespoke for their mistress's comfort. She and Mark usurped Lady Appleton's place to remain here without her. God only knew what conditions prevailed inside those grim prison walls so close at hand.

Sir Walter had sent them to this inn. To wait.

"You need to sleep," Mark murmured. "To rest. Tomorrow we will be able to think more clearly."

But Jennet's trouble was that she already saw matters far too well. They were in terrible trouble. All of them. If Lady Appleton were found guilty, everything she owned would be confiscated by the Crown. And everything Jennet and Mark had worked for over the years would be gone. Even if new owners decided to keep the household at Leigh Abbey intact, life there without

Lady Appleton did not bear thinking about.

Tears slowly rolled down Jennet's cheek at the thought. Sensing her distress, Mark gathered her close, kissing the unwanted moisture away.

"We must do something." Her voice broke on the words.

"What can we do?" He held her tight, as worried as she.

"Rescue her?"

Jennet had been trying to think of ways to break Lady Appleton out of prison from the moment Sir Walter's messenger had intercepted them on their way to London. He'd told them the terrible news and also delivered the letter Lady Appleton had written just before she was taken to Newgate.

"In some prisons," Jennet whispered, thinking of a tale she'd heard about the gaol in Gloucester, "the very walls do crumble away from age. Prisoners have only to step through gaping holes between the stones and walk away."

"A prisoner might also creep out over the roof, or escape by rushing the gates, or contrive to cut holes in walls," Mark ventured, "but I do not see Lady Appleton doing any of those things."

They had both gotten a good look at Newgate when they journeyed from Sir Walter's lodgings in Blackfriars to the Saracen's Head. The stones seemed solid, the entire huge complex daunting.

With a sigh, Jennet snuggled closer to her husband's warmth. "Well, then, we wait until the trial is over and rescue Lady Appleton on her way to Tyburn to be executed."

Shocked, Mark went stiff in her arms. "No. 'Twill not come to that."

"It may." Lady Appleton always said it was better to face the truth, no matter how bad it might be.

"Sir Walter—"

"Sir Walter is but one man. If it lay in his power to free her, she would already be out of that dreadful place. We cannot let her be executed." Jennet choked on more tears, but this time when Mark sought to wipe her face, she jerked away and sat up in bed. "Will you help me?" she demanded.

"You know I will, love. When you have a plan that has any hope of success."

"I have told you my plan already. We will rescue her on her way to Tyburn. We will gather all the servants from Leigh Abbey and rush the dead carts and free her."

"And then?" Jennet heard his skepticism, but at least he was listening.

"Then we flee the country. All of us. We will send the children on ahead, to Sir Robert's sister in Scotland." Lady Glenelg was devoted to Lady Appleton. She was also young Kate's godmother.

"Let us pray," Mark said after a long silence, "that it does not come to such a pass."

Chapter 8

Roused from a doze by the tolling of the great bell at St. Sepulchre, Sir Walter Pendennis could not, for a moment, remember why he was sleeping in his chair rather than in the comfortable bed in the next chamber. Then, in the act of rubbing his knuckles against eyes gritty with sleep, his bleary gaze fell on the jumble of papers covering his work table.

Susanna.

He'd been striving most of the night to discover some means to save her. The coded message her servants had brought him had been no help. It did naught but prove she *should* have been the woman supping with Robert in that tavern.

He had managed, just before he dozed off, to think of a way to secure her temporary release. It would, however, take another day or two to arrange.

With an utterance of disgust, Walter shoved the mess away from him and stood. A piece of parchment tumbled to the floor. The Lady Mary's letter. He left it where it had fallen.

Seizing his warmest cloak, he abandoned his lodgings and hurried through the frigid dawn toward Newgate. He knew what he would see, knew he did not want to witness it, and yet he could not seem to stop himself. He felt compelled to make the grim pilgrimage, as if by doing so now he could become inured to what might come after.

As it was Monday, the usual execution day, the clamor of the bells began at six. It would continue without letup as an accompaniment to the condemned procession. Walter arrived in time to see three two-wheeled carts emerge from the gatehouse. Each had a guard of halberdiers and in each rode a half dozen prisoners, shackled and fettered and sitting atop their own coffins.

There was not much of a crowd. Only a few hundred spectators and a handful of ballad sellers and hawkers. Walter took that to mean there were no celebrities among the condemned, no highwaymen to be mobbed for locks of hair and bits of clothing. He did not understand why anyone would want such mementoes, but apparently some folk did.

How long, he wondered, until he stood in this selfsame spot to watch Susanna brought out of Newgate? She had already slept five nights in that evil place. If he did not find a way to help her soon, the charges lodged against her would produce this inevitable result.

So far, his efforts to determine the identity of Robert's real killer had fallen short. He'd pulled strings. He'd called in favors. He'd spent more than one late night studying reports from his agents, for he'd ordered every intelligence gatherer in his employ to learn all they could about

48

the current activities of every political enemy Robert Appleton had made over the years.

There were a goodly number of them, all with sufficient reason to want him dead. No less a person than the regent of France, old Catherine de' Medici, who was said to know more about poisons than anyone, even Susanna, might have ordered his death. Another suspect was the king of Spain. He had little fondness for Robert after the debacle eighteen months earlier.

Had some foreign power ordered Robert Appleton's death? Or was his killer someone he'd angered since his disappearance? What had he done during those months? What person had he offended? Had his continued existence threatened someone? Walter had no answers, only dozens of questions.

The dead carts traveled north, moving slowly past St. Sepulchre. The death knell continued, emanating from the church which stood diagonally opposite the prison, its square tower distinguishable even from a distance by its four corner spires. As each condemned man was carted past, charitable members of the congregation handed out brightly colored nosegays. No one knew why. The origins of this particular tradition had long been forgotten. They also offered mulled wine containing a narcotic. That needed no explanation.

"Sir Walter!"

At the sound of his name, Walter glanced around. The Saracen's Head lay just beyond the graveyard adjacent to the church. Coming toward him from that direction at a fast clip was Leigh Abbey's steward, Mark Jaffrey.

"Any news?" Jaffrey asked.

"No." Together they fell into step behind the procession, following it along Giltspur Street and Snow Hill and across Smithfield to Cow Lane. The intent of the meandering four-mile-long route was to allow the greatest number of persons to gape at the prisoners, in the hope they would be deterred from committing similar crimes. Walter doubted the sight had any such effect. Most folk regarded executions as just one more spectacle provided for their entertainment, a cross between bull or bear baiting and a rousing Sunday sermon.

At length, the carts turned west to begin the steep descent into Holborn. Walter lifted a sweet-scented pomander ball to his nose as he crossed Holborn Bridge over the Fleet. Once Fleet Ditch had been a river flowing into the Thames. Now it was an open sewer, clogged with refuse and the bodies of dead animals.

The procession paused for refreshment outside the Half Way House, a tavern in Holborn. Another tradition, but one in which Walter was in no mood to indulge. The rest of the way to the place of execution was rough and unpaved, through countryside where houses were few and far between and hedges and brambles lined the lane.

"We have come far enough." His abruptness startled Jaffrey but the other man continued to keep pace, and silence, as they turned back. Walter was grateful he did not ask why they'd been following the procession in the first place, for he had no rational answer.

When Newgate's heavily decorated arch loomed once more before them, Jaffrey's steps faltered. He stopped to stare at the imposing edifice, made more impressive by the weight of time. For centuries, prisoners had vanished behind its high, thick walls. This vile place swallowed them, spitting them out again only to be carted off and killed.

"We will not let her be executed," Jaffrey said. "We talked it over. Jennet and I, and Fulke and Lionel, too. We're all of us willing to do anything we must, even if that means breaking the law ourselves."

Walter narrowed his eyes as he looked at the steward. "For the nonce," he warned, "tell me nothing more."

But the idea of arranging for Susanna to escape stayed with him. He began to think about where they might go afterward.

And wonder if she'd agree to marry him.

Chapter 9

Susanna attempted to block out the mournful clang of the Great Bell at St. Sepulchre in the Bailey by putting her hands over her ears. It was no use. The sound was too loud.

At least, since this was Tuesday, the tolling did not signal more executions. When silence fell, sudden and final, Susanna swallowed hard. Then she shivered, although the chamber in which she was confined boasted both a hearth and a charcoal brazier.

She had been in Newgate less than a week, but it seemed an eternity. Since she'd been bound over for trial and committed to gaol, she'd heard nothing more from Walter, and she'd had no visitors save for the keeper of Newgate and his wife. Twice, she had been invited to sup with them, an event enlivened by music for entertainment and the consumption of a great deal of wine on the part of the keeper.

Restless, Susanna wandered about her quarters, finally stopping before a single narrow window. She had discovered, on her first day in prison, that the casement was rusted. It did open, but forcing it was scarce worth the effort. Although the view encompassed the broad market street that ran from Newgate into West Cheap, the long rows of butchers' stalls in the Shambles were located at this end. It did not take much imagination to understand why Newgate Prison was also called "The Stink."

The sound of a key in her lock startled Susanna. She had lost track of time, staring blankly at the leaded glass panes and the wavery view beyond. She turned just in time to see the door swing open.

Walter Pendennis had never been so welcome. A rush of warmth engulfed her as he ducked under the lintel and entered the chamber. She moved toward him, arms outstretched, her eyes drinking in every detail of his appearance even as tears threatened to blur her sight.

He was taller than she, as Robert had been, and as broad-shouldered as her late husband, but somehow Walter had always been more approachable. Perhaps, she thought as she was engulfed in his embrace, it was that little paunch that showed even beneath his exquisitely tailored doublet, or the fact that his sand-colored hair was beginning to thin.

He had disillusioned her only once, by deceiving her about how much he knew of Robert's schemes, but she had long since forgiven him for that. In a choice between personal desires and duty, perforce he had been obliged to choose his allegiance to the Crown. Since then, he had shown himself to be a good and loyal friend, a man she could trust.

Encompassed by his strength, savoring the feel of thick velvet beneath her cheek, she allowed herself the luxury of remaining locked in his arms until he moved his hands from her waist to her shoulders and set her away from him. She saw that his blue eyes were troubled. His haggard appearance made her heart catch. He looked worse than she did.

"Will they not let me leave?" Until she whispered the question, Susanna hadn't realized just how much she had been counting on Walter to secure her release. The plans she'd made would be for naught if she did not regain her freedom.

"There are conditions," he said.

Relief surged through her. "I'll accept them gladly, no matter what they are."

"You are to be released on furlough. For the payment of twenty pence a day, a guard's wages, you will be permitted to go anywhere you please, but you will have to return for trial. And the guard will stay with you at all times, to assure that you do come back."

"How long do I have? When is my trial?"

"I have arranged for the case to be adjourned until the next quarter sessions. That gives us until seventeen days after Easter."

"Bless you, Walter. And Easter comes late this year." She calculated quickly. "We have nearly four months to discover who poisoned Robert. Surely that will be enough time."

"I also arranged for Robert's burial at Leigh Abbey." Walter removed his hands from her shoulders.

"I am indebted to you, Walter."

The words did not begin to convey her gratitude. It had troubled her, not knowing what had been done with Robert's body. In the ordinary way of things, she'd have prepared him for burial, participated in the rituals, the formalized grief and mourning. No matter how contradictory her feelings toward Robert had been, she'd owed him that much—the ceremonial respect of a proper funeral.

"I only wish I could have done more. Discovered more. Robert carried a few coins. Nothing else. Not even a forged passport. Neither have I had any success in discovering whether he had lodgings in London at the time of his death. Or a horse."

"He will have had a horse." Robert always had a horse.

"I have been considering who might want Robert dead."

"So have I." As she spoke, Susanna gathered up the pages she'd spent the last interminable days covering with notes. "I remember a time, in Warwickshire, when Robert was attacked by two ruffians. He told me then that he had many enemies, that there were any number of persons who might want to kill him, though he never specified who they were."

She'd suspected he was exaggerating. He often did, making himself out to be more important than he was. And in that particular instance, it had turned out to be something she had done that had led to them being set upon.

"You have been making lists." Walter's smile was fleeting.

"I've had little else to do." She handed him the most important one to study while she fetched her cloak.

A moment later, a bemused look on his face, Walter returned the paper. "I am sorry. I had hoped you were unaware of them."

"Robert may have been an excellent intelligence gatherer, but he was never clever at hiding his mistresses."

She should have known, Susanna realized, that Walter would recognize all three names.

Before Robert's disappearance, she'd believed Walter was just another of her husband's colleagues. In truth, Walter had been his superior, answerable only to the queen herself. He wielded considerable power in the government, though not enough, it appeared, to save her from the necessity of proving her innocence.

"It seems likely to me," she told him, "that Robert would have contacted at least one of his former mistresses during the last eighteen months. Those three are the ones whose names I know, but I suspect there are others. At least one more."

"When?"

Susanna hesitated. Walter had known her husband longer than she had. "In the early days of our marriage, I came upon Robert and a woman.

They were locked in a passionate embrace in one of the gardens at Durham House. I do not know who she was. I only saw her from the back."

Walter looked so uncomfortable that Susanna suspected he did know, or could guess, the woman's identity. For the moment, however, she chose not to press him to reveal it.

"I mean to talk to each of these three women, Alys and Annabel and Eleanor. Question them. I want to know if they had any contact with Robert, and I want to learn where each of them was when he died, for a discarded mistress, like a discarded wife, might have motive for murder."

"Alys is in Dover," Walter said, tacitly agreeing to her proposal, "but Annabel lives in Scotland. Leaving the country may be a problem. As for Eleanor, I've had no reports on her whereabouts for more than two years."

"I know where Eleanor is," Susanna told him. "She came to me after she gave birth to Robert's daughter."

Walter's surprise was evident in the way he fumbled for words. Normally one of the most articulate of men, he needed a moment to phrase his questions. "How old?" he asked first. And then, "Where is she now?"

"Rosamond was born during Robert's sojourn in Spain. Unable to reach him, her mother came to me at Leigh Abbey. I arranged for both of them to be installed at Appleton Manor. It seemed appropriate." The Lancashire property was Robert's inheritance from his father, as Leigh Abbey was Susanna's from hers.

"Did Robert know?" Walter took Susanna's cloak and draped it over her shoulders. He watched her face as he fastened the clasp.

"Not for a long time."

She had been considering where he might have gone after his disappearance. Why not Lancashire? He knew that county well, for he'd spent his childhood there. And would a man not want to meet his only child?

Susanna had also done a good deal of ruminating about what Robert had intended to do with the money she was bringing him. Run off with Eleanor and Rosamond? Perhaps. She suspected that, if they could find his bolt-hole in London and his belongings, they would have the answer to that question.

Pulling on her gloves, she moved toward the door. "We have much to do," she declared as she lifted the latch. Determined to remain optimistic, she sent a brave smile over her shoulder. "If you will introduce me to my guard, we can begin."

Chapter 10

Jennet paced nervously, waiting for Sir Walter to bring Lady Appleton to the Saracen's Head Inn.

"She'll soon put things right." Lionel, who had boundless confidence in their mistress, towered over Jennet. In the last year he'd begun to fill out. It seemed only yesterday he'd had but half Fulke's strapping bulk. Now Lionel was full grown, and the two men were of comparable size.

Fulke's lugubrious expression conveyed stoic acceptance rather than optimism. Jennet frowned. What did he feel about Sir Robert's death? Even though Fulke had chosen to remain with Lady Appleton, he'd been Sir Robert's man for a long time. He'd accompanied him on journeys into Scotland and to Spain.

Mark's voice interrupted her speculations. "They are just coming now," he announced from his post by the window.

Jennet rushed to his side and looked down with relief upon the familiar figure of Lady Appleton. Even cloaked and hooded, she was easy for Jennet to recognize. She had a long, self-confident stride and a proud carriage.

Sir Walter, as was his wont, wore bright peacock plumage. Part of his doublet showed beneath his scarlet cloak, a blaze of apple-green velvet in the morning sun. His tawny-color bonnet boasted a huge black plume, held in place by an equally ostentatious red jewel.

A third person accompanied them. A stranger. A short, stocky fellow whose head seemed a bit too big for his body. Lank brown hair hung just past his ears, its shade a match for the leather jerkin he wore over a sheep's-color doublet. A guard, Jennet realized, and from that instant did much dislike him.

A few minutes later, Lady Appleton entered the inn chamber. Her composure seemed unruffled as she greeted her faithful retainers, though her face had the pinched look it sometimes got when she'd received bad tidings.

She discouraged Jennet from rushing into speech with one quick, warning glance and refused Mark's offer of refreshment. Then she introduced Bernard Bates.

Up close, the guard's appearance did not improve. A unkempt beard shadowed the lower half of his pockmarked face. The remainder was dominated by a pair of dark, deep-set, watchful eyes.

Sir Walter accepted a cup of ale and instructed Bates to wait without. Bates went as far as the door but remained inside the room. He leaned against the frame, arms crossed over his chest, as if daring anyone to object.

"What we cannot change, we must accept," Lady Appleton murmured. "Come, my friends.

Gather around this table. We have plans to discuss."

Lady Appleton produced several sheets of paper filled with writing, proof she'd not lost heart during her imprisonment. Jennet smiled, but her mistress's next words quickly erased the expression.

"We must visit a number of persons during the next few weeks," she said. "I hope to determine which of those who might have had reason to wish Robert harm were away from home on the day he died."

"Visit?" Jennet echoed. "You mean travel? In winter?"

"Bad roads and cold weather did not deter Robert's murderer. In truth, the slowness of travel at this time of year may be to our advantage. It would take a number of days to reach Westminster from any distance. If one of these suspects has been absent from home, it will have been noticed. By servants. By neighbors. Someone will tell us this, and we will have our poisoner."

She made it sound simple, but Jennet was not deceived.

"More travel," she grumbled. Her backside had scarce recovered from the trip into London.

"More travel." Lady Appleton sounded almost cheerful. "You need not come with me, Jennet. I'll not ask it of you."

"You need not ask, madam. My place is with you. Just do not expect me to be pleased that I must ride."

"I would never think to. And I anticipate that you will grumble all the way. I should fear you were ill if you did not."

"All the way to what place?" Mark asked.

Lady Appleton's voice was controlled, her expression serene as she tapped the pages on the table. "The tavernkeeper at the Black Jack saw a woman meet Robert, greet him familiarly with a kiss. She is the most likely person to have added poison to his meal, but to want to kill him, she must have had some connection to him. The most logical suspects are, therefore, his former mistresses, one of whom he may have contacted during the last year and a half. We will visit Dover first, as that place is close at hand."

Jennet saw the sense in this proposal at once. For years, Sir Robert had kept a mistress in Dover. Alys Sparcheforde. He'd even set her up in her own house. She'd not taken it well when he ended their association.

Sir Walter cleared his throat, then withdrew a piece of fine, thick parchment from inside his doublet. "There is one person upon whom you must call before we journey into Kent. When the Lady Mary Grey heard of Sir Robert's death, she wrote to me. She fears the entire story of his disappearance will come out. At this late date, she prefers the queen not learn what was kept secret from her eighteen months ago."

The Lady Mary had lied to her royal cousin, Jennet remembered. Lied to help Lady Appleton.

"I have taken the liberty," Sir Walter continued, "of arranging a meeting between you, tomorrow morning in a private place."

"Could she have done it?" Jennet asked. "Could the Lady Mary have poisoned Sir Robert?"

"I think it doubtful," Lady Appleton replied.

But Jennet was not so sure. The Lady Mary was a maid of honor to the queen and, according to what Sir Walter had told them when they first arrived in London, Queen Elizabeth and all her court had been at Whitehall Palace on the day Sir Robert was murdered.

Jennet bit her lower lip to keep from pointing out that Whitehall, like Charing, was part of Westminster.

No doubt Lady Appleton was right, Jennet told herself. She usually was. And it made sense that one of Sir Robert's mistresses had killed him. The only thing that surprised Jennet, now that she thought about it, was that one of them had not done so sooner.

Chapter 11

Lady Mary Grey had a particular reason for choosing the lodgings above the water gate at Whitehall as a meeting place. She could trust the discretion of Master Thomas Keyes, the gatekeeper.

Her position at court was precarious. By the accident of her birth, she was the queen's heir, but that near relationship had proven more curse than blessing to Lady Mary's sisters. Jane had been executed by Queen Mary for attempting to usurp the throne. Catherine would live the rest of her life a prisoner, confined for daring to wed without Queen Elizabeth's permission.

"My lady," Keyes said, "here is Lady Appleton to see you."

"Thank you, Thomas. You may leave us."

He was tall, the tallest man in England, some said. He towered over Susanna Appleton, even though she stood higher than most women. From behind Lady Appleton's head, Keyes had the audacity to wink at Lady Mary. She had to fight not to smile.

Only after his footsteps had faded away on the stairs did Lady Mary realize that a stranger had accompanied her guest into the chamber. A low sort of fellow, to judge by his dress. He stationed himself by the door, looking ill at ease but determined.

"Who is this man?" she demanded. "I asked to speak with you alone."

"My apologies, my lady." Lady Appleton's expression was rueful. "I fear I am not permitted to go anywhere without my guard."

"From whom does he guard you?" But even as she asked, she suddenly understood the true nature of his duties.

With a grimace of sympathy, she resigned herself to the fact that he must stay. She led Lady Appleton to the east-facing window opposite the door. Unfortunately, it was also far from the fire in the hearth. Pure, clear winter sunlight would have to do to warm them while they talked.

"Does he know who I am?" she asked.

"He may guess."

The words were diplomatic, but Lady Mary was no fool. She could scarce help but be aware of how easy she was to recognize. Only a bit over four feet tall, she had enough of a deformity to be called "Crouchback Mary" by the cruelest of the queen's courtiers. Those distinctive features, combined with the bright red Tudor hair and a profusion of freckles, made it difficult for her to hide her identity.

At court, she was often overlooked, in both senses of the word, but here, with none but Lady Appleton for company, she stood out. The guard would doubtless remember her.

When she wished, Lady Mary could call up every bit as much regal dignity as her royal cousin

Elizabeth. In an authoritative voice, she ordered Lady Appleton's unwelcome escort to remain by the door, then turned her back on him.

"I read the letter you wrote to Sir Walter," Lady Appleton said. "You need have no concern, my lady. Your name will not come into the matter of Robert's death."

Although Lady Mary trusted few people, she believed Lady Appleton. "Your discretion does you honor, but I fear others may know of our connection. Your husband contacted me a few weeks ago. He threatened to reveal the secret you and I and Sir Walter agreed to keep between us. He asked to be paid for his silence."

Audacity had never been a trait Sir Robert Appleton lacked. Even though he'd been the cause of all her difficulties, he'd believed he could persuade her to give him money and some of her jewelry.

"I was to have met him on the day after his appointment with you, Lady Appleton. If you killed him, I do thank you. He was a troublesome man. Dangerous and clever."

"Someone else was more clever." A sigh escaped the new-made widow. "I did not poison my husband, my lady."

"Then who did?"

"Mayhap someone else upon whom he made demands. If he had other victims, I mean to discover them, and I will find out who killed him." Her lips twisted into an ironic smile. "I have little choice in the matter. The threat of being burnt at the stake if I fail does provide wondrous fine incentive to succeed in my quest."

"You are remarkable calm."

"There is no profit in swooning or tearing out my hair. My time is better spent asking questions."

"What if you discover I killed Sir Robert? You have already sworn to tell no one of my involvement."

"I think it unlikely you did so, my lady."

"Why? I cannot account for my time at the hour your husband was poisoned." She'd taken pains to learn all the details of the case and this was unfortunately true. Should she be obliged to prove she was not in Charing that evening, she'd have to reveal an even greater secret than the one Lady Appleton had just now promised to keep.

"Forgive me, my lady, but it is most doubtful you and I could ever be mistaken for one another, even cloaked and hooded. I am . . . overlarge."

Diplomacy again. Sir Robert had been a master of pretty speeches, but his widow possessed a sincerity he'd lacked. She chose her words not to flatter, but to avoid causing distress.

"Tell me your plans." Lady Mary's peremptory tone brooked no dissembling.

Lady Appleton hesitated only long enough to convey that she complied because she wanted to, not from any sense of obligation. "One of Robert's former mistresses seems the most likely person to have poisoned him." She summarized the itinerary she intended to follow in order to discover the whereabouts of each of three women on the day Sir Robert died.

"You must have a care for your own safety," Lady Mary warned. She glanced at the guard, then pursed her lips in thought. "If this woman met your husband in your stead, then mayhap she knew you were expected. What if she meant you to be blamed? As you were. Indeed, why else choose poison? Why else dress as you would be dressed?"

"Robert's poisoner wants me dead, too?" The idea that the murderer might have plotted against them both seemed to startle Lady Appleton. "I assumed Robert was the only intended victim, but what you say makes sense. I will consider it further."

Pleased to have contributed something new to the gentlewoman's thinking, Lady Mary was emboldened to offer another piece of advice. "Before you proceed to Dover, stop at Lady Northampton's house in Blackfriars."

"For what reason?"

"Your excuse will be a visit to a dying woman, but—" She broke off at the look on Lady Appleton's face. "You did not know? She has suffered for some time from ulcers in the breast and now grows weaker day by day. But seeing the marchioness is not your true purpose. You must seek out her waiting gentlewoman, Mistress Constance Crane."

"I do not know the name."

"Mistress Crane has been in Lady Northampton's service for many years. As far back as the wedding of my sister Jane to Lord Guildford Dudley . . . at Durham House."

Comprehension dawned in Lady Appleton's shrewd blue eyes. "She and Robert—?"

"I was a mere child at the time, but I can remember seeing them together. You saw them there, too, I do think." Lady Mary had caught a glimpse of Lady Appleton that day, leaving the gardens. Her face had been uncommon pale, her manner so agitated that Lady Mary had gone looking for the cause of her distress.

Regret tinged Lady Appleton's voice. And sadness. And resignation. "We were all much younger then."

Chapter 12

"Goodman Bates," Susanna said as they entered the enclosed precinct of Blackfriars, "I am about to visit a dying noblewoman. I am certain you can have no wish to accompany me into her bedchamber. Will a testoon persuade you to wait outside?"

Bates was a man of few words. He extended one hand, palm up. When she'd laid the coin upon it, his thick fingers curled lovingly around the silver sixpence. Susanna wondered why she'd not thought to bribe him sooner.

Lady Northampton was one of old Lord Cobham's daughters. Susanna did not know her well, but they had met several times when they were both mere girls and Susanna's father had visited Cobham Hall. Years later, during the heady days before the duke of Northumberland's plots on behalf of the Lady Jane Grey had brought them all close to ruin, Susanna had met her again.

The woman propped up against down pillows bore little resemblance to the vibrant creature Susanna remembered. She was pale, emaciated, and obviously failing. Her elaborate bedstead, hung with green velvet lined with green sarcenet and trimmed with gold lace, only emphasized her pitiful physical condition.

Scattered across the counterpane were a variety

of abandoned needlework projects. Piles of lace, thimbles and thread, a velvet pinpillow, and a silver needle case had been shoved to one side. The latter now rested against a copper warming pan.

"If you are here to suggest some potion or elixir to cure me, I fear you came too late." The voice, at least, was as Susanna remembered it, a musical alto.

"I offer naught but the distraction of my company."

Susanna had observed more than once that bracing honesty was often more welcome in a sickroom than a surfeit of sympathy. She did feel sorrow for the pain the woman in the bed must suffer, but she saw no need to dwell on her misery or encourage her to feel sorry for herself. Nor did Lady Northampton seem to want her pity. Susanna refused to offend her by offering it.

"I thought you might have heard I was desperate," the invalid said. "I did undertake a futile journey to Antwerp to consult physicians there."

"Had I known that, I'd never have dared cross your threshold," Susanna said with mock humility. "How could a simple country herbalist hope to compete with the most renowned doctors in the world?"

Lady Northampton's chuckle was appreciative. She waved Susanna toward a small chair drawn up beside her bed. Made of wicker, it was lined with green cloth and comfortably padded.

From a nearby window alcove came the soft

strains of a song King Henry had written in his younger days. Susanna narrowed her eyes as she glanced toward the woman playing the lute. Constance Crane? It seemed likely. Her brown hair matched what Susanna remembered of the woman in the garden.

How odd, she thought, that the Lady Mary should have known about her. More peculiar still had been her insistence that Susanna intrude upon Lady Northampton. It was not as if they had been close friends. Susanna was several years younger than the woman in the bed.

"Most of my visitors bring me nostrums to dull the pain," Lady Northampton said, reclaiming Susanna's attention, "but I do not wish to waste my last days in drugged sleep."

Some of these gifts were piled atop a small, square table near at hand. Susanna could scarce make out its inlaid-work top for all the little ointment pots and wooden boxes scattered across that surface. She sniffed, but no pungent aromas reached her.

"That holds dragonwort." Lady Northampton indicated the nearest container. "I am told it has the magic power to heal any wound or ulcer as soon as it is applied. One of those others is filled with Green Oil of Charity."

Made from adderstongue leaves, Susanna thought. Neither remedy would do Lady Northampton a bit of good.

"You might enjoy one of my favorite sweetmeats," she suggested aloud. "'Tis made from elfwort. I use only roots from three year old plants, dug in autumn. They become aromatic and slightly bitter when ground, but make a tasty treat when tempered with eggs, saffron, and sugar."

"Anything would be better than milk of almonds." That food was frequently prescribed for invalids. "I abhor almonds."

Lady Northampton did not seem to be aware of Robert's most recent death or Susanna's arrest. She did not mention the past. Instead she shared several anecdotes, stories of attempts by well-meaning friends to take her mind off her pain.

Susanna listened with only half her attention. The other half was on the waiting gentlewoman, who continued to strum her lute, providing background music without calling attention to herself. The woman was almost as thin as her mistress. Light brown hair framed a face distinguished by a sharp blade of a nose and a slight droop at the corner of one of her blue eyes.

As ailing persons were wont to do, Lady Northampton tired herself out with talking and, between one word and the next, fell deeply asleep. A moment later, Constance rose from the window seat, gesturing for Susanna to follow her into an anteroom.

As soon as the door to the adjoining bed-chamber was closed, Constance turned to face Susanna, staring at her with disquieting intensity. She was several inches shorter than Susanna.

That did not surprise her. Robert had disliked excessive height in a woman. What was unexpected was that Constance appeared to be older than she.

"You killed a good man." Constance said.

"You are wrong, on both counts." Susanna made no attempt to pretend she did not know they'd shared Robert's attentions a dozen years earlier.

Neither did Constance. "You never appreciated his finer qualities. You belittled him."

"'Tis plain you did not know him well. Or recently."

Constance's wince confirmed the latter.

"You were his mistress years ago." Susanna did not mean to be cruel, but she doubted Robert had continued the liaison after Northumberland's fall. That had occurred only a few months after her discovery at the Lady Jane's wedding.

"He was a bright light in my younger days." Constance's voice broke. "A comet, streaking through my universe, bringing color and excitement." A single tear flowed silently down her cheek. Then another.

Memories coated with nostalgia were a potent force. Susanna experienced a pang of sympathy for Constance. "We all had grandiose dreams back then," she murmured.

"He might have married me, had Northumberland not forced you upon him."

Startled, Susanna voiced her first thought.

74

"A pity he did not."

Constance's eyes widened.

"None of us had control over our choices."

The duke of Northumberland, Leicester's father, had been her guardian. He'd arranged her marriage to Robert, one of a number of gentlemen attached to his household. Walter Pendennis had been another. How different things might have been, she thought, if Northumberland had matched her with Walter Pendennis. Would Robert have wed Constance? Since they would never know, such speculation would not only be painful, but fruitless, as well.

"Why did you come here?" Constance demanded. "Why did they not keep you in prison?"

"I am released on my promise to return for trial. In the meantime, I intend to find out who killed Robert. I did not, Constance, but whoever did knew him well. Perhaps a woman, someone he trusted. A former mistress, mayhap?"

"You think I poisoned him?" Aghast, she backed up several steps, knocking into a small table and setting a mortar and pestle to rattling.

"The thought did cross my mind." Susanna spared a glance for her surroundings. They were in a storeroom of sorts. Medicines of all kinds, in flasks and bottles and pots of assorted sizes, lined the open shelves of a large cupboard, together with a box containing a bone ear-picker and toothpick set.

Constance cleared her throat. "I believed

Robert died of the plague more than a year ago. I grieved for him."

Susanna rounded on her. "When did you last see him?"

Constance hesitated, refusing to meet her adversary's eyes.

"Did he ever visit you again after Northumberland's arrest?"

Susanna felt certain now that her earlier guess had been accurate. Soon after she'd seen Robert kissing Constance in the garden at Durham House, the duke of Northumberland had been executed and Robert, for a short time, had been imprisoned. The marquis of Northampton, more deeply involved in the plot, had been deprived of title, land, and income. Lady Northampton had lived for years in near poverty. If Constance had remained with her, Robert would have gone out of his way to avoid any contact with her. He'd been most eager to prove himself a loyal subject of the new regime.

"I am sorry," Susanna said, and meant it.

Constance swiped angrily at the tracks of her tears. "How did you know about me?"

"I saw you and Robert together. In the garden at Durham House."

Constance sighed deeply. "That was the last time I was with him. Robert Appleton was the one great temptation of my youth, and my great folly. I thought if I gave myself to him, he would fall so deeply under my spell that he would defy

Northumberland, renounce his pre-contract with you, and marry me."

"But that day in the garden—that was after he and I were wed."

Constance's expression was unreadable. "What you saw, Lady Appleton, was my farewell to your husband."

Chapter 13

The kitchen at Leigh Abbey was almost as large as the manor's great hall and was connected to it by a long range containing a small parlor and the buttery, pantry, and scullery. Beneath them all were underground cellars. Above were servants' lodgings.

The vast room was still warm when Jennet entered, even though it was the middle of the night in winter. The heat came from the fire still burning in one of two huge hearths built side by side against one wall.

Traceried windows high on those same walls let in slivers of moonlight, but greater illumination came from the lantern on the cook's long, narrow, recently scrubbed worktable. At the sound of Jennet's footsteps on the stone-flagged floor, Lady Appleton unbent from her position next to a gently steaming kettle, round-bellied like a small cauldron, that hung over the flames.

"I see I was not the only one too restless to sleep," she said.

"I am hungry." Mark had eaten all the tidbits Jennet had squirreled away in their privy lodgings in the east wing. She'd left him snoring to forage for food.

Late that afternoon, three days after Lady Appleton's release from Newgate, she and her servants and Bernard Bates had returned to Leigh Abbey. First thing in the morning, she would journey to Dover, seven miles distant.

Lady Appleton had never met Alys, the mistress Sir Robert had acquired during the last years of the reign of Queen Mary. Jennet, who had, was not eager to repeat the experience.

"Have you slept at all, madam?"

"I was confined away from mine own home much too long, and the quest we begin tomorrow may occupy many weeks to come. Is it so surprising that I feel the need to indulge in a pastime I may never be able to pursue again?" A small smile played about her lips. "I had a greater craving for milk of almonds than for sleep."

Jennet saw that Lady Appleton had been occupied with this particular task for some considerable time. The sweet almonds waited in a bowl, blanched, peeled, and pounded. The pounding was a long and tedious business, but every good housewife knew that what was sold in shops as ground almonds was more often made from peach kernels. The only way to be sure of the quality of the ingredients was to prepare them at home.

Lady Appleton also preferred to make her own barley water, which she'd done by boiling a handful of barley three times. As Jennet watched, she combined a beaker of the stuff with the ingredients already in the pot, added the almonds, and left the mixture to simmer.

Jennet spared a glance for the containers neatly

lined up next to the lantern as she cut herself a wedge of cheese, added a heel of bread, and began to munch. Sorrel. Violet and strawberry leaves. The tops and flowers of borage. Bugloss. Endive. Succory. Pansies. Marjoram. Rosemary. She frowned. "I thought milk of almonds was made with onions."

"One sort is. Yet another has no onions, nor any salt, but contains a great deal of sugar. This is a more complex recipe, one I have tried but once before. 'Tis a pity Lady Northampton does not care for almonds, else I'd send some of it to her along with my gift of sweetmeats."

"You have said little of your visit to her." Jennet took possession of a convenient stool, first displacing a long-haired cat. That characteristic marked it as one of a litter sired by Bala, the odd-looking feline their nearest neighbor had brought back with him from foreign parts.

"There is little to tell. Lady Northampton is dying."

"There's more to it than that." Jennet polished off the cheese and licked her fingers. "Sir Walter had a worried look on his face when you told him where you'd been."

Then he'd asked Lady Appleton if she'd talked to Lady Northampton's waiting gentlewoman, and Lady Appleton had admitted she had. Jennet had been mulling over that exchange ever since.

Lady Appleton strained the milk of almonds and poured it into two goblets, offering one to

Jennet. As the beverage cooled, she supplied sketchy details of the two visits she'd paid before they left London. It had been the Lady Mary Grey who'd told her where to find Constance Crane, yet another of Sir Robert's mistresses.

Relishing her role as Lady Appleton's confidante, Jennet listened attentively to every word, then asked if Constance could have killed Sir Robert.

"Possible, but not probable. She's far too busy nursing Lady Northampton. And why wait almost a dozen years to take revenge?"

"Mayhap she lied about not seeing Sir Robert again."

"Mayhap she did. If she did, I will find her out. In the meantime, I mean to question other suspects."

"Alys?"

"Alys. I chose to ignore her existence when Robert kept her, but I knew about her. A grocer's daughter. Young. Pretty. And after Robert evicted her from the house he'd kept her in, I could scarce avoid hearing that she swore he'd regret having treated her so callously."

"But if Alys meant to murder him, would she not have done so in the heat of her anger?" Jennet sipped thoughtfully at her almond milk. "Alys is the sort to act on impulse. I do not think she'd have either the patience or the cleverness to plan for Sir Robert to die the way he did, let alone arrange that the blame should fall on you."

Lady Appleton's eyes narrowed. "You have met her?"

"In a manner of speaking."

"When? Where?"

"'Twas the first July after Mark and I returned to Leigh Abbey from Lancashire. We had gone to the Dover fair. Alys was nearby when someone spoke to me, addressing me in such a way that 'twas obvious I was in service at Leigh Abbey. The next thing I knew, Alys had stuck out her foot and sent me sprawling to the ground."

"The July after—but you would have been great with child."

"Aye, and she could not have helped but notice. My son was born that October."

"Do you tell me she intended to trip you, even though doing so might harm an unborn babe?"

"Oh, aye. I knew it had been deliberate even before I heard someone mention Alys's name."

"What happened after?"

Jennet snorted derisively. "She offered her hand to help me to my feet and made a great show of apology and remorse. I did not believe a word of it. Faith, I could see the deceit in her eyes and the hatred there, too. 'Twas plain she did much dislike anyone connected to Leigh Abbey or the Appletons. But she acted in the heat of the moment, not after careful planning. That, too, was obvious."

"You should have told me of her behavior straight away," Lady Appleton said.

But Jennet shook her head. "What could you have done? And 'twas a busy time just then. Right before Sir Robert left for Spain. And that same week, you met Master Baldwin."

A small smile played across Lady Appleton's face at the mention of her stormy first encounter with Bala the cat's master. It vanished a moment later, when she recalled they had been speaking of Alys's assault on Jennet.

"A woman who would do what she did to you, Jennet, is capable of other violent acts."

"Alys is vicious. That is true enough. But she seems an unlikely poisoner. Then, too, though it pains me to argue for her innocence, it would be passing difficult to mistake her for you. She lacks your height."

"Chopines strapped to her shoes can add as much as three inches to a woman's height." Lady Appleton stood and began to clear away the goblets and containers of herbs. "Even if Alys had naught to do with Robert's death, she may still know something about his movements during the last eighteen months. Mark told me Robert was here. He may well have stopped in Dover."

"I suppose there is no help for it, then. You must meet Alys face to face."

Another faint smile drifted across Lady Appleton's features. "Thanks to your warning, I will know to watch my step with her. And her feet."

As Jennet helped her mistress carry the heavy kettle into the scullery, she could not help thinking how convenient it would be if Alys were the poisoner. The beginning of an idea came to her as she scrubbed a thin scum of almond milk off the inside of the iron pot.

"What poison was used to kill Sir Robert?" she asked.

Lady Appleton gave her an odd look. "It is difficult to be certain."

Encouraged by Jennet's interest, she began to discuss the possibilities. Before long, her voice took on what Jennet privately called her lecturing tone. She left off discussing poisonous herbs and spoke instead of how one might determine the cause of a person's death.

"In Italy, doctors are permitted to cut open the bodies of those who have died and study their innards, but such enlightened practices are called barbaric here in England and banned by law."

Jennet's shudder was only partly due to the encroaching chill from the winter night beyond the walls. "There must be other ways—"

"Oh, yes. Analysis of symptoms. I observed Robert's last moments and the condition of his body after death. A man might react as Robert did if he were given aconite."

"Is this aconite easy to obtain?" For all her long association with Lady Appleton, Jennet knew little of herbs. In the usual way of things, she did not care to learn more.

"Aconite can be extracted from several plants. One of them, monkshood, grows in my herb garden here at Leigh Abbey, since it also has medicinal value. And aconite is used to kill pests. Many people place cakes made of paste and toasted cheese and powdered monkshood root near rat holes to rid themselves of vermin."

"This monkshood, madam . . . what if Alys were found to be in possession of some of it?"

Lady Appleton went very still. "That signifies nothing unless we can prove she was in London on the day Robert died." Her gaze sharpened, suspicious and probing. "What are you plotting, Jennet?"

Jennet twisted her hands in the towel she'd just used to dry the kettle. "Nothing," she mumbled.

"I think, Jennet," Lady Appleton said in a quiet, uninflected voice, "that it would not be wise for you to accompany me to Dover."

Chapter 14

With a jaundiced eye, Sir Walter Pendennis surveyed the weathered signboard announcing that the premises up ahead were called the Star with the Long Tail. An unfortunate choice for a name, he thought. Comets always brought bad luck. Not just ill fortune. National disasters. Supernatural plagues. Famines. Droughts.

Leonard Putney doubtless felt he'd survived several such since his marriage to the buxom young woman who'd once been Robert Appleton's mistress. And the fair-haired, full-figured Alys? Was she content with her lot?

He thought not.

Walter had left Leigh Abbey ahead of the others. He wanted time in Dover to ask certain questions, questions he'd as soon Susanna not overhear. She might put on a show of not caring what her husband had done, but it must hurt her to confront the stark reality of his unfaithfulness. Walter wanted to spare her as much as he could.

Susanna had been distressed by meeting Constance. She would find it even more difficult to deal with Alys. There was no help for it, he thought. He'd have to confront her first.

He cast a longing look toward the Dover anchorage, struck by the enormous appeal of taking ship across the Narrow Seas. On a clear day, he'd have been able to glimpse the distant hovering line of the French coast.

This day was overcast, appropriate to Walter's dismal thoughts. Winds swirled down from the North Sea, causing the salt water of the Straits to leap high and giving the sea and the town and the castle above a grim and gloomy aspect.

A man wrapped in a dark cloak came out of the inn just as Walter reached the door. A neighboring shopkeeper called out a greeting, revealing that this was Leonard Putney. Walter stopped and stared, struck by how slight Alys's husband was. He watched the fellow until he disappeared from sight, wondering if he could have been mistaken for a woman in the darkness of the Black Jack.

The notion seemed far fetched, involving as it did Robert's permitting Leonard Putney to kiss him in greeting. And yet, stranger ruses had been enacted by those seeking to hide their true activities.

But would Robert have involved Putney, of all people, in his schemes? The man had a better reason than Alys did for wanting Robert dead. Jealousy. Putney had taken Robert's leavings. If he believed she still lusted after her former lover, that gave him motive for murder.

Walter's usefulness to the queen lay in his ability to gather information, much of it trivial. He'd kept track of Alys over the years. For their own reasons, his agents made it a practice to frequent all of Dover's inns, which numbered at least ten besides the one Putney owned, and the town's dozens of victualling houses, many of which offered beds as well as food. Any gossip repeated in those places got back to him, and the Putneys had played a prominent role in some of it.

Leonard Putney, despite his profession as an innkeeper, had a reputation as an unfriendly sort. If he had disappeared for three or four days at the beginning of January, no one would have paid particular attention to his absence. Not when Putney owned a second inn in Folkstone, farther west along the coast. He was also reputed to be a smuggler.

Walter had heard that Alys, too, left Dover from time to time, though with her the disappearances were usually in the company of some man. She was regularly beaten for straying, straightaway upon her return. He frowned. The gossips also speculated that it might be Putney himself who arranged the trysts . . . and profited from them. Such practices were not uncommon. Many an innkeeper dabbled in the business of procuring women for his customers. Wives and maidservants alike sometimes did double duty as prostitutes.

If Alys was one of them, Walter thought, watching the woman herself come forward to greet him the moment he entered the inn, it was doubtful she'd been forced into it. Alys had never been the simple, obedient, grateful mistress Robert had supposed she was. Walter's old friend had possessed a talent, mayhap even a penchant, for selecting women who were out of the ordinary.

No other patrons occupied the common room this early in the day. Walter saw an avaricious expression skate across the cold blue ice of Alys Putney's eyes as she noted the finery in which her new customer was dressed. It altered to something even more calculating when her gaze lifted to his face and she realized she knew him.

"Master Pendennis." Her voice came out as a sultry purr. "It has been a long time."

Not long enough, he thought. "'Tis Sir Walter now, Alys."

She bobbed a mocking curtsey and waited. No doubt she expected him to order a meal or bespeak a room. He did neither, but simply stared at her, remembering.

What had first drawn Robert to Alys Sparcheforde was not in question. She'd set out to lure him using a ripe body and a tart tongue. She'd soon gotten what she wanted from him—a house to call her own, money for clothes and sweetmeats. She'd been sixteen when Robert first met her, and she'd held him for three years, longer than any of his other woman.

Robert had severed his ties with Alys abruptly, following his return from a sojourn in Lancashire. He had tried to provide for her, after his own callous fashion, by offering her to Walter. Unfortunately, he'd done so in Alys's presence, right after he'd told her he was selling the Dover house. Walter had made matters worse by declining to take her on as his mistress.

"You have done well here," Walter said, the comment designed to be a deliberate reminder that she'd married Leonard Putney within a month of the day Robert ended their association.

She was still as fair-haired as he remembered her, but breasts that had formerly jutted out, firm and high and just begging to be fondled, now sagged alarmingly. Her once ripe mouth looked pinched.

"Well enough," she agreed. Her fingers strayed to her face, where Walter's sharp eyes picked out a small scar, a mark such as might have been made by a blow from a hand wearing a ring.

He knew better than to waste pity on her. Even if Susanna had not told him what Alys had done to Jennet, he had an instinctual understanding of the little ways women like Alys used to give themselves the illusion of having power over others. She was the sort who'd offer to sew a tear in a doublet and manage to stick her needle into the wearer a dozen times before the mending was complete.

But could she have killed Robert, even contrived that Susanna be blamed, as the Lady Mary suggested? She was devious. Cunning. Venal and vengeful. But not the most clever of women. Robert's other mistresses had all possessed greater intelligence. And more education, too.

Mayhap that was why Alys had lasted longest.

"Have you had many lodgers here from London these last few weeks?"

"Men keep at home when the days are cold."

"And you, Alys?" he asked. "Did you travel during Yuletide?"

"Progresses are for royalty, Sir Walter." She almost smiled. "Have you some reason for these questions?"

"I had thought news from London might have reached you ere now."

"What news?" Impatience sharpened her words. Annoyance radiated from her narrowed eyes.

"News of Sir Robert Appleton's death."

"Sir Robert has been dead for many months," she informed him in haughty tones. "Died of the plague, they say. In France."

"That appears to have been a case of mistaken identity, but he is dead now. Murdered. He was killed ten days ago in London."

He'd hoped his blunt announcement would cause her to betray something—shock, dismay, guilt—but her face did not alter in the least. Nor did she blurt out any telling revelations. A full minute passed before she spoke. "'Tis naught to do with me."

"Did he contact you during this last year?"

"I thought him dead, I tell you."

"When did you last see him?"

"Not since before I married Leonard."

"And Leonard?"

"What about Leonard?" She sounded belligerent now, but he heard an edge of fear beneath the bravado.

"Has he been here in Dover throughout the last fortnight?"

"'Tis rare Leonard ever leaves Dover. The world comes to us."

"Lies, Alys. I know better."

The clatter of horses' hooves in the innyard spared her the need to answer. With a last, fulminating glare, Alys bustled past him to greet the arriving travelers. She did not even stop for a cloak, but hurried outside, as anxious to escape his questions, he thought, as to welcome new custom.

On a silent curse for the newcomer's bad timing, Walter followed her out. Another few minutes, time to make her angry enough, and she might have let slip some useful information.

Or not.

There was an innate craftiness about the woman. She was also predisposed to assume she might be blamed for something. Thus, she loudly proclaimed her innocence even before she was accused. That particular combination of characteristics meant she'd be a hard nut for anyone to crack.

As soon as Walter exited the inn, he realized his trip to Dover had been futile. Alys had been resistant to helping him, but she was adamantly opposed to assisting Susanna. Powerful emotions had turned Alys's face ugly. She glared at the small party of still-mounted riders.

That she recognized Robert's widow and hated her was plain as the chill in the air. But how did she know this was Susanna? Where, Walter wondered, had Alys seen her before?

In London, perhaps? Kneeling beside her dead husband beneath the Eleanor Cross?

Chapter 15

"Goodwife Putney?" Susanna asked.

A short, yellow-haired woman scowled up at her. Her kirtle was of substantial woollen cloth, dark blue in color and banded with black velvet. Her apron and cap were what any respectable tradeswoman might wear, but her bodice buttoned up the front only as far as a turned-over collar cut low to reveal a good deal of flesh.

"Yes, Lady Appleton," the woman replied. "I am Alys Putney." Her tone conveyed not just disrespect but outright loathing.

Susanna stared with intense curiosity at her husband's former mistress. Alys was a very different sort of female from Eleanor or Constance. They had been gently born and well educated, taught not only the social graces but how to delve into intellectual matters. Alys seemed more earthy. No doubt she possessed her fair share of native intelligence, but it was plain just to look at her that she was accustomed to relying on physical charms to get what she wanted. She was almost . . . coarse.

It seemed more of a betrayal, somehow, that a woman so common should have been the one with whom she'd shared Robert for such a long time. A foolish thought, Susanna chided herself. What did it matter now?

Susanna glanced at Walter, unsurprised to find

him already at the Star with the Long Tail. When she'd been told he'd left Leigh Abbey a half hour ahead of her, she'd assumed he'd come here to talk to Alys first alone. She wondered why, and how much he'd told the woman about Robert's death. From his sour expression, he'd not had much luck getting information out of her.

"A word with you in private?" she suggested to the innkeeper.

Where they were now, everything they said to each other could be overheard by Fulke and Bates, as well as by the ostler lingering at the door to the stables.

Despite the fact that Alys was shivering in the cold morning air, she made no effort to move inside. "We've no need of your sort of custom. Be off with you."

"I perceive, then, that you know my husband is dead and I am accused of killing him."

Alys's eyes widened.

Her reaction gave Susanna pause. The woman struck her as sly but not clever. Did she have the wit to feign innocence of recent events in London? Or had she, in truth, heard nothing of the charges against Susanna until this moment?

"How?" Alys moved forward to lay one hand on the pommel of Susanna's saddle. "How did you kill him?"

"He died of poison but not by my hand." Susanna gave the fingers near her knee a pointed look.

Alys loosed her grip and backed away. Her mouth worked soundlessly for another moment, causing her face to take on an unfortunate resemblance to a fish, before she sputtered a denial to Susanna's unvoiced accusation. "I had naught to do with any poisoning. You'll never prove I did."

Her voice was shrill enough to attract the attention of passersby on the street. A crowd began to gather.

Determined to grill Alys further, Susanna freed her right knee from the purpose-cut hollow in her sidesaddle. She had every confidence that she could convince Alys to answer more questions. If flattery did not work, there was always bribery. And, as a last resort, threats. Half an hour in private with the woman should be enough.

The velvet sling that took the place of a stirrup on a man's saddle made reaching the ground unassisted a hazardous process. Before Susanna could dismount, let alone try any method of persuasion, a man barreled in through the gate.

"Tell them nothing!" he bellowed.

Alys's glare shifted from Susanna to the newcomer.

Leonard Putney, Susanna presumed. He was short, a few scant inches taller than his wife. As he advanced upon them, his cloak swirled away from his body. He had little flesh on his bones, but by the pained expression on Alys's face when he seized her arm, his grip possessed a bruising strength.

"They are here to cause trouble," Putney told

96

his wife. "They seek someone else to blame for her crime."

"We seek the truth," Walter objected.

Putney spat.

Cold, salt-tinged air eddied all around them, carried in off the Narrow Seas, but it was the look in Putney's eyes that caused Susanna to shiver. She had witnessed powerful, irrational emotions before, but this was the first time such intense hatred had been directed at her. It seemed to fill the space between them with a palpable force.

"Begone!" Putney rasped. Spittle dotted his beard.

Alys flinched. Susanna could not tell if she was reacting to her husband's harsh voice, or to the increased pressure of his fingers on her arm, or out of fear for what he would do when they were alone. Leonard Putney hated Susanna, but he also despised everyone else in the innyard, including his own wife.

"I know why you came here!" he shouted." You'll not put the blame on us. We were here in Dover and together when Appleton was killed."

Susanna's mare shied away, sidestepping nervously. Walter had gone for his horse as soon as Putney appeared and now, mounted, seized Susanna's reins to lead her out of danger. The innkeeper's enraged and rapidly purpling face convinced her to go quietly. The man was not about to confess, or allow Alys to. For now, they had reached an impasse.

With a farewell nod to Alys and a final glance that was not devoid of sympathy for the woman, Susanna rode out of the innyard.

"I will have my men investigate further," Walter promised when they'd left the walls of Dover behind. "Such a heated denial smacks of a guilty conscience. When Putney found you had come to his inn, he was quick to assume the worst."

"Knowing what he does of his wife's past, he might react the same way if he'd only just heard of Robert's murder. Some traveler may have brought word of it to Dover."

"We will learn, I think, that they were not in Dover ten days ago. They are lying about something, Susanna. I am convinced of that much."

"Yes," she agreed, "but I am not certain that means they had aught to do with Robert's death. We came to Alys first, after Constance, only because she lives nearest to London. There are others with far better reasons to want Robert dead. Others with more recent cause to hate him."

Walter hesitated, then asked, "Is it necessary that you be the one to go to Lancashire to question Eleanor Lowell?"

"It was beneath an *Eleanor* Cross that Robert died."

"True enough, but what purpose does it serve for you to travel so far? You might instead leave the task to others. You have already agreed to let Catherine ask questions for you in Scotland."

"Only because I am not permitted to go there

in person. Besides, I have no one I trust to do the task at Appleton Manor."

"What about that man of law Robert employed? The one from Manchester."

"Matthew Grimshaw?" At the thought, Susanna grimaced. "He would either bluster at Eleanor, demanding answers and trying to frighten her into agreeing to whatever he suggested, just to escape his badgering, or he'd cave in without getting anything out of her, thwarted the moment she took offense at his attitude and refused to talk to him."

"I could go north in your stead."

"No, Walter. I think it best that I visit Appleton Manor myself."

Curiosity drove her, as well as the need to investigate. Eleanor Lowell did not live there alone. With her was Robert's only child.

Chapter 16

In common with most visitors who passed through Dover's Walgate, Jennet's eyes were drawn left, to the hilltop castle some quarter mile distant.

Her goal, however, was much more modest, a certain grocer's shop. From the exterior, the half-timbered house did not appear to be a very prosperous place. Tucked away on a side street, its windows had wooden shutters hinged at the top and bottom but, contrary to the custom followed by most shopkeepers, they had not been opened to form a counter on which to display goods.

Jennet ventured cautiously into the dimly lit interior of the shop, inhaling a musty smell that did little to reassure her about the quality of the herbs and spices the place offered for sale. Sniffing cautiously, she could distinguish the scent of mint, which kept its aroma even after it was dried.

"What lack ye?"

The sharp-voiced question made Jennet jump, for she'd thought herself alone in the shop. The speaker emerged from an inner room, moving slowly and ponderously through the door.

Widow Sparcheforde, Jennet thought, noting the sour expression on her deeply lined face.

Alys's mother was dressed in plain dark wool, the bodice well fitted with rolled shoulder pieces and sewn-in sleeves. She wore a goffered ruff and a crisply starched apron and had a money pouch suspended from her waist. Jennet felt dowdy in comparison.

"Well?" The old woman sounded irritable. "What do you want?"

"I have come to buy spices." Like most of those in his trade, the late Grocer Sparcheforde stocked an assortment, though he'd also sold sugar, confectionery, crystallized fruits, honey, wax, and herbs.

Suspicion lurked in the widow's eyes as she watched Jennet's movements. She made no effort to wait on her. "If you want aught from a high shelf," she said when she observed Jennet's interest in items stored above her head, "you'll have to wait for it."

"Have you no one to help you here? No one to look out for you?"

"A lazy apprentice. He went off to run an errand for me an hour since. God only knows where he's got to."

"No family?"

"Oh, aye. An ungrateful daughter."

Jennet smiled to herself. Alys's mother was stooped. She hobbled when she walked. Her hands had the gnarled look of one whose joints had stiffened with age. Jennet permitted herself the uncharitable hope that Alys would one day look just like her mother. 'Twould serve her right. The only fate more just involved her execution for the crime of murdering Sir Robert Appleton.

The subtle offer of a sympathetic ear was all it

took to start Goodwife Sparcheforde talking. She seemed to welcome a fresh audience for an account of all her woes. Jennet soon learned, as she'd hoped she might, that young Alys had been trained by her father in the preparation of herbs and spices.

Grocers were not supposed to usurp the work of apothecaries but the two trades did sometimes overlap. Just how much, Jennet wondered, had Alys learned at her father's knee? Enough to select and prepare an effective dose of poison?

"Raised his own herbs, he did," the widow bragged.

Sparcheforde had purchased spices—grains of paradise and cloves and ginger and pepper—but in the last years before his death, he'd also planted an herb garden behind his daughter's inn and saved himself the expense of buying those he could grow.

"What herbs?" Jennet asked.

"Peppermint, spearmint, and thyme." She named a dozen others, too, but not the plant Jennet was looking for. More direct measures seemed called for.

"Monkshood?" she asked.

As soon as the word was uttered, Jennet knew she'd gone too far. Goodwife Sparcheforde's eyes narrowed. "Who are you?" she demanded. "Why do you ask me that?"

"Faith, I am but a simple goodwife like yourself."

But the grocer's widow did not believe her. She realized Jennet did not intend to buy anything, either, since she had put nothing in the wicker basket she'd brought with her. Enraged, Goodwife Sparcheforde heaved herself toward Jennet with a menacing growl that sent the younger woman running into the street.

As she fled, imprecations and curses followed her. Pedestrians paused to look, wondering what was amiss.

Her cheeks flaming with embarrassment, Jennet hastened toward the spot where she'd instructed Lionel to wait for her. From the look of alarm in his eyes as he watched her approach, the old woman was still after her.

"I know who you are," Widow Sparcheforde shouted just as Lionel caught Jennet's arm and hauled her up onto the pillion behind his saddle.

Jennet had to abandon the basket.

It was not a graceful escape, but she was beyond caring. She clung to Lionel's waist as they rode hard for Walgate, burrowing her overheated face into his strong back.

"She knows who you are," Lionel said when they were clear of the town, "and I know who she is." Jennet heard suppressed excitement in his voice . . . and something more. Deviltry? Anticipation? Fear?

"She's Widow Sparcheforde. Naught else." Still winded from her precipitous flight, her words had a breathy quality.

"More than that." Now Lionel sounded like a man hoarding a delicious secret.

"What more?" Jennet was in no mood for games. Her attempt to help Lady Appleton had not been the resounding success she'd anticipated.

"Some folk say she's a witch. And she did curse you, Jennet."

For a moment, Jennet's chest tightened and her breath stopped. Then she sucked in air and rewarded Lionel with what she hoped was a painful pinch, though her fingers closed around more fabric than skin.

"Stop trying to frighten me."

"I tell you true." He sounded almost cheerful at the prospect of her coming misfortune. "That is what they say in Dover and have done for years. Widow Sparcheforde can cast spells. Why, just last month, a man's cow died but two days after he spattered old Mother Sparcheforde with mud. He rode past her at too great a speed. She cursed him for it on the spot. I suppose it must have been a mild curse," Lionel mused, "else he'd be dead now, not just his cow."

"Nonsense," Jennet declared.

That was what Lady Appleton would say.

But on the way home, Jennet ordered Lionel to stop at a farm cottage she knew. When they continued on, they were leading a scrawny old cow. She'd stopped giving milk, and the farmer had intended to slaughter her.

Jennet had a better use for the beast. A precaution only, she assured herself, just in case Lionel's story was true. She saw no profit in taking unnecessary risks. If the old woman *was* a witch, then let it be Jennet's animal, not Jennet herself, who suffered the effects of her cursing.

Chapter 17

The entire household at Leigh Abbey rose early on Sunday to attend morning services in the parish church. Everyone above the age of six walked there through the frigid dawn.

During Susanna's detention in Newgate, Robert had been brought home and buried. There was not an inhabitant for miles around who had not heard that his widow was suspected of poisoning him, and Susanna hoped for some sign of support from her neighbors. After all, her family had lived in this part of Kent for generations and had always been good masters, paying well for services rendered and treating their retainers with fairness. Nearly everyone in the parish depended upon Leigh Abbey in some way.

Instead, she observed subtle evidence that the parishioners believed she was guilty. She resolved to hold her head high and pretend she did not notice.

Jennet was not so restrained. She had to be prevented by brute force from accosting the carpenter's wife when that woman stepped aside in order to avoid any accidental contact between her skirts and those of an accused murderess. The snub was too obvious to be misinterpreted.

"She has no call for such rude behavior," Jennet complained, furious on her mistress's behalf.

"Ignore her. Less said, soonest mended."

But this was not some dispute over who made the best bread. Susanna's neighbors, the honest, hard-working people she had known all her life, believed her capable of killing her husband. Throughout the service, those covert glances which did not condemn her out of hand, surveyed her with morbid curiosity. They were as bad as carrion crows.

Beside her, Jennet fidgeted during a psalm, glared at those around them through the lessons from the Old and New Testaments, and was restrained only by Mark's hand over her fist when whispers during the litany were not sufficiently masked by the coughing of parishioners suffering from catarrh. The words *murder* and *poison herbs* were clearly audible.

"Where is their loyalty?" Jennet muttered, but she managed to seethe in silence through the decalogue, epistle, and gospel. The Nicene Creed was read, another psalm sung. Then came the sermon.

Since he owed his living to Leigh Abbey, the preacher chose a subject with no connection whatsoever to Susanna's present troubles. While he railed against the evils of allowing revelers to have free reign during the holiday season and turned that into a diatribe against mummers, players, jugglers, musicians, and other masterless men, her thoughts drifted.

Was there a connection between the Eleanor

Cross and Eleanor Lowell? Susanna had met Eleanor for the first time shortly after Rosamond's birth. Unable to contact Robert because he was in Spain on the queen's business, Eleanor had brought the child to Leigh Abbey.

The discovery that Robert had yet another mistress had not surprised Susanna, but she had been shocked to learn there was a child. In all the years they had been married, she had never conceived, and Robert had gotten no other bastards, or at least none Susanna knew of. Until Rosamond, she'd assumed the fault for this lack might lie with him. Rosamond had been proof it was Susanna's failing.

Refusing to dwell on her inadequacy as a wife, Susanna forced her wayward thoughts back to the matter at hand. There were several mysteries surrounding Robert's death. One involved the reason he'd made his way to the cross at Charing. Had he gone there in order to call attention to the mother of his child?

If he had, that did not necessarily mean she had killed him. It might rather indicate that he had gone to see her at some point during the preceding eighteen months. Robert's activities then were still unaccounted for, despite Walter's best efforts to trace them.

Had he spent part of that time with Eleanor and their daughter in Lancashire? Might he even have brought them with him to London? Susanna knew only one certain way to find out. On the morrow, she would leave Kent and journey northward. The answers to many questions might be found at Appleton Manor.

More psalms followed the sermon. An infant was baptized at the font. Susanna paid little mind, scarce aware of her surroundings. Oblivious to the cold bench beneath her, she barely noticed that her feet were icy. Her warm cloak staved off the worst of the shivers.

On the other hand, she mused, the Eleanor Cross might have nothing to do with Eleanor Lowell. The name was not uncommon. The second Lady Madderly had also borne it. She'd been murdered, too, though not by poison. Was that the message Robert had been trying to convey? That someone had murdered him?

It was also possible, she supposed, that he'd not intended to leave a dying clue at all. It could have been sheer happenstance he'd died where he did.

At last, the worship service was over. A glance at Jennet showed her ready to exit the church and do battle on her mistress's behalf.

"Keep your temper under control," Susanna warned her, and steeled herself to do likewise. She expected to face further condemnation, but the first person they encountered outside the church was Nicholas Baldwin, their nearest neighbor.

"Lady Appleton. Well met." Baldwin greeted her with a respectful little bow and a smile, making plain to all who witnessed their meeting that he had no doubts about her innocence.

Nick Baldwin was as solid as one of his own merchant ships. Although he was a London man and a relative newcomer to Kent, he had quickly shown himself to be a generous benefactor of local causes. Susanna expected he'd be made a justice of the peace for the area before much longer.

Walter studied Baldwin with wary eyes, then introduced himself. Odd, Susanna thought. She'd always assumed it had been Walter who'd provided Baldwin with information about the inhabitants of Leigh Abbey, Walter who'd told him that she, in particular, could be trusted. It was apparent to her now that the two men had not met before. Someday, she thought, she would have to inquire of Nick Baldwin just who had recommended her to him. At present she was preoccupied with more pressing matters.

"I held you well rid of Sir Robert the first time he was reported dead," Baldwin said bluntly. "I have not changed my opinion, but I am sorry for your trouble over this. If I can help in any way, you've only to say the word."

"I ask no more than your continued friendship," Susanna told him, placing one hand on his arm. They'd spent many a pleasant hour together since their first, rather acrimonious encounter. Nick Baldwin had traveled widely, to such exotic places as Muscovy and Persia, and had brought back all manner of souvenirs, including the male cat, Bala, whose long fur had begun to crop up among the shorter-haired felines in this part of Kent.

Walter took her elbow to ease her away from her neighbor. Startled, Susanna glanced his way in time to catch a fleeting glimpse of an unguarded expression before he carefully blanked it. He'd looked, she thought, as if he'd just bitten down on a sour persimmon.

Bidding Baldwin a fond farewell, she motioned for Jennet and Mark to join her for the walk back to Leigh Abbey. None of the other neighbors, she noted, had chosen to follow the London man's lead. The rest of them seemed to prefer to believe the worst.

"I do think," she murmured as they left the churchyard, "that we will hold afternoon prayers in private in Leigh Abbey's chapel."

Chapter 18

Jennet fumed all the way home. Disloyal villains! Self-righteous fools! How could anyone know Lady Appleton and think her capable of such a heinous crime?

While she was busy packing for their departure, even when she was playing one last time with her children, Jennet continued to stew about the narrow-minded stupidity of their neighbors.

"Running off to Scotland has begun to have more appeal," she told Mark when he came to fetch her. Lady Appleton wanted to see both of them in her study.

They found her at her writing table, a ledger open before her. Her expression was as somber as Jennet had ever seen it.

She looked first at Mark. "I must leave someone I trust in charge of Leigh Abbey while I am gone. My steward is the most logical choice."

"But, madam—"

She cut short Mark's protest. "What happened at church today may be only the beginning of our troubles. I will not compound them by placing the demesne farm in inexperienced hands. It is only natural that there be a certain . . . unease about my fate. Creditors will doubtless begin to demand all payments in cash. You are the only one who can make sure the manor continues to run smoothly. I rely upon you to ensure that these accusations against me do not undermine all we have built here."

Mark glanced at Jennet, then away. The previous evening, after her return from Dover, they'd talked far into the night. Lady Appleton was right. Rumors were already flying, in town and countryside alike. Few besides Appleton Manor's loyal house servants wished to be tarred with the same brush now being used to blacken Lady Appleton's good name.

Jennet chewed on her lower lip and fingered the talisman she'd attached to the loop that held her housekeeper's keys. She'd hoped the contents of this little leather pouch would be powerful enough to negate Widow Sparcheforde's curses. It contained wood betony (said to have power against evil spirits), a sprig of rowan (always good to scare away the supernatural), and a bit of Saint-John's-wort (to ward off witches and fairies).

Her bad luck, however, had already begun. The cow she'd bought still lived but Jennet had stabbed her finger on a cloak pin while sorting her mistress's belongings. It throbbed painfully when she twisted her hands together.

And now Lady Appleton meant to leave Mark behind.

"January and February are hard, hungry months in the best of times," she told him, though both Mark and Jennet knew that very well. "This winter has been uncommon cold. There have been problems with foxes raiding the henroosts. Cattle usually fed on leaves, mosses, vines, and young shoots will have to be kept alive on loppings from trees until the snow melts."

"You cannot mean to go to Lancashire alone," Jennet objected and gave Mark a sharp kick to the ankle to encourage him to speak up.

"Others can supervise the work here," he said with satisfactory promptness. "My place is with you, madam."

"Others can, but I want you to do it, Mark. Someone in authority must set folk to their tasks. Woodcutting. Winnowing and grinding of grain. Lambing will soon begin and at Candlemas it will be time to plough, harrow, and spread manure, to set trees and hedges, prune fruit trees, and even sow oats and beans, if the weather permits."

"Who will accompany you, then, madam? It is a long, hard journey to Appleton Manor."

"Sir Walter goes with me. And Fulke. And Bernard Bates."

Her guard dog. Jennet grimaced.

"Not Lionel? If you will not take me," Mark protested, "then he—"

"I need Lionel here." Lady Appleton tapped the ledger again. "He knows my herb garden. He must oversee that work. Sow spike, coriander, and white poppy in the new of February's moon, aniseed and fennel under the full moon, which will occur on the fifteenth day of that month. And beneath the old moon, plant holy thistle, hartshorn, and burnet. Then, in March—"

"Madam," Mark interrupted, "if Lionel is to stay, let him do all. My place—"

"Your place is with your wife and children. Jennet, you will remain behind, as well."

"Oh, no, madam," Jennet protested. "Where you go, I go."

"But your children—"

"I go with you, madam," Jennet repeated. "Mark's sister will care for them, as she did during the time we were in London." Young Robert had still been in swaddling clothes back then, but Jennet had not hesitated to be parted from him and her daughters. She did not hesitate now. In truth, having thought about the matter while Lady Appleton was discussing her herbs, Jennet had realized that leaving Mark behind would serve to relieve her sole maternal concern. This way, when the time was right, he would already be in place to pack up the family and make a run for the border.

"This is a long journey, as Mark has said, and I have no way to know how it will end." For a moment, Lady Appleton sounded discouraged.

It would end close to Scotland, or so Jennet hoped. Aloud she repeated what she'd said before. "Where you go, madam, I go."

Lady Appleton turned aside, as if her emotions had of a sudden come too close to the surface, and she did not want anyone to know. She was quick to recover her composure, however, and to bestow upon Jennet a faint smile. "I know better than to order you to remain behind when you are this determined."

Had she heard about Dover? Guilt assaulted Jennet, but she held her peace, unwilling to acknowledge her disobedience if that was not Lady Appleton's meaning.

"But consider one other matter, Jennet, before you commit yourself to going with me," Lady Appleton continued. "Can you bear to be parted from your little ones?"

"My place is with you." Jennet stifled a twinge of regret and told herself that the coming separation would not last long. One way or another, matters would be settled before the next quarter sessions met in London.

"Then I will be glad of your company," Lady Appleton said. Jennet thought the interview over, but at the last minute her mistress called her back. "One more thing, Jennet."

"Yes, madam?"

"You must promise me there will be no more of going off on your own to ask questions."

Jennet's hand clasped tight around her talisman. "How did you—"

"I overheard Lionel telling the head gardener how he'd gulled you."

"Gulled—?"

"Even if that old woman believes herself to be a witch, Jennet, her words cannot harm you."

"But, madam, she is a grocer's widow. She knows what herbs to use to cast her spells!"

"Superstitious nonsense," Lady Appleton declared. "And Lionel has admitted to me that he made up the story about the man with the dead cow."

Jennet was not convinced, but she did not argue further. Instead she gave Lady Appleton an edited account of her conversation with Widow Sparcheforde. "There is an herb garden behind the Star with the Long Tail. Is that not suspicious?"

"Most goodwives grow herbs, Jennet. You know that."

"But Alys—"

"Sir Walter's intelligence gatherers will keep watch over Alys Putney and her husband. Do not trouble yourself about them. But if you wish to accompany me north, Jennet, you must promise that from now on you will tell me about any plans that have to do with my troubles before you implement them."

"Are you wroth with me?"

"No, Jennet. I know your intentions were good. But, please, from now on, share your plots and schemes beforehand."

Lady Appleton must have seen a flash of guilt in Jennet's eyes. Certes, Mark did, for he came to stand at her side, his posture defensive. "She's done nothing," he said.

"Yet." Lady Appleton knew her too well. "Tell me. Now."

"How far is Lancashire from the Scottish border?" Jennet asked instead.

"A few days journey. But you know what Sir Walter said. I am not permitted to leave England. I have written to Catherine, asking her to act on my behalf in Edinburgh."

"Lady Glenelg can question Sir Robert's Scottish mistress," Jennet agreed, "but why not confront the woman yourself? We could all of us go to Scotland. It cannot be too difficult to slip quietly across the border. There Lady Glenelg will keep us safe."

Astonished, Lady Appleton took a step away from Jennet. "Do you suggest I flee the country? Live in exile for the rest of my life? Never!"

"Is not living, anywhere, better than dying at Tyburn?" Tears filled Jennet's eyes. "I could not bear it if aught happened to you!"

To Jennet's astonishment, Lady Appleton hugged her. "Your love and loyalty humble me, Jennet, but you must not give up hope that we will find out the truth. I will be cleared of the charges against me."

"But—"

"We will not talk of failure unless we must. Certes, I do not want to be executed, but you must never put my welfare ahead of that of your family."

"Family first," Jennet promised.

But Lady Appleton *was* family, and Jennet silently vowed she would do whatever she had to in order to keep her mistress safe . . . even if it meant taking that stubbornly independent gentlewoman into Scotland by force.

Chapter 19

Susanna brought Walter Pendennis a posset as he sat in the inner chamber beyond the dining parlor, a room with a view of the gardens and the fish ponds beyond. He was not displeased to have his brooding interrupted.

As he took the steaming cup from her hands, he marveled at her resilience. She'd been the one shunned at church that morning. She was the one facing a trail for murder. And yet she sought to bring him greater ease. He sipped the fragrant brew, savoring the combination of herbs she'd chosen. Calming ingredients. Something to settle the stomach and strengthen the heart and give them both the will to go on.

"Chamomile," he guessed, relying partly on his keen sense of smell, partly on his knowledge of Susanna's favorite nostrums. "What else?"

"Some might hesitate to ask," she murmured, taking a swallow from her own portion. "For all you know, there might be henbane in the drink. Or deadly nightshade. Or—"

"Susanna!"

At her startled look, he realized he'd never spoken so sharply to her before. "I'll hear no more of such talk," he said. "You have dedicated your life to preventing people from being poisoned. You are not likely to change into a heartless killer overnight."

"I wish everyone had your confidence in me."

Her voice trembled slightly, alarming Walter. He'd rarely observed any sign of weakness in this woman. The lack of support from her neighbors had unsettled her more than he'd realized.

Even as that thought passed through his mind, Susanna managed a smile and reached out to pat the back of his hand. "Drink it all down," she advised. "You look as if you had the troubles of the whole world on your shoulders. The posset contains blessed thistle and borage to purge melancholy, together with a bit of thyme and a dash of St. John's wort. 'Twill do you only good."

"My cares cannot so easily be lifted." But he obeyed her, draining the cup.

"Shall I give you jet to wear? 'Tis said to ward off phantasms due to melancholy."

"Jet I will wear but not for that purpose." Some folk criticized him for his love of lush fabrics, bright colors, and fine jewelry. Susanna never had.

"You did not need my troubles to add to your own burden." She wandered away, crossing the room to stand by a window.

When Walter came up beside her, he saw that she was staring at her pride and joy, the herb garden close to the house. Even at this time of year, there were a few medicinal and pot herbs growing there. Come spring, it would be alive with color and scent.

"My burden, as you call it, has become far weightier of late, but not because of your troubles.

I grow weary of the work I do for the queen."

It was unlike Walter to confide in anyone, but this felt right. He trusted few people, yet from the moment he'd met Susanna Appleton, he'd sensed she was different. She was someone quite unique in his experience. Someone he could rely upon.

"I have begun to doubt the usefulness of sorting through and decoding every shred of gossip, every intercepted message, every movement of recusants and suspected traitors. Someone else could do the job as well, and with more enthusiasm. I am tired, Susanna. Tired of knowing other people's secrets. Tired of trying to decipher what poses a true threat to the queen and what is simply some pathetic soul's cry for attention. I have begun to see plots and treasons in every meeting of two men on a street corner. I have no judgment left."

She set aside her posset and turned away from the window. "You push yourself too hard, my dear. And you are right. The world will not stop spinning if you let go its reins. But I think you would soon miss the intrigue, the challenge."

"Just now, my work has but one value to me. It allows me to help you. I will utilize all my resources on your behalf and when they are no longer needed for that purpose, gladly abandon them." He took both her hands in his. "When you are free of these absurd charges against you, I mean to make some changes in my life. I've often thought of returning to my native Cornwall. I have

121

land there, land I acquired years ago but have never had leisure to enjoy." He clasped her fingers more tightly and waited until she met his eyes. "Come with me, Susanna. Leave here. Leave these folk who do not believe in you as I do. You are free to remarry now. And you must know I lo—"

Her hand, jerked free from his, gently covered his mouth to cut off the word before he could complete it. "Oh, my dear," she said sadly. "Let us not spoil our friendship by making more of it than there is."

He wanted to object, to declare that he had long had powerful feelings for her, feelings that were much more than mere friendship. But she was already moving away from him, drawing into herself, gathering that inner strength he so admired.

She did not want a husband, did not need one. So she had always said. But until this moment, Walter had never entirely believed her.

A great sadness engulfed him. Without Susanna in it, his life in Cornwall would be as empty of meaning as his days in London seemed.

"I will understand," she said, "if you no longer wish to travel north with me." Her intent gaze was fixed on his expression, making him wonder how much of his inner torment she could guess.

"Have we not just agreed naught can spoil our friendship?"

She nodded but her expression was bleak as she contemplated their coming journey. "What if I cannot prove I am innocent, Walter? We could fail."

"I'll not permit such a miscarriage of justice." Disappointment in love did not alter his determination to save Susanna's life. Whether she shared her future with him or not, she deserved to have one.

"Can you stop it?"

"I have influence at court. The queen can pardon even a convicted murderess."

"But will she? And if you tell her the whole truth about Robert, she'll not be in charity with you. Indeed, she will be most put out with us both."

"If that is the only way—"

"No, Walter. We promised our silence on the matter to the Lady Mary."

"Would you rather burn? Provide a spectacle for members of the royal court? Tyburn is within easy walking distance of Westminster, convenient for any courtiers who wish to make their way across the fields northwest of Charing."

A vivid picture of the gallows came into his mind. Giant elms had at one time grown thick there, alongside Tyburn Stream. There was still a dense wood running north beyond the high road to Tottenham. But where once the dead cart would have been drawn up beneath a tree, the rope set, and the cart drawn away again to let the prisoner hang, these days Tyburn "tree" consisted of two stout oak uprights, a crossbeam, a platform, and a ladder. There was even talk of constructing a permanent gallows on the site.

But Susanna would not have the mercy of death by hanging.

Walter's stomach lurched in spite of the soothing posset he'd just imbibed. After she had been brought to the gallows, she'd have a rope put round her neck, but that was mere symbolism. For the crime of killing her husband, her lord and master, she'd be burnt alive, not hanged.

If it came to that, Walter vowed, he would bribe the hangman to strangle her. Anything to spare her the flames. He'd provide the customary alms given by a condemned prisoner for swift and painless dispatch and a handsome bonus besides.

Then he realized that he would not.

If the law demanded Susanna's death, he would instead find some way to spirit her out of England. "I will bribe Bates if I must," he vowed, "and obtain false passports. We can escape to the Continent." They could spend their lives together, even if she would not marry him. "I traveled much in Italy in my younger days," he added. "I would enjoy showing you the sights of that ancient land."

Though she smiled, Susanna shook her head. "Does everyone want me to run away? Have you no faith in my ability to find the real murderer?"

"Certes, you are clever and resourceful, but—"

"And I have sworn to present myself at the Sessions House in Old Bailey Street on the ninth day of May," Susanna reminded him. "No matter what happens between now and then, I mean to honor my word."

Chapter 20

Edinburgh Castle
January 17, 1565

Solemnly treading couples, the gentlemen in hats, cloaks, and gloves, followed the notes of sackbutt, shawm, and pommer to perform the steps of a courtly pavane. Formal, processional, and dignified, it required gliding steps that kept the feet on the ground.

Catherine, Lady Glenelg was grateful for small favors. She was still a novice when it came to dancing and self-conscious about her ability. This particular skill had not been considered important enough to study in Susanna Appleton's household, where Catherine had lived before her marriage. She'd have made a fool of herself and disgraced her husband here at the Scots court had she not been blessed with a new friend patient enough to teach a beginner.

Catherine forced a smile for Gilbert as her husband bowed to her, his weight on his right foot while he pointed the left. Her *reverence* was a curtsey in which she bent both knees.

Those knees ached. So did her head. Her feet hurt, too. Much as she loved him, at this moment Catherine wished she'd never agreed to accompany Gilbert to Scotland. For hours, she had been obliged to participate in energetic dancing accompanied by over-loud music: galliards, where men laid aside their cloaks and danced in doublet and hose; the coranto, which used the same steps as the pavane but substituted running and jumping for walking; the cinquepace, a still livelier form of the galliard.

These were all well and good in moderation, but Queen Mary of Scotland did not comprehend that concept. A frantic quality laced her endless celebrations. Worse, she seemed oblivious to the grumblings of the strait-laced Reformers who watched her every move. A clash seemed inevitable. When it came, England would be involved. The Glenelgs would be forced to face up to their divided loyalties.

Heels together, Catherine turned her body gently to the left, then to the right, a movement called "the branle." Although it was winter, her court dress felt too warm. The fitted bodice and tight sleeves constricted her movement.

Next she was required to execute a *simple*. Take one step forward with the left foot on the first beat, she reminded herself, then bring the right foot up beside the left on the second.

Tired as she was, Catherine had to force herself to concentrate, to count the steps and think ahead. She repeated the *simple* and followed it with the required *double*—three steps forward, then the right foot up to join the left on the fourth beat. After two more *simples* came a *reprise*, which consisted of standing still and moving her knees from side to side.

During the dance, the participants toured the entire hall, past elegant tapestries of gilded leather and brocaded green velvet and cloth of gold. As they repeated the steps in varying combinations, backward and sideways, endlessly, Catherine stumbled only once. Gilbert was there to catch her.

"We have stayed long enough," he declared when the tune finally faded into silence.

She protested, but not with any enthusiasm. She had no wish to weaken Gilbert's position at court, but she suspected that no matter how many activities they joined in, the two of them would never be more than tolerated.

Catherine was English through and through. Her husband had been born and bred in England, the only child of an English father and a Scots mother. He'd pledged reluctant allegiance to Scotland only when he'd inherited his maternal uncle's lands and title.

An hour after leaving the castle, the Glenelgs were back in the privacy and blessed quiet of their own bedchamber in their own house in Canongate, an area just outside the city walls of Edinburgh. Gilbert looked tired, Catherine thought, watching him pour them each a cup of wine. He worried too much. And he worked too hard. Even this late, one of the servants had been waiting up with dispatches for him to read.

"Leave those until you've rested, *caro sposo*."

Catherine glided toward him to place one hand on his arm. With the other she removed her small velvet cap and shook her hair free of net and pins. If all else failed, she could always distract him by discarding bits of clothing until she wore nothing but her long white shirt with its smart white collar.

"One of these letters is for you, sweeting."

At the sight of a familiar seal, an apple pierced by an arrow, Catherine forgot her objections to reading the post. "Why has a letter from Susanna come by packet?" she demanded as she grabbed it. "Something must be wrong. Why else would a private message be sent through official channels?" Her first sharp, skittering sense of panic increased tenfold when she skimmed the letter. "Susanna says Robert is dead. Murdered. And that she stands accused of the crime!"

The first revelation did not shock her. She'd suspected there was something odd in the earlier report of her half brother's death. But how could anyone think Susanna could kill?

"There is a letter here from Pendennis," Gilbert told her, extracting it from the others. "In code."

It took him a few minutes to translate the message, time enough for Catherine's vivid imagination to conjure up a dozen alarming possibilities. Although Susanna had written that it would be months yet before she came to trial, Catherine could not help but be frightened for her. What if she could not prove her innocence?

If Gilbert's deepening frown was any indication, he did not like what Pendennis had written. He handed the transcription to her as soon as he'd finished the decoding. It confirmed that Robert's death by plague had been a contrivance to cover up activities better kept secret.

"I do not know why I should be surprised that he was murdered the moment he came back from the dead," she murmured. "Robert always did have a flair for making enemies."

"No wonder, either, that Susanna is a suspect. She has good reason to want him to stay dead."

"She'd never have killed him. Never."

"Guilty or innocent, it is an ominous sign that she has been charged with the crime."

The more negative Gilbert's comments, the stronger Catherine's avowals became in Susanna's defense. "She has until May to catch the real killer."

As soon as the words were out, Catherine realized she believed in Susanna's ability to do just that. As fast as it had earlier engulfed her, her panic dissipated. Susanna had brought murderers to justice ere now. She could do so again.

"Susanna intends to journey to Appleton Manor to ask questions," she told Gilbert.

"Lancashire? That is a long way for a killer to have traveled. Sir Robert was slain in Westminster."

"That woman is at Appleton Manor. Eleanor. And her child."

Gilbert took back his translation of Sir Walter's

letter and reread it. "Susanna suspects one of her husband's mistresses. Logical. I suppose she wants us to question Annabel Mac Reynolds."

Taking the wine Gilbert held out to her, Catherine gave him Susanna's letter. While he read it, she crossed to their bed, pulled aside the crimson velvet hangings, climbed two little steps, and settled herself atop the counterpane with her legs tucked up beneath her, tailor-fashion.

"She's asked you to discover Annabel's whereabouts on the day Robert was poisoned."

"Annabel left court before Christmas," Catherine mused. "She went to visit her family, or so she said. I did not see her tonight. Therefore, she has not yet returned. She's had time to go all the way to London."

"How did Susanna learn Annabel had been her husband's mistress?" Gilbert sat beside his wife, turning her chin with the help of one large finger so that she was obliged to meet his eyes.

He had removed his gloves. The touch of flesh on flesh sent an anticipatory shiver straight to her womb, and for a moment, that sensation eclipsed all thought of Susanna's troubles.

He had also removed his cloak and his doublet, Catherine noted. Unlike Susanna's marriage to Robert, her union with Gilbert was a love match. They could talk about this troubling situation, plan and scheme and share ideas together. They could also share much more, comforting and soothing one another in perfect harmony.

"Catherine? How did Susanna hear about Annabel?"

"I told her," Catherine admitted. "In a letter." At the time, she'd thought it her duty to report what she'd learned upon first coming to the Scots court.

"Robert had gone back to England by the time we arrived here. He was unlikely to return or take up with her again." Gilbert sounded disapproving.

Catherine frowned down at her hands, which were tightly clasped around the cup balanced in her lap. "It did not seem right that everyone here knew of their scandalous trysts and Susanna did not."

"Scarce everyone." Gilbert slung one arm around Catherine's shoulders and tucked her in close against his side.

"More than one person felt obliged to report Robert's dalliance to me."

"Mayhap they did so in order to discover what relationship existed between the two of you."

That they were related was obvious to anyone who met both Robert and Catherine. She had her half brother's dark brown eyes and hair, his narrow face, and his high forehead. The characteristics, in combination, were distinctive.

"I understand that you were angry on her behalf," Gilbert continued, "but what if your rash revelation gave Susanna additional cause to hate her husband?"

"She did not hate him!" Catherine twisted out of her husband's embrace to glare at him. "She knew he had mistresses and accepted that fact. She also taught me that it is best not to try to keep secrets."

Catherine had to admit, however, that if she had it to do it over again now, two and a half years later, she'd not be so quick to share the rumors she'd heard bandied about at the Scots court.

"One section of Sir Walter's letter puzzled me," she said when she was snuggled close to Gilbert's side once more. "He hinted that Annabel may be more than she seems. What does he mean by that?"

Gilbert hesitated before he answered, as if weighing how much to tell her. She could feel the increase in tension in his chest and shoulders. "It is possible Robert first knew Annabel in France, years ago, when Walter Pendennis was there as part of the English delegation. Annabel was in Queen Mary's retinue then."

"I know the Scots queen lived at the French court for most of her childhood." For a brief time, during her late husband's short reign, Mary Stewart had worn the crowns of both France and Scotland. "But what could that have to do with Robert's murder?"

"I suspect he thinks Annabel might have acted on orders from Catherine de' Medici. There have long been rumors that she recruits beautiful young women as spies."

"And she is reputed to be a poisoner. How

convenient." She shut her eyes for a moment, then lifted her lashes to give Gilbert a direct look. "I do not believe Annabel went, or was sent, to England to poison my brother. She's never been at all interested in hearing about him. Why should she even suspect he was still alive?"

"You read Susanna's letter. She speculates that he might have contacted her, perhaps even tried to extort money from her."

"That seems most doubtful." Catherine downed the last of her drink and handed the empty cup to her husband.

Looking thoughtful, Gilbert set it next to his own on the bedside table. When he took her in his arms again, Catherine felt him smile against her forehead. "I think you are right. If Robert had asked Annabel for help, she'd have told him about Vanguard."

"How clever of you!"

Soon after Robert's alleged death, Susanna had sent his favorite horse, Vanguard, to Catherine as a gift. The arrival of the big, black stallion with the white blaze on his forehead had caused a stir at the Scots court. It seemed that during Robert's time in Edinburgh as a special envoy from England, Queen Mary had tried to persuade him to make her a gift of the courser. It would have been politic of Catherine to do so when Vanguard came into her possession. She had chosen instead to follow her brother's example. She doted on the horse, just as Robert had.

"Since we still have Vanguard, it follows that Robert never contacted Annabel. If he knew we had the animal, he'd have lost no time coming here and reclaiming him, by theft if necessary." Gilbert bent his head, lips ready for kissing her, but paused when he caught sight of her expression. "Now why do you frown?"

"Because, in spite of your logic, I must still do as Susanna asks and question Annabel."

Before they'd met, Catherine had not expected to like Robert's former mistress. But Annabel had turned out to be clever and lively, and she noticed little things that others at court did not. Amusing things. She had also flattered Catherine by asking her help. She'd wanted someone with whom to practice her English. Annabel was fluent in French and also understood Gaelic and Inglis, the language of the lowland Scots, but although she'd learned to read Catherine's native tongue, she had great difficulty pronouncing English words. As did Queen Mary. In exchange for dancing lessons, Catherine had been endeavoring to teach Annabel the correct way of speaking.

Gilbert began to undo Catherine's laces. "You can do nothing until she returns to Edinburgh." He lowered his head to taste the slope of her breast. As a distraction, it was most effective. Worry over the danger facing her sister-by-marriage could not compete with the lure of the marriage bed. Giving in to her own desires, Catherine consigned all thought of murder to the future and threw herself with blissful abandon into Gilbert's eager embrace.

Susanna would discover the truth before she had to stand trial. Catherine was convinced of it. That being so, she did not give the matter another thought until well after Gilbert had left her bed the next morning.

Chapter 21

The journey from Leigh Abbey to Appleton Manor took ten days in the best of conditions. Susanna's party progressed at a snail's pace. Frozen roads were easier riding than those mired in mud, but excessive snow was always a problem. By the time St. Paul's Day dawned, they had twice been delayed by fresh accumulations and were still in Cheshire.

Although they'd spent the night in a comfortable inn, safe and warm and cozy, Susanna's leg ached from an old injury. Cold weather always made it worse. And even before she and Jennet joined Walter, Fulke, and Bates in the common room to break their fast, Susanna sensed that Jennet, too, had woken stiff and sore. In her case the condition was the result of having to ride long hours on a pillion attached to the back of Fulke's saddle.

The prospect of yet another day on horseback made Jennet surly. Her temper was already fraying when she heard Bernard Bates knock on a table and call out "Put!"

"I see it," Fulke answered.

The two of them were engaged in a game of cards. This time Bates won the round and the game and collected the stakes. Fulke shuffled and dealt three of the inexpensive, block-printed cards to each of them.

"Wastrels," Jennet grumbled.

"They must do something to pass the time," Susanna reminded her. Travel was nine parts boredom and one sheer panic, as when horses bolted or rivers had to be forded.

"But that game has a low reputation even in alehouses. And I'll wager Bates cheats." She spoke loudly enough to be overheard.

Bates glowered at her but said nothing. He rarely broke his silence, though once or twice Jennet had provoked him into speech.

For some reason, Jennet had taken an intense dislike to Susanna's official escort. She complained that he was always hanging about, that she all but tripped over him every time she turned around. Susanna had given up trying to convince her that Bates was only doing his duty. Since he did not know her as well as Jennet did, he could not be certain she would not try to escape. He had to stay close.

Fulke looked up from the card game with a grin. "Have a care, Jennet, lest we wager for your company. Loser takes the pillion, eh, Bates?"

But Bates refused to gamble for those stakes. At the end of the next game he collected the cards and stored them inside his doublet, then went to look outside. "Fair weather," he said from the door. And then, succinct as ever, "Fair year."

He referred, Susanna realized, to the old superstition that the weather on St. Paul's Day was an indicator for the coming year. If she remembered correctly, a windy day predicted war, a cloudy day a visitation of the plague. She wished it were that easy to guess what the next months held for her.

They were on their way within the hour, Walter and Susanna in the lead. Fulke, with Jennet behind him, rode in the middle. Bates led the pack horse and guarded their backs. They had ridden thus all the way from Leigh Abbey, stopping some nights at inns, others at the estates of friends. Cold as it was, they'd been able to use frozen rivers and streams as roads. That was preferable, in Susanna's opinion, to traveling them by boat. She had no tolerance for choppy water and even on a short crossing took the precaution of dosing herself with ginger or peppermint, either of which helped soothe an unsteady stomach.

★ ★ ★

Two days later, when they had been on the road just under two weeks, they at last came to a rise in the land and looked down upon Appleton Manor. Not a creature stirred in the barren white landscape, but the house, in contrast to the first time Susanna had seen it, deserted and desolate, greeted them with a welcoming spiral of smoke rising from its central chimney. When a crisp, cold breeze carried the scent of burning gorse their way, Susanna felt some of her uneasiness wane. She had been sore afraid they'd arrive to find Eleanor and the child gone to London and the manor abandoned.

Sitting a little straighter in her saddle, Susanna

guided her mare over a double-arched stone bridge across what, in more hostile times, would have been called a moat. She was nervous, she admitted to herself, worried about meeting Robert's daughter. Since his death, she'd felt a growing need to see his child again. Irrational, she supposed, but there it was. She had come to Appleton Manor as much to spend time with Rosamond as to question Eleanor.

The little girl was Robert's heir, whether or not Susanna was executed for killing him. She intended to take steps to insure that the child's illegitimacy did not bar her from claiming the Appleton estate. She could do that much, at least, for the child who should have been hers.

They rode into the cobblestone courtyard a few minutes later, setting up a great clatter. The heavy oak doors of the main entrance at once flew open. Beyond, Susanna could see into the lofty room at ground level that was Appleton Manor's great hall, but her gaze quickly shifted to the small figure in the foreground.

The child was scarce two years old, but she was fleet of foot and already showed signs of having inherited her father's impetuousness. She wore neither cloak nor gloves to keep the cold at bay. No cap covered her dark tumble of hair.

Susanna reined in. Bold as a pirate captain seizing a prize, Rosamond stared up at her. Dark eyes set in a narrow face marked her as Robert's offspring. Frown lines wrinkled her high forehead, another legacy from her father.

"I not know you," Rosamond declared in a clear, high voice. The frown turned into pout.

Susanna swallowed hard and slid from her saddle to the ground, landing off balance so that she had to grasp the pommel to steady herself.

Rosamond giggled. "You clumsy."

Susanna heard Jennet gasp at the audacious remark but paid no attention. Instead, she knelt next to the child, bringing their faces level. Maternal instincts she'd been certain she did not possess cried out to her to gather Robert's daughter into an embrace.

She resisted the urge.

"Good day to you, Rosamond," she said instead. "You have grown since I saw you last." She had been a newborn at the time but she'd already had those distinctive Appleton eyes. Susanna had never doubted her paternity.

"I not know you," the child repeated.

She wanted Susanna to introduce herself, to give her name. A simple enough task . . . except that Susanna was not sure what their relationship was. "I suppose I am your stepmother," she said, hesitant to make the claim.

Two years earlier, Susanna had acted on impulse, certain she wanted to see as little of Rosamond as possible. She'd packed mother and child off to distant Lancashire and tried her best to forget their existence.

"Lady Appleton. You do us honor." The soft-spoken words were tinged with irony. Eleanor Lowell had emerged from the house and crossed the courtyard to her daughter's side.

"I am pleased to find you at home." Susanna stood. "I ask your pardon for descending upon you without warning, but we have come on a matter of considerable importance."

Like her daughter, Eleanor had dark hair, but her eyes were hazel and her face a perfect oval. Her turned-up nose was the only thing Rosamond seemed to have inherited from her mother. In all else, the girl was pure Appleton.

As the others dismounted, Susanna introduced them to their hostess, careful to give the impression that Bates and Fulke were both manservants.

"Come in out of the cold," Eleanor bade them.

She scooped Rosamond into her arms. The child howled in protest but Eleanor paid no attention to the noise. Carrying her was the most expedient way to get her inside. The moment the door closed behind them, she released the little girl but bent to whisper in her ear. Whatever she said, threat or promise, prevented any immediate display of temper.

The great hall had been modernized during Susanna's last visit to Appleton Manor. It boasted a new fireplace and chimney and had several woven tapestries hanging over cold stone walls to keep the heat from escaping. Pale sunbeams shone through an oriel window to light the dais end of the hall, including the stairs that led to the great chamber above. Eleanor ordered Susanna's belongings taken up the high, curving staircase at the opposite end of the hall, which led to a chamber with its own fireplace.

"Jennet shares my room," Susanna told her. "Fulke and Bates will be comfortable in the lodgings above the stables." Walter, she realized, presented a problem. She glanced at her old friend, then looked again.

Walter stared fixedly at Eleanor Lowell. His face wore a most peculiar expression. Not suspicion, which might be expected.

Something quite different.

Chapter 22

Walter could not stop staring.

This lovely, self-contained creature was Eleanor, the woman who had caused Susanna so much distress?

He knew the surface details of her life. She was older than Alys or Annabel, younger than Constance or Susanna. She'd been born in Westmorland. Her father, a knight possessed of only a small inheritance, had died when she was young. Her mother had remarried and sent Eleanor off to a cousin as soon as she was old enough to enter service. For a period of less than six months, Robert had carried on a dalliance with Eleanor, meeting her in a chamber at the Crowne, an inn situated just beyond the church-yard of St. Botolph-without-Aldgate.

None of those facts had prepared Walter to meet the angel smiling up at him, an invitation in her eyes.

"You must sleep in my chamber, Sir Walter."

His heart tripped at the words, though he was certain she intended no double meaning. Color seeped into his face, something that had not hap-pened since he was a schoolboy. When he looked away from Eleanor in embarrassment, he encoun-tered Susanna's amused and sympathetic gaze.

By God! He did not wish to be pitied!

Eleanor cleared her throat. "You misunderstand me, Sir Walter. Appleton Manor boasts few private chambers. I mean to move, with Rosamond, into the cook's lodgings off the kitchen. You must have the great chamber, as befits your rank."

"A tight squeeze," Susanna commented. "I recall the cook as a woman of ample proportions."

Guilt flashed in Eleanor's eyes before she looked away from Walter to address Susanna. "If you mean Mabel, she is no longer here. She left some time ago, Lady Appleton."

"Who does the cooking?"

"I supervise mine own kitchen."

Walter's sharp eyes moved from face to face. Eleanor looked defensive, her expression betraying concern, even trepidation. Had she had a falling-out with a servant Susanna had hired and sent her away? Or had this Mabel left of her own accord? Either way, Susanna should have been notified, since she paid for the maintenance of this household.

Susanna's countenance gave away less than Eleanor's. Walter could not begin to guess her thoughts. But all Jennet felt was there to be read—suspicion, irritation, exhaustion after the long days of riding. And something more. Relief?

Eleanor forced a smile. "It will take no time at all to move my belongings and Rosamond's." She strode toward the stairs, as if anxious to escape.

"I'll not turn you out of your quarters," Walter protested. "I can use the cook's room. Or sleep here, by the hearth." In bygone days, half the household would have placed their pallets there.

Eleanor allowed herself to be persuaded, then left her guests to their own devices while she devoted her attention to supervising the servants, sending one maid scurrying to fetch fresh bedding and ready sleeping quarters and another to check the food supply.

A delightful woman, Walter thought as he watched her bustle out of the hall. Her soft voice drifted back to him, giving instructions for the preparation of a hearty evening meal.

She was not conniving like Alys, nor duplicitous like Annabel. She must have seemed a heaven-sent respite to Robert, until he found out about the child.

At the thought of his old friend's by-blow, Walter stopped staring at the mother and searched the hall for the daughter. To his surprise, he discovered Susanna once more crouched beside the girl, this time in the rushes before the hearth. From her earnest expression, she was attempting conversation with the child.

Walter could not make out their murmured words, though it looked to him as if Rosamond was doing most of the talking. He'd not had much to do with children, but she seemed an unusual child, bolder and more articulate than most girls twice her age. The combination was jarring.

When Rosamond scampered off in the direction of the kitchen, Susanna glanced up and caught

Walter staring. "I cannot tell what she thinks of me. Are all children so difficult to comprehend?"

Walter was at a loss to answer, but Jennet had experience aplenty to draw upon. Three little ones, Walter recalled. The youngest must be about the same age as Rosamond.

"Treat her like a small adult," Jennet advised. "Ignore any tantrums. She is too young to always make sense but old enough to prattle on and on, well pleased with the sound of her own voice. A most vexing combination. If you want her to like you, you have only to offer her bribes."

Susanna looked stricken. "I should have thought to bring her a present."

Once again, Jennet came to the rescue, producing a square of cloth. A knot here and a fold there turned the handkerchief into a poppet.

Delighted, Susanna went off in search of Robert's daughter. "We will postpone both questions and revelations until the little one is asleep," she said as she went past Walter.

"Certes," he called after her. But he did not understand her sudden fascination with the little girl and fervently hoped the child would be fed and put to bed early.

His wish was granted. It seemed that Rosamond's mother was a sensible woman as well as a beautiful one. Her manner with her little girl was firm and direct. She put up with no nonsense.

At supper, Walter sat between Eleanor and Susanna at the elegant refectory table on the dais.

The repast was modest but skillfully prepared. It was plain Eleanor knew a thing or two about cooking. He'd suspected as much when he'd stepped into the kitchen earlier and found her roasting a chine of beef, a loin of pork, a dove, and a chicken, all at one fire.

The pork, basted with sweet butter, was tender and delicious, the chicken superbly seasoned with a sauce made of onions, claret wine, lemon peel, and the juice of an orange. Where she'd gotten such things in winter, he did not ask, but he assumed the funds Susanna allotted for provisioning the manor were in accord with her usual generosity. He was not surprised that she wanted her husband's daughter to have the best.

When the ginger cake had been served and more wine poured, Eleanor was the one who shifted their conversation away from insubstantial banter. "No one travels for pleasure at this time of year," she said. "Did some particular reason prompt you to pay a visit in winter?"

"We came to discuss Robert," Susanna said.

Alert for any indication Eleanor was aware of what had occurred a few weeks earlier in London, Walter watched her carefully.

"Robert is dead," Eleanor protested.

"How did he die?" Walter asked. If she was innocent, she'd answer "of the plague."

Eleanor started to speak, then caught herself. Confusion reigned on her delicate features, making Walter wonder if she thought Robert dead because she'd been told he died in France, or because she'd had a hand in his recent murder.

"You wrote to me, Lady Appleton," Eleanor said at last. "You said he was dead but you promised I could go on living here with Rosamond. You promised." Her voice went breathy with emotion on the last two words.

"Robert is indeed dead," Susanna assured her, "but his demise was much more recent than you suppose. For the last eighteen months, he was still alive, although his movements were unknown to us. Was he here during any of that time?"

Eleanor's eyes widened at the question, but this time her hesitation lasted no longer than a heartbeat before she denied it. Her voice dropped to a tremulous whisper. "He's dead now? You're certain?"

"Aye," Susanna said. "In London, on the third day of January. I saw him die. There is no mistake this time."

Something was wrong here, Walter thought. Eleanor was distressed, but not in the way someone who'd lost a loved one would be. Her face was pale as snow. She twisted agitated hands together in her lap, indicating to him that strong emotions were at work. But he was uncertain which ones. Fear? Guilt? Was she lying to them? Had she believed Robert was still alive? Or had she known already that he'd been killed in London?

Walter held his silence and let Susanna explain that she'd come to Appleton Manor in the hope

148

of tracing Robert's movements. She omitted the fact that Robert had been poisoned and did not mention that she had been accused of the crime.

"I would help you if I could." Eleanor did not ask what had caused Robert's death. Because she did not care? Or because she already knew the answer?

Walter had trained himself to be suspicious of everyone, to dissect every word he heard uttered, but when Susanna did not press Eleanor to answer questions, Walter was glad to follow her lead. For the moment, they let the subject drop. When Susanna asked instead about Rosamond, Walter stopped listening.

The permanent residents of Appleton Manor were accustomed to country hours and retired early. The travelers did likewise, exhausted after so many long days in the saddle. Walter settled himself on the pallet in front of the hearth in the great hall expecting to fall instantly asleep, but mind and body conspired to betray him. Eleanor's image crept into his consciousness.

Walter sat up, appalled by the direction of his thoughts. How could he have such a strong reaction to Eleanor Lowell? She was Robert's cast-off mistress. She had borne his child. She might even be a murderer.

None of those things seemed to matter. He desired her.

Walter beat his pillow into shape, wrapped his blanket more tightly around himself, and vowed to think of something else, to focus on anything but the way Eleanor Lowell stirred his blood and provoked inconveniently lustful thoughts. Two weeks earlier, he'd wanted to marry Susanna, loved her. It was disloyal to want another woman so soon.

But he did.

His body paid no mind to his conscience.

At length, Walter fell into a restless sleep. It seemed to him that he'd only just closed his eyes when he opened them again to see someone creeping down the stairs in the early morning gloom.

Eleanor.

Telling himself this was an ideal time to question a suspect, he added breeches and doublet to the shirt and hose he'd slept in and followed her into the kitchen.

She knelt by the hearth, stirring embers she'd preserved in a pottery fire cover, bringing them back to life. He moved closer, until her perfume, sweet marjoram, one of his favorite scents, began to scramble thought processes that had always before functioned in a rational and orderly manner. His intention to interrogate her forgotten, he asked, "Will you share a morning cup of ale with me?"

"I have too much work to do, Sir Walter." She would not look at him after her first, startled glance. "You must realize that your arrival nearly doubled the size of this household."

When the fire had been restored and she'd

hung a pot of water over it to boil, Eleanor left the kitchen, rolling up her sleeves as she went. She came back a moment later bringing ale for him to break his night's fast. Then she fetched ground meal and a container of ale barm and, ignoring him, began to make bread, first bolting wheat meal through a fine bolting cloth, then dumping it into a waist-high wooden trough secured to a thick, short-legged stand.

Walter sipped his ale, watching in silence while she warmed the ale barm then poured it into the hollow she'd made in the flour. When she'd added salt, she plunged both hands into the meal and began to knead.

He found the process surprisingly sensual. "Have you no servants to make the bread?"

"They have other duties. One maid is milking, the other gathering eggs."

"Then let me help."

Eleanor stopped molding and shaping to stare at him. "You? Bake bread?"

"Why not? Am I so useless?" The thought of plunging his hands into the malleable dough tantalized him and made him think of other soft things he might enjoy kneading.

"You are . . . an important personage."

Her tone of voice snapped him out of his trance. Just what, he wondered, did she mean by that? It had not sounded like a compliment.

"Have you finished so soon?" he asked when she left off kneading and wiped her hands on her apron.

"For the nonce." She closed a wooden lid over the trough and piled warmed sacks on top. "The dough must lie here an hour to swell before I take it forth and shape it into manchets. And they must rise again before they are baked."

An oven, which had yet to be fired, had been built into the wall next to the hearth. Faggots of furze and blackthorn, tied in bundles, had been stacked nearby. If they were kept extremely dry, they would burn fast and intense, as was necessary for baking bread.

Eleanor moved on to her next task, selecting the whitest and youngest bacon in her larder and cutting away the sward. She sliced the collops thin, placed them in a dish, and poured hot water over them. "They must stand thus an hour or two," she explained, "or you will taste naught but salt."

"What did you see in him?" Walter's abrupt question escaped before he could stop it.

Accepting the sudden change of subject, Eleanor turned slowly toward him, bracing her back against the stonework by the hearth."You are blunt, Sir Walter."

She looked so troubled that he had to fight a nearly overwhelming urge to offer comfort, to take her in his arms and assure her all would be well if she'd just tell him the truth.

But then, instead of answering his question, she posed one of her own. "Why did Lady Appleton believe Robert came here?"

"This was his childhood home."

"He hated it here."

"How do you know that?"

Closing her eyes, Eleanor gave a sad little sigh. "I know a great deal about Robert Appleton. I even knew he did not die in France. I . . . heard from him after Lady Appleton wrote to tell me he'd succumbed to the plague. He sent me a letter."

"He wrote to you to say he was still alive?" That spoke of less caution than Robert was accustomed to use, but a woman like Eleanor might well have that effect on a man.

"I thought he might mean to make some provision for his daughter," Eleanor continued. "He knew I was here with her. I had no desire to see him. You must believe that." She gave a short, bitter laugh. "I'd learned he was not to be trusted. I had no wish to be deceived again."

Walter moved closer, keeping his voice gentle. "How did he deceive you?" Part of him did not want to hear her answer. He had to remind himself that this was why they'd come to Appleton Manor. To question Eleanor. To find out all she knew and if she had a motive for murder.

Eleanor sighed again, more deeply this time. Her eyes were open but averted from his. "I met Robert some three years ago, when I accompanied my cousin to court. She wanted an audience with the queen."

"You were her waiting gentlewoman," Walter recalled.

"She treated me more like a slave." Again, he

153

heard the bitterness, but she did not dwell on her treatment in that household. "Robert offered me an alternative. He made promises. A house of my own. Even marriage. By the time I discovered there was already a Lady Appleton, I was with child."

"You did not tell him." Walter knew Susanna had been the one to break that news to her husband. "Why not?"

"Pride, I suppose. I was far enough along by the time he left England that he should have noticed the changes for himself. He did not." She stirred the fire, her gaze fixed on the flames. Walter could not guess what she was thinking.

"He brought disgrace upon you. You must have hated him for that."

But she shook her head. "I do not blame him for anything, but neither do I mourn him. I brought disgrace upon myself. I met Robert at a moment in my life when I was desperate enough to do anything to break free of the constraints forced upon me by my situation. I have had a good deal of time to think since then. I am the one at fault for what happened."

Had she met him instead of Robert, matters would have turned out differently. The thought came out of nowhere, startling Walter. He shoved it away before it could breed more like it.

"How did you manage after he left? Robert was sent to Spain. You vanished from London soon after." Her cousin, an unpleasant individual of advanced years, still had no idea what had happened to Eleanor. She'd told Walter's agent that she had no further interest in her wayward young relative.

"Robert gave me a purse, a generous gift of gold coins. He said he would come to me when he returned, but he would not tell me where he was bound or how long he would be away, so I put little faith in his promises. I left my cousin's house the next day. She suspected my condition. If I had not gone on my own, she'd soon have thrown me out."

"Where did you go?" Walter moved close enough to inhale her scent, his admiration for her growing with every new detail she supplied.

"I lived a simple life in a small town just outside London. Until Rosamond was born, I thought I might manage on my own. I prided myself on being frugal. Then the bulk of the money Robert had given me was stolen. I sold other presents he'd given me, but those funds did not last long. I soon realized I had only two choices. I could seek a new protector, becoming dependent upon another man, or I could throw myself on Lady Appleton's mercy."

"You made the right decision." Walter reached out and caught her hand, giving it an encouraging squeeze.

Eleanor's gaze dropped to their joined fingers, and she frowned. As if she feared allowing the intimacy might be misinterpreted, she pulled free. "Robert taught me many valuable lessons."

"I am certain he did. When did you last see him, Eleanor?"

"Before Rosamond was born."

Walter wanted to believe her. That worried him. It was not in his nature to so thoroughly lose his objectivity, out of character for him to be influenced by a soft voice and a beautiful face.

He should inform her Robert had been murdered. She thought they'd come to Appleton Manor only to try to account for his whereabouts during the last year and a half. She did not know that Susanna believed one of Robert's mistresses had poisoned him or that Susanna would have to stand trial for murder if she could not prove her own innocence.

But Walter was unable to decide what to say to Eleanor. He felt a coward's relief when her two maidservants interrupted them by arriving in the kitchen to take up their morning chores. As soon as Eleanor was distracted by their chatter, he slipped away.

Chapter 23

Jennet was not happy.

It should have been a simple task to pry information out of Blanche and Lettice, the two maid-servants employed at Appleton Manor. Jennet had once held the post of housekeeper here, for more than a year. During that same time, Mark had served as steward. Their first child had been born in the chamber in which Eleanor Lowell now slept.

"None of the servants I supervised are still in service at Appleton Manor," she reported to Lady Appleton. "All of those here were hired less than a year ago."

"She does not keep very many servants," Lady Appleton observed.

"Only four live in." Jennet finished untangling her mistress's long, thick hair and returned the mother-of-pearl inlaid comb to the top of the little table that held the Venetian mirror. "Two maids, a manservant, and the groom." The current steward, who also oversaw neighboring Denholm Hall, lived there with his family.

Jennet held up a clean bodice already loosely joined to a stomacher stiffened with wooden busks. Lady Appleton stood still while Jennet dropped the garment over her head, took a moment to readjust the ankle-length chemise beneath, then held her arms out to the sides so that Jennet could tighten and tie the ribbons that held the pieces together.

"Did anyone know where Mabel went?"

Jennet was glad Lady Appleton could not see her face. She had not asked. Mabel Hussey, who had been both cook and housekeeper before Lady Appleton's first visit to Lancashire, had been the bane of Jennet's existence throughout her tenure at Appleton Manor. The two women had clashed over every detail of running the household and although Jennet had been the one Lady Appleton left in charge, Mabel had resisted all Jennet's attempts to drive her away. She'd taken unholy delight in staying on as cook after Lady Appleton returned to Leigh Abbey. She'd known Jennet wanted her gone and refused to cooperate just to torment her.

Why, then, would she have let Eleanor send her packing?

"I do not know where Mabel is." It was the simple truth.

"Did you ask if Eleanor was here throughout Yuletide?"

"Aye, I did. They claim she was, but they also showed all those signs of nervousness you told me to watch for—eyes shifting away, fiddling with skirts and aprons, a hesitation before answering."

By the time Jennet finished giving a full account of her conversation with the maids, most of the details so trivial as to be useless, Lady Appleton was fully dressed and ready to begin her day.

"They may be telling the truth about Eleanor's presence in Lancashire," she said. "It is possible their nervousness stems from another cause. A pilfered bit of food from the pantry or some similar minor offense."

"She may have paid them to lie. Or threatened them if they did not."

"You do not care for Eleanor, do you, Jennet? What do her servants think of her?"

Jennet had deliberately saved one damning bit of information until the end of her account. "According to Blanche, the dairy maid, two different male guests have stayed here during the past year."

Bundling her unruly hair into a caul, Lady Appleton handed Jennet a French hood to arrange over it. "You think one of them could have been Robert?"

"Aye, and since none of these servants were at Appleton Manor five years ago, when Sir Robert last visited here, none of them could have recognized him."

"Did the maids give you names?"

Jennet nodded. "Aye. One I recognize and one I do not."

"Names can be assumed." She sounded calm, but Jennet sensed she had Lady Appleton's full attention.

"John Secole was one name. He lived here nigh onto six months and left during this past summer."

"What appearance had he?"

"Dark haired. Bearded."

Lady Appleton fingered a small, jeweled case she wore as a pendant. Inside was a miniature of Sir Robert. Like most portraits Jennet had seen, it had features so stylized as to make the subject almost unrecognizable. The man painted in little with beard and mustache could as easily be mistaken for Sir Walter or Lord Robin as Sir Robert.

The sound of a horseman approaching drew Jennet to the window. She was unsurprised to recognize the rider.

"What is he doing here?" Lady Appleton asked, coming up behind Jennet to stare down into the courtyard.

The shutters had been opened at dawn to let in the bright winter sun, but the light was accompanied by eddies of cold air coming in around the leaded panes.

As they watched, Eleanor Lowell, cloaked and hooded, emerged to greet her visitor. "Never tell me Master Grimshaw is her other suitor," Lady Appleton whispered.

"Both before and after the mysterious Master Secole." Jennet relished the moment. It was rare anyone could confound Lady Appleton.

Matthew Grimshaw had changed little in the years since Jennet had last seen him. Tall and gaunt, he was almost bald, with small dark eyes, no beard, and a long, pinched face.

As if he sensed he was being watched, he glanced nervously up at the house. Lady Appleton drew back from the window, pulling Jennet with her. She was limping, Jennet noticed. The leg she'd injured five years earlier still pained her when the weather was as cold and damp as it was this morning.

"Matthew Grimshaw," she muttered, shaking her head. "I thought Eleanor had better taste in men. After Robert, even with all his faults . . . Grimshaw?"

"He has been a regular visitor since she arrived here. Blanche thinks he wants to marry her mistress. Lettice is sure Eleanor has ruined her chance to become Mistress Grimshaw by granting him her favors before marriage."

"I wonder if she sent for him when we arrived?"

"She may have had no need to. He is in the habit of paying regular visits."

Jennet was more curious about Grimshaw's opinion of Rosamond. He'd had naught but unkind things to say to her when she'd given birth to Susan. Master Grimshaw's meddling opinion had been that servants should neither marry nor have children, since a family might interfere with the efficient performance of household duties.

Lady Appleton had returned to the window and surprised Jennet by chuckling. "Our stay here will not lack drama," she remarked.

Jennet peeked out. Sir Walter had joined the two figures in the courtyard. "What do you mean? Does Sir Walter already know Master Grimshaw? Are they old enemies?"

"Say rather that they are new rivals. I vow, Jennet, every time Eleanor and Walter looked at each other last night, I could almost see the air heat in the space between them. It is possible neither has yet acknowledged the attraction, but it is only a matter of time before they must."

"Eleanor Lowell and . . . Sir Walter! But, madam, how can you sound so pleased?"

"I want my old friend to be happy."

"He would be happy with you."

"You know I never intend to remarry."

"But he does not believe you when you say so. He hopes to persuade you to become Lady Pendennis one day. I know he does." And of all the gentlemen Jennet had met, she thought none so fit as Sir Walter to teach Lady Appleton the joys of marriage.

"He believes me now." Lady Appleton made Jennet sit on the window seat beside her. "Sir Walter asked me to become his wife before we left Leigh Abbey. I refused him."

"Faith, he's quick to shift his interest!" Jennet glanced again into the courtyard.

"Eleanor might suit him well, always assuming she did not kill Robert."

But Jennet could not share her mistress's sentiment. In truth, this unexpected development left her feeling most uneasy.

Chapter 24

Susanna's first full day at Appleton Manor was hectic but satisfying. Pretending to believe Matthew Grimshaw had come to pay his respects to her, she questioned him about several matters of business he'd attended to for her during the previous two years.

She did not mention Robert.

Neither did Grimshaw.

When Grimshaw left, Walter joined her. Ill at ease, he reported that Eleanor had admitted to knowing Robert had not died in France. She'd received a letter from him but denied any other contact.

After dinner, a quiet meal during which no one seemed to feel much like talking, Susanna closeted herself with her steward, then interviewed each of the servants. By the time she dismissed the dairy maid, she was in need of solitude. She sought it in the stillroom.

The changes Eleanor had made there suggested she had little interest in medicinal herbs. Curious, Susanna began to explore. She found only a few common remedies, stored in stoppered pots and small vials. Horehound drops for coughs. A salve made of saffron, lettuce seed, white poppy seed, and woman's milk to induce sleep. A small ceramic container bore the label, "for hemorrhoids." Removing the thin skin tied over its mouth, which appeared to be coming loose, Susanna sniffed, then eyed the mixture inside. At a guess, it contained dill, dog fennel, and pellitory of Spain, beaten with sheep's suet and black soap.

Most of the space in the stillroom was filled with the tub Eleanor used to cool down vaporized infusions and the results of this process, all in neatly labelled bottles—water of wormwood, water of strawberry, lavender water, even orange water. Several jars contained rose petals steeped in salt, which formed an aromatic paste that would eventually be made into rose water.

Susanna found evidence that Eleanor also used the stillroom when she made vinegars and pickles and jams and jellies. Glass basins, tumblers, and salvers, sweetmeat and syllabub glasses, tin biscuit pans, and a copper preserving pan had been added to the utensils she had installed five years earlier, the copper pot for boiling ingredients for cordials, a pair of brass scales and weights, and the cone-shaped pewter alembic. A layer of dust covered the latter.

"I overheard them talking," Jennet announced from the doorway.

"Eleanor and Grimshaw?" Susanna retied the cover of the salve pot and returned it to the niche where she'd found it.

"Aye."

Susanna knew she should not encourage Jennet to eavesdrop but her ability to listen in on other people's conversations often proved useful. "Close the door behind you and tell me what you learned."

"Most of what they said was in whispers and I could not make out any words. But then they stood right in front of the place where I was hiding and I heard Eleanor say that she expects her daughter to inherit Appleton Manor." Jennet looked outraged at the idea.

"A not unreasonable hope. Rosamond is Robert's only child." Susanna had anticipated Eleanor's desire for an inheritance for the girl. It seemed natural that a mother would be concerned about her two-year-old's welfare.

"She is a bastard. A by-blow. A merrybegot."

"Robert's child, all the same."

Stiffening at the reprimand in Susanna's sharp tone, Jennet was quick to shift the thrust of her dislike from Rosamond to Eleanor. "If the daughter inherits, the mother also profits."

"Meaning?"

"The maidservants tell me that Rosamond has, for the most part, been in the care of a woman called Nurse Bond. Her mother ignores her."

"A wet nurse?" It was not uncommon for a gentlewoman to employ one. Jennet, Susanna recalled, had done so herself for her third child, so that she might live in London with Susanna while the baby remained at Leigh Abbey with Mark.

"Nurse Bond moved here to Appleton Manor after her own babe died. She was in residence, using the chamber we now occupy for herself and the child, until two months ago, staying on even after Rosamond was weaned. Then she went off with mother and child on a trip to Manchester, and they came back without her. The maids say Mistress Rosamond cried for her nurse for weeks afterward. Doubtless she found her mother's inattention a poor substitute."

Years of experience with Jennet's vivid imagination told Susanna what she was thinking. She was wondering if the wet nurse had seen something she should not have and been disposed of to keep her from telling anyone about it.

Susanna agreed it was peculiar that Eleanor did not seem to keep servants long. "I know where Mabel is," she told Jennet. "It was no great mystery. She moved to Denholm Hall to cook for the steward's family."

"Then why did Eleanor not say so?" Jennet sounded more suspicious than ever. "She did not want us to question Mabel. That is why."

"Is it not possible Eleanor just found Mabel difficult to deal with? As you did, Jennet?" She did not allow time for a reply. "No matter. We will find out the truth of it when we talk to Mabel."

But any visit to Denholm Hall would have to wait until the next day. Dusk came early at this time of year and was already upon them.

★ ★ ★

Matthew Grimshaw joined them at supper that evening. Since Eleanor seemed pleased to have his

166

company, Susanna made an effort to be civil to the man, though his conversation bored her to tears. She supposed she could tolerate him for the duration of one meal and an evening's entertainment.

"I've told Matthew why you are here," Eleanor announced when the first course had been served.

"Excellent." She'd expected this. No doubt that had been the part of their conversation Jennet had not been able to overhear.

"You might have mentioned your suspicions when we spoke this morning," Grimshaw chided her.

"I was certain you would volunteer the information if you'd had recent contact with Robert." Besides, since the direct approach had not produced useful results, she'd thought to try a new technique. Instead of blurting everything out, she'd waited to hear what Grimshaw had to say.

He'd said nothing then. He said nothing now.

Susanna contained a sigh.

"Did Sir Robert Appleton contact you at any time during the last eighteen months?" Walter asked. "Write to you? Visit you? Make demands on you?"

"I've had naught to do with Sir Robert for years," Grimshaw declared. "He had no reason to write to me. It has always been Lady Appleton who managed estate business."

"That is true enough." Robert had not cared for the man and the feeling had been mutual, even though Robert had once done Grimshaw a great favor. He had kept silent about certain matters that, if widely known, might have cost Grimshaw his commission as a justice of the peace.

Thinking of events five years past, Susanna reached for a bit of mutton from the trencher she shared with Walter. Eleanor was paired with Grimshaw.

"I do wonder . . . ." Grimshaw's words trailed off, as if he'd changed his mind about sharing his concern.

"Speak up, man." Walter sounded out of temper. "If you know something of Robert Appleton, then tell us."

Fussing with his napkin, the lawyer hesitated. Weighing his words, no doubt. Susanna could not fault his sense of caution. "You will forgive me, Lady Appleton, if this subject is painful to you, but may I ask how Sir Robert died?" Her hesitation produced an unexpectedly sharp look from Grimshaw. "Was he, perhaps, murdered?"

"What makes you think so, Master Grimshaw?" Walter asked.

"Why, the very fact that you do not wish to answer my question."

"He was poisoned," Susanna said.

"Indeed? By whom?"

"That is something I intend to find out, Master Grimshaw. No doubt something Robert did during the last months of his life led to his death. That is why we are attempting to retrace his steps."

"I do not know why you think he came here," Grimshaw grumbled. "This would be the last place he'd show his face, saving only Leigh Abbey. Too many people hereabout could recognize him."

"So you might think, but my husband had some small skill with disguise."

She decided not to mention Master Secole just yet. She wanted to talk to Mabel first. Then she would broach the subject of her visitor with Eleanor. Time enough to get the lawyer's reaction later.

"Sir Robert was an intelligence gatherer for the Crown," Eleanor said into the small silence that had fallen among those seated at the table on the dais.

Everyone turned to look at her.

"He told you that?" Walter sounded shocked.

She met his gaze and Susanna saw again the sparks she'd witnessed the previous evening. "Aye, and some few things about those he worked with, too."

"I thought he refused to reveal his destination when he was about to leave for Spain. Did you not tell me that you did not know if he would come back?"

"I did not mean to imply that he told me nothing, Sir Walter. Early in our acquaintance, when I confessed to him that his insistence on secrecy made me fear he was involved in something criminal, he reassured me by explaining that he often undertook secret missions at the queen's behest.

He mentioned your name, Sir Walter, as one of his fellows."

Interesting, Susanna thought. Was it possible Walter's arrival at Appleton Manor had upset Eleanor more than the sudden appearance of her lover's widow? Had Eleanor's initial denial of any knowledge that Robert was alive been an attempt to protect herself? If she'd once suspected Robert of being involved in illegal activities, it was not so far-fetched to imagine she might fear so again. Had she worried that admitting she knew he was not dead would lead to her own arrest? For all Susanna knew, Eleanor had jumped to the conclusion that Walter was at Appleton Manor to accuse her of treason.

Matthew Grimshaw cleared his throat. "Whatever he was in life, Lady Appleton, if your husband was poisoned, it follows that you must be suspected of murdering him. You were an expert on poisonous herbs five years ago. No doubt you know even more ways to kill a man now."

"Matthew!"

"Be careful what you say, Eleanor. She is here to find a scapegoat. If she can convince the authorities that Sir Robert spent time at Appleton Manor, she will attempt to build a case against you. She will say that something he did while he was here prompted you to follow him to London and kill him."

"But I did not." Eleanor turned to Walter. "Is this true? Is that why you came here?"

"We are investigating everyone connected to Sir Robert."

Reaching for Grimshaw's hand, drawing on his presence for strength, Eleanor glared at both Walter and Susanna. "I did not go to London. I did not kill Robert. If you will not take my word for it, then ask my servants. They will swear I have not left this place in months."

"I can vouch for her, as well. I was a guest here at Appleton Manor during Yuletide." Grimshaw's attitude was protective toward Eleanor, making Walter glower.

Susanna was a trifle surprised by Grimshaw's staunch support. In the past, she'd felt he lacked backbone. He'd always been easy to browbeat. A stronger man would never have put himself in a position to be manipulated by Robert. She had herself coerced him into drawing up certain legal documents, even though he disapproved most heartily of their contents.

"Was he here throughout the holidays?" Walter directed his question at Eleanor, but she was not looking at him.

"Matthew, it is not necessary—"

"Hush, my dear." He patted her hand, then addressed Walter. "You need not take my word for it. Call in the servants. Ask them."

It was time to resume control of the situation, Susanna decided. She stood, drawing everyone's gaze to her, and gestured for Eleanor's manservant to come forward. Every word spoken at the table on the dais had been overheard by the others in the hall, not only those serving the food, but also Fulke and Jennet. And Bernard Bates, who sat with the two of them at the lower table, a constant reminder of what Susanna's fate would be if she did not succeed in finding Robert's killer.

"Leek, is it not?" Susanna had met him earlier in the day. She'd questioned him then, as she had all the other servants, about Eleanor's whereabouts during Yuletide, but she had not thought to ask about Grimshaw.

"Aye, madam." He looked terrified.

She smiled to reassure him. "All I want is the truth, Leek. Was Mistress Lowell at home throughout the holidays?"

"Oh, aye, Lady Appleton." The man stumbled all over his words in his eagerness to reassure her. "And Master Grimshaw did come to visit, just as he's said."

"On what days was he here?"

A frantic blinking answered her. "What days?"

"On what day or days was Master Grimshaw at Appleton Manor?"

"I do not remem— Oh! I do remember. 'Twas Twelfth Night. Yes, it was. Was it not, Master Grimshaw?"

And so it went. One by one, Susanna called the servants in. One by one, they confirmed what Eleanor had said and agreed that Grimshaw had visited Appleton Manor. With Grimshaw glaring at them, they were nervous about answering, but

172

Susanna had seen this reaction before. Grimshaw might be easily cowed by his betters, but he had a tendency to bully servants and anyone else he considered his inferior. In the end, there could be no doubt. It was impossible for Eleanor to have been in London when Robert was murdered.

"Can you have any doubt now?" Grimshaw demanded when the groom of the stable had added his account to those of the others. "You have Eleanor's word. You have the servants' corroboration. And my presence confirms her presence here during the crucial period."

"Matthew," Eleanor objected. "There is no need to defend me so fiercely. I am innocent of poisoning Sir Robert."

Susanna sighed. She believed Eleanor. And because she did, her prospects looked that much more bleak. It did not reassure her to glance up and once again meet Bates's implacable gaze. Unless she made some progress in her investigation, he would soon be escorting her back to Newgate.

★ ★ ★

Early the next morning, Susanna and Jennet set out for Denholm Hall. Jennet rode apillion behind the ever-present Bernard Bates.

Catherine's childhood home had changed little since Susanna had last seen it, but its atmosphere was much improved, enlivened by the presence of the steward's merry wife and a half dozen children.

Mabel Hussey had seen more than fifty summers and begun to show her age. Her once fair hair was streaked with white. Her face had gone from being round and rosy-cheeked to fleshy, the bags beneath her eyes giving her the look of a sorrowful hound. Her hearty laugh remained unchanged. She greeted both of them like long-lost kin, embracing first Jennet, then Susanna.

Crushed to Mabel's ample bosom, Susanna felt truly welcome for the first time since coming north. Meaty hands seized her shoulders to hold her a little apart and look at her. "'Tis glad I am to see ye, madam," she declared.

"I am glad to see you, too, Mabel. And delighted to find you so near at hand."

"Who's he?" she demanded, giving Bates a considering look.

"He's come to inspect the dovecotes," Susanna told her. She'd already bribed him to go off with the steward so that she and Jennet might speak with Mabel in private.

A short time later, when they were seated around the kitchen worktable on high stools, cups of perry in hand and a plate of Mabel's famous gooseberry tarts in front of them, Susanna asked the cook why she'd left her post at Appleton Manor.

Mabel gave a snort. She never troubled to hide her feelings. Her answer was blunt and forthright. "She were up to no good with that John Secole."

"And you disapproved?" Susanna hid a smile

174

with her cup. What she knew of Mabel's youthful adventures seemed to argue against the notion of prudery.

"There be a young girl child in that house."

"You were concerned for Rosamond?"

"I do remember me what Sir George got up to," she said in ominous tones. "And Secole did watch the girl. Stared at her sometimes, though to be fair 'twas not often he'd go near her."

Robert's father, Sir George, had developed a fondness for young women in his later years. Very young women. "Rosamond is a mere baby," Susanna pointed out.

"He were odd, this Secole." Mabel drained her cup and poured more perry into it from the jug.

"Odd how?"

"Skulked about. I never did get me a good look at his face, and that be the Lord's own truth."

"So he might have been disguised?" Unable to contain her excitement any longer, Jennet blurted out the question. "Could he have been someone you knew?"

"Could Secole have been Sir Robert?" Susanna saw no point in hiding their suspicions. Interrupted by the cook's frequent questions, she told Mabel the surface facts of Robert's three deaths and explained her present dilemma.

Unfortunately, Mabel had never gotten close enough to the mysterious Secole to have more than a vague impression of his appearance.

"He come in November," Mabel recalled.

175

Five months after Robert's death by drowning in the Solent, Susanna thought. "Was Master Grimshaw a regular visitor to Appleton Manor by then?"

"Aye. Took him but one look at Mistress Eleanor to be smitten."

"How did she react to him?"

"Encouraged him. 'Twould be a proper match."

"Encouraged how?"

"The way any sensible woman does," Mabel said. "Give a bit. Promise more. Hold back enough to make him offer what she wants."

"Did he stay at Appleton Manor overnight?"

"A time or two, but there were no harm in it. I were there to make it respectable." Mabel grinned, showing all her big yellow teeth.

"Did the two men ever meet?" Susanna asked. "Secole and Grimshaw?"

Mabel shook her head. "I do not think so. Mistress Eleanor took care that they should not. But, then, I left while Secole still lived at Appleton Manor. Could be they met afterward."

"When did Secole leave?"

"He were gone by the last midsummer."

Some seven months past, Susanna calculated. Plenty of time to journey to London . . . or just about anywhere else.

"That Lettice, one of the new maids, told the steward's wife that Secole went to sea."

"Was he a mariner then? Or a ship's captain?" It was difficult to imagine mistaking Robert for a lowly sailor, but seemed even less likely that Eleanor would take a real one into her bed.

"What of Matthew Grimshaw?" she asked when it appeared Mabel could not tell them any more about Secole. "When did he resume his courtship of Eleanor?"

"Why, as soon as Secole were gone," Mabel said. She chuckled. "So soon after that there were talk he'd paid to have Secole pressed into service on a ship bound for the Indies. He may never have met the man, but I wager he knew about him and were not pleased to have him living at Appleton Manor with Mistress Eleanor."

Susanna rode back to Appleton Manor in thoughtful silence. When she learned Grimshaw had gone back to Manchester, she decided it was time to have a talk with Eleanor. A short time later, the two women met in the upstairs chamber Eleanor had assigned to Susanna.

"Have you been happy here, Eleanor?" Susanna gestured for her to take the room's single chair.

"Why, yes, Lady Appleton. Most happy." She did not sit. She looked flustered, but she had already been agitated before Susanna asked to speak with her. Not surprising, after the discussion at last night's supper table.

"You treat this house as if it were your own," Susanna observed.

Eleanor did not reply, but Susanna sensed no guilt in her.

"Tell me about Master Secole."

One hand, straying to her throat, betrayed Eleanor's sudden alarm, but although she might have been startled by Susanna's knowledge, she was quick to regain control of herself. "That gentleman visited me here some time ago."

"And who is he?"

"A friend. An old friend." Eleanor did not meet Susanna's eyes. "John Secole is the youngest son of a gentleman of Westmorland. As children we were neighbors."

"How did he know you were in Lancashire?"

"A chance meeting in Manchester."

"And you invited him to stay here with you?"

"Good country folk keep open house," she reminded Susanna in a prim voice.

"Not for seven months."

"I took pity on an old friend, Lady Appleton. He was down on his luck."

"And where is this old friend now?"

"Halfway to Muscovy to earn his fortune, or so I suppose."

Muscovy? Susanna had not expected that answer but was pleased by it. Master Baldwin, her neighbor in Kent, had many contacts within the Muscovy Company. If Eleanor was telling the truth, Baldwin could verify it.

Silence lengthened between them, a deliberate ploy on Susanna's part. Eleanor fidgeted, went still, then at last burst into nervous speech. "I do not wish to cause Master Secole any trouble. I took him in without your permission, Lady Appleton, and I am sorry for it, but that was not his fault."

"And you sent old servants away. Mabel is under the impression she chose to leave, but I suspect she was subtly encouraged to do so. Why, Eleanor?"

"I . . . I do not know what you mean."

"Your actions make perfect sense, if John Secole was really Robert Appleton."

Color swept into her face. "I . . . no."

"No?"

Eleanor advanced across the chamber until she stood face to face with Susanna and only an arm's length apart. "Lady Appleton," she said, "I learned several hard lessons from your husband, the first of which was to trust no one. The second was to depend only on myself. If you mean to expel me and Rosamond from this place, then say so. I will accept Matthew's offer of marriage and move to Manchester."

"I'd not wish that fate on anyone."

"You have no right to judge me."

"I do have an interest in your daughter's future."

"Do you want her? Take her! I know well enough that I am not cut out for motherhood. I have no patience for the task."

"I suspect I would have had much the same reaction to a child," Susanna admitted. "I am told the first few years are passing difficult, although I must confess I find Rosamond most interesting."

"You were not here all day to hear her fuss and

wail. Her tantrums were what drove Matthew back to Manchester."

"A useful talent."

"Spare me your sarcasm, Lady Appleton. The child is wilful, with the devil's own temperament."

"Or her father's?"

"I have seen how you watch your husband's child."

"Indeed?"

"You envy me. Resent me. Because of her."

"Perhaps," Susanna agreed, chagrined that although she'd gone out of her way not to seem jealous of the other woman, something of her feelings had leaked through.

Take Rosamond? The idea tempted her, but she had no wish to separate mother and child, and no desire to make Eleanor part of her permanent household.

She supposed she did begrudge Eleanor Robert's child. By rights, she ought to much dislike both Eleanor and Rosamond. After all, the little girl was nothing so much as a living reminder that Susanna had failed in her duty as a wife. She had been unable to give Robert a legitimate heir.

Chapter 25

Holyrood Palace
January 29, 1565

Catherine attempted to be objective as she watched Annabel MacReynolds cross Queen Mary's hall toward her. She'd had twelve days to brood about her friendship with Annabel, to wonder if the Scotswoman's warmth and charm might have fooled her into seeing affection where only political advantage existed. Had she been taken in by flattery? She did not like to think so.

But Catherine had grown up in the remote Lancashire countryside, living at Denholm Hall with only her irascible mother and the maids for company. In Lady Appleton's household in Kent, she'd filled the role of younger sister to the mistress of the house. Most of the other women she'd encountered there were much older than she, or servants, or visitors who did not stay long enough to establish more than a slight acquaintance.

She'd not had a close female friend until she came to the Scots court as Lady Glenelg and met Annabel, one of Mary of Scotland's eleven lesser ladies. In spite of what Catherine had heard about Annabel's involvement with Sir Robert Appleton, she had been drawn to the Scotswoman's cheerfulness and her outgoing nature. Catherine had convinced herself that Robert, who had collected mistresses the way some men acquired hats, must have seduced Annabel.

The friendship between the two women had deepened upon Catherine's discovery that Annabel would tolerate Bede, the foul-tempered pet ferret Catherine had brought with her from England. After Bede's unexpected death the previous summer, Catherine and Annabel had buried him in the garden in Canongate with a brief ceremony and copious tears.

But as much as Catherine wanted to believe her friend innocent of any involvement in Robert's murder, doubts tormented her. Sir Walter did not make mistakes. Not about this sort of thing.

The red-haired, green-eyed beauty embraced Catherine, engulfing her in a cloud of musky perfume. "I have missed you," she declared, speaking in her charmingly accented English, the English Catherine had been coaching her to speak.

"You were gone a long time," Catherine said. "Why you could have gone all the way to London and back in the span of your absence from Edinburgh."

"Whyever would anyone want to?" Annabel laughed at the idea, but her mirth vanished when she sensed Catherine's reserve. Stepping back, she regarded the Englishwoman with a solemn expression. "What has happened, Catherine?"

Once, Catherine thought ruefully, she'd thought

herself skilled at finding out secrets. Now she could not even hide her own doubts.

"Perhaps I long to return home." She made the suggestion as a delaying tactic, a diversion, but as soon as the words were out she realized she meant them.

Annabel gave Catherine's hand a squeeze. "I can understand why. You love your Gilbert well but Scotland not at all."

"And for the most part, I do not care for the Scots." Catherine was careful to keep her voice too low for anyone to overhear.

Dour and quarrelsome by nature, and judgmental, too, many of those she had met in last two and a half years had been unwelcoming or intolerant. She was shunned, if not for being English, then as an educated woman. Annabel alone had seemed to be open and affectionate, accepting Catherine for who and what she was.

"I know what you are thinking," Annabel said. "If life here in Edinburgh is scarce tolerable, then Dunfallandy, where Gilbert is laird, will be unspeakable."

"Even Gilbert's mother, who was born there and wanted to return, fled back to her comfortable house in London after a fortnight."

"Never fear, Catherine. We will keep you here at court and you and I will find ways to enliven our days."

"I must speak with you in private." Catherine could no longer keep up social pretense. "'Tis a matter of great importance touching on my brother."

"As you wish." Annabel no longer smiled.

They met in the Canongate house an hour later. Catherine offered wine and marchpane and honesty. "There are questions which must be asked and I mean to ask them, no matter how painful they are. If what we have is true friendship, it cannot easily be rent asunder."

Without giving Annabel a chance to interrupt, Catherine told her everything she knew about Robert's death and Susanna's plight.

Annabel went still. When she spoke, her voice was somber. "My kinsmen will tell you I was here in Scotland all this time but you have no reason to believe them. They would lie for me if I asked them to."

"Would you lie to me?"

"I do not lie to my friends. But why should you believe that denial? Trust no one, Catherine. That is a great truth, one I learned when I was little more than a child."

"You are not so old now." Catherine bit down hard on a piece of marchpane, the third she'd devoured. She tended to eat when she was nervous or upset.

Annabel sighed. She seemed about to pose a question of her own, then appeared to think better of it.

"Do you know Sir Walter Pendennis?" Catherine asked.

"I know his name. A friend of Robert's."

"He seems to know a great deal about your time in France."

"It is no secret that I was in France with the queen."

"Are you an intelligence gatherer for the French queen mother?"

Annabel frowned. "I would be a great fool to admit it if I were."

"And I a greater one if I have allowed you to use me to spy on my husband."

"I like you, Catherine. And your Gilbert. I never betray the confidences of a friend."

"Was Robert not—?"

"A friend? Never. But neither was he mine enemy. I have never killed anyone, Catherine, nor wanted to. Not even Robert Appleton."

Frustration brought Catherine to her feet, scattering the marchpane crumbs that had fallen onto her skirt. "Someone did! I must go to England," she added a moment later. "I am not sure what I can do there, but this talk of friendship makes me see that Susanna needs her friends now, and needs them near her."

"I understand this. She befriended you long before you knew me." Annabel gave a brisk nod and rose to go. "Yes, you must go. And when you see her, tell Lady Appleton I do not believe Robert was . . ." she paused, searching for the right word, ". . . important enough that anyone in France or Scotland would want him dead."

"How do you—"

"That is all I will say on the subject." Annabel left in a rush, before Catherine could insist on questioning her further.

By the time Gilbert returned home a few hours later, Catherine was almost packed. She'd also given orders that Vanguard be prepared for a long journey.

Gilbert took one look at the capcases and trunks spread around their bedchamber and reached for her.

"Susanna needs me," she whispered against his neck. "If I leave at once, I can catch up with her before she leaves Appleton Manor."

"I cannot go with you."

"You will be with me in my heart."

Gilbert said nothing. Catherine freed herself from his embrace and studied his face. "What is it? What is wrong?"

"How can I ask you to return here? I know how much you miss England."

"So do you."

"My lands are here."

"We could live at Denholm Hall. It became yours when we wed."

"Your brother was content to take over his wife's properties and live off her inheritance. I'd not emulate Robert."

Two men more different Catherine could not imagine. "I will return," she promised, "because we vowed to become one, to abide together. But

186

think about Denholm Hall while I am gone, Gilbert. We could be very happy there. You could serve at the English court as easily as at the Scots."

"Work for Sir Walter perhaps? As Robert did?"

"Not as Robert did." It was Catherine's fervent hope that no one would ever want to murder her Gilbert.

Chapter 26

Appleton Manor
February 10, 1565

After supper, Eleanor Lowell seated herself on a stool by the kitchen fire and prepared to read to her maids. This was a custom also practised at Leigh Abbey and on occasion during the past two weeks, any hope of departure put off by bad weather, Jennet had joined them to listen to chapters of *A Proper New Book of Cookery,* a volume so old that the pages were torn and the cover tattered.

Tonight, at Sir Walter's suggestion, he and Lady Appleton joined the circle settled on stools and benches around the hearth. Opening *The Book of the Courtier,* which Lady Appleton had brought with her from Leigh Abbey, Eleanor smiled at Sir Walter. "I understand this author does not hold silence a virtue in women, as most men seem to."

"Tom Hoby's a sensible man blessed with a clever wife," Sir Walter replied. "There's talk he'll be named ambassador to France when Sir Thomas Smith is called home. A nice position, with a stipend of twelve hundred pounds per annum."

"Did you ever consider becoming an ambassador?" Eleanor watched him the way a cat pondered a juicy mouse.

Sir Walter made a dismissive gesture but looked thoughtful.

If she'd dared, Jennet would have made a rude noise.

"Robert was in France with Hoby once, was he not?" Lady Appleton asked. "Long ago?"

Recalled to the presence of others besides Eleanor in the room, Sir Walter nodded. "Very long ago. I had just left my studies at Cambridge and gone to Italy at that time. Robert traveled to France with one of the earl of Leicester's brothers."

Struck by the fact that she already knew this, Jennet searched back through her memories. It had been a short while after she'd first come to Leigh Abbey as the lowliest of the maidservants, before her mistress had married Robert Appleton, though they were already betrothed. The servants often gossiped about where their betters had gone off to and what they were up to while they were there.

"The delegation was led by the marquis of Northampton," Sir Walter continued. "Lady Northampton accompanied him to France."

The woman dying in Blackfriars, Jennet remembered. Constance Crane's mistress. Had Constance also gone to France? From what Lady Appleton had said, Constance must have began her dalliance with Robert Appleton by then.

"In fact," Sir Walter added, "if memory serves, 'twas that very Lady Northampton who inspired Hoby to begin this translation. Just think, if not

189

for her encouragement, we would have to hear you read in Italian, from the original version by Master Castiglioni."

He affected a mock-Italian accent for the last phrase and twirled one end of his mustache with his fingers. The jest was well received. Everyone knew Italians were untrustworthy and villainous. Jennet had not forgotten Lady Appleton's account of how they cut up dead bodies to find out what had killed them.

Under cover of more laughter, Jennet slipped unnoticed out of the kitchen. She'd been hoping for just such a chance. This was the only time of day when she could be certain where everyone was, even Bates and Fulke. They were in the stable, teaching Eleanor's menservants to play that dreadful card game, Put.

Jennet hurried along the passage that connected the service rooms and kitchen to the hall. At most she'd have an hour to search undisturbed.

In Jennet's opinion, Eleanor Lowell was a liar and a cheat. She might not have gone to London and killed Sir Robert, but she knew more about him than she'd admitted. Jennet was sure of it.

What she expected to find, Jennet did not know, but she hoped for letters from Sir Robert. Eleanor claimed she'd received only one and that she'd burnt it. Jennet did not believe that either.

She crossed the hall, lit only by rushlights in the wall sconces, her ears cocked for any sound. She heard nothing. She should be able to search

Eleanor's belongings without fear of being caught. A grim smile on her face, Jennet climbed the stairs and entered Eleanor's chamber.

It was not unoccupied. Jennet had not thought it would be since Rosamond shared her mother's bed. Jennet had, however, been counting on finding the child asleep.

Old Widow Sparcheforde's curse still appeared to be at work.

As soon as Jennet entered the room and lit a candle, Rosamond peered out from behind the blue velvet hangings. "Mama?"

"I am not your mama. Go back to sleep."

Rosamond slipped out of bed to see what Jennet was doing.

Jennet tried to ignore her as she searched for letters or other incriminating documents. If anyone questioned her, she decided, she'd say she'd heard Rosamond cry out in her sleep and had come in to check on her.

Eleanor possessed a great number of chests and boxes. Shivering in her thin chemise, Rosamond hovered at Jennet's side like a miniature ghost as she investigated the contents of the largest one. Jennet made the mistake of glancing her way.

Lady Glenelg's eyes looked back at her.

Jennet sighed. She wanted to dislike Rosamond, to see in her only a feminine echo of her faithless father. But Rosamond was also much like Sir Robert's half sister, and Jennet had been fond enough of her to ask her to be the godmother of her second child.

"Want Mama," Rosamond said, and stuck her thumb in her mouth.

"She is busy now." Without warning, Jennet felt a powerful longing for her own little girls. She'd tried not to miss them but sometimes, when she let down her guard, the ache to hold them in her arms again as well nigh unbearable.

"Mama's." Rosamond pointed to the chest Jennet was rifling.

"Yes. Well, I am helping your mama." Jennet pawed through sleeves and collars, ruffs and gloves. "Your step mama," she clarified in a low mutter.

Rosamond sucked harder on her thumb and continued to watch while Jennet closed the lid of one chest and opened the next.

It was full of fabric. Velvet. Brocade. How had she come by such fine stuff? Jennet wondered as she ran loving fingers over one luxurious, textured surface. Presents from some man? From Grimshaw? From Secole? From Sir Robert.

Eleanor Lowell had expensive tastes, and that she could indulge them struck Jennet as suspicious. There were even two mirrors in her bedchamber, both silvered, not the cheaper sort of polished metal.

She was a sly one, Jennet decided, a conniver as bad as Alys Putney, able to make others think she needed them to take care of her. She was angling

192

to wed Sir Walter. That was plain as day. And she'd chosen him over Master Grimshaw not because he was the better man, but because he had more material advantages to offer her.

Twelve hundred pounds per annum, indeed!

A woman like that was capable of bribing servants to swear she'd never left Appleton Manor. She was hiding something. Jennet was as sure of that as she was that Sir Walter was smitten with the woman. Lady Appleton had been right about that. All the signs were there. He sighed and toyed with his food. And he stared at the object of his affection to the exclusion of all else.

Lady Appleton's behavior was almost as puzzling. She'd asked no more questions since Master Grimshaw returned to Manchester. In spite of the constant, looming presence of Bernard Bates, she acted as if she had come to Lancashire to visit an old friend. She and Eleanor spent hours together without ever mentioning what awaited one of them back in London. They'd made candles and traded recipes and seemed to have developed a rapport between them that passed Jennet's understanding.

Jennet thought it a good thing she was at Appleton Manor to look out for her mistress. Someone had to. She closed the lid of the second chest and moved on to a small enameled box, prepared to go through every one of Eleanor Lowell's possessions with a fine-toothed comb.

"I help." Rosamond broke a lengthy silence to

plunge both hands into a collection of embroidery silks. Before Jennet could stop her, she had them in a hopeless tangle. In an attempt to avert total chaos, Jennet picked the child up and carried her to the window seat opposite the door.

"I need you to help me another way, Rosamond. You will be my lookout. If you hear anyone coming, you must tell me."

She'd scarce turned back to the boxes before Rosamond gave an excited squeal. She was on her knees on the window seat, nose pressed to the panes of glass to see into the stableyard below. "Papa!" she cried.

Jennet hurried to Rosamond's side. For a moment, she half expected to see Sir Robert, back yet again from the dead.

"That is Sir Walter," she told Rosamond, hearing the relief in her own voice. She could see why the child had made the mistake. Sir Walter's face, illuminated by naught but the lantern he held in one hand, appeared to be dominated by his beard and mustache. He'd trimmed them to the same style Sir Robert had favored.

"Not Papa?" Rosamond asked.

"No. Not your papa." But had he been here? Could Rosamond confirm that the mysterious Master Secole and Sir Robert Appleton had been one and the same? "Do you know who your papa is, Rosamond?"

The question was too direct. Rosamond was, after all, only two years old. Instead of answering, she pouted. Tears welled up in her dark eyes. "Want Mama."

Jennet gave up trying to get answers out of the child. Much as she wished she could believe Rosamond would remember, she knew it was unlikely. Even if the child's father had been here for six or seven months, even if he'd told her to call him papa, he'd left Appleton Manor the previous summer. Another seven months had passed since then. After that much time, no child Rosamond's age, not even this unsettling little girl who often seemed so much older than she was, would remember the details Jennet needed to know.

What made more sense, Jennet decided, was that Rosamond had begun to use the name "Papa" for any man. Her own Susan had done that for a few months when she was about Rosamond's age, to Mark's great embarrassment.

A pity, Jennet thought. She had liked the other interpretation better.

So absorbed was she in her speculating that she did not hear footsteps on the stairs. Rosamond, curled up on the window seat, had fallen asleep, her duties as lookout forgotten. Jennet had no idea anyone had come into Eleanor's chamber until Lady Appleton spoke.

"What are you doing here, Jennet?" By her tone, she already knew the answer . . . and did not approve.

"I heard Rosamond stirring."

"Ah. I see."

Rosamond's mother had followed Lady Appleton into the room. Neither one of them challenged Jennet's lie, but Eleanor Lowell believed it no more than Jennet's mistress did.

Jennet's spirits sank. They were ranged against her. A friendship had developed between the two gentlewomen that excluded her.

Hurt, resentful, Jennet decided Widow Sparcheforde might not be the only one who was a witch. What else could explain why Lady Appleton, as well as Sir Walter, had stopped suspecting Eleanor? Eleanor must have bewitched them both.

And if that were true, it followed that Eleanor could have killed Sir Robert without ever leaving Lancashire. Everyone knew a witch had only to cast the right spell and, wherever he might be, her intended victim would fall down, dead.

This solution so terrified Jennet that she fled from the chamber before Lady Appleton could dismiss her. On the morrow, no matter what the weather, she would have to seek out the local cunning woman and buy a charm for unwitching.

Chapter 27

Lady Glenelg's escort, four outriders and a tiring maid, had not shared their young mistress's enthusiasm for travel when they set out. After nearly three weeks on the road, making their way over steep terrain and wild landscape, part of the time on packhorse trails but more often following narrow, meandering footpaths, the men held themselves stiff in their saddles, stoic expressions on their faces as they soldiered on. Wynda, the older woman Gilbert had insisted accompany his wife for propriety's sake, was close to exhaustion. She clung to the rider in front of her with a feeble grip and alternated coughs with whimpers.

"That is Manchester," Catherine said, waving her arm toward the substantial cluster of buildings in the distance. The spire of St. Mary's glinted in the winter sun.

Wynda took one look and began to wail. After a moment, Catherine realized what the trouble was. She could see cart after cart streaming out of the town. The sight had convinced Wynda that something was amiss behind Manchester's walls, a plague at the least.

"It is Monday, a market day." Exasperation made Catherine snap at the woman. She was not unsympathetic, but now that the journey was almost done, Wynda might try to be a bit more optimistic. "Ride on," she ordered, ignoring the loud, reproachful sniffle behind her. "We will be there by nightfall."

And none too soon. February was almost gone, and they were still a day short of reaching Appleton Manor. Catherine would have gone straight there if she'd thought she could arrive before sunset.

They clattered across the stone bridge over the River Irk and into the center of the town just as Manchester's watchman, with his jack and sallet and bill, began his rounds. Catherine swiveled her head as they rode toward her cousin's house, trying to see everything at once. Manchester appeared to have gotten smaller in the last five years. Things were much closer together than she'd remembered.

How strange, Catherine thought. Going away had changed her perceptions. She had known that London dwarfed Manchester but now she had to admit that even Edinburgh was grander and more sophisticated.

The Manchester house Catherine had inherited from Randall Denholm had been leased to a large family, which was sensible from a financial standpoint but left her in a quandary. She'd considered bespeaking a room at the inn in Withy Grove, which had been making travelers welcome since the time of King Edward III, but it made more sense to go directly to her cousin, Matthew Grimshaw, and ask for news as well as beds for the night.

Grimshaw's two-story house seemed unchanged, with its two gables and glass in every window. She'd never realized before what a prosperous-looking establishment it was.

"Knock at the door," she ordered, remaining in the saddle while her servant did so. She knew better than to show any weakness in front of Matthew. She intended to assert herself the moment she saw him.

She'd been fourteen when she'd last encountered her sour-tempered, much older cousin. For the most part, he had ignored her and she had been able to observe how he acted around others. He'd cravenly bent to the will of anyone with a more forceful personality than his own—Catherine's mother, for example.

Cousin Matthew's housekeeper, Judith Mosley, answered the door. Her eyes widened at the sight of Catherine, mounted astride on Vanguard, her limbs encased in boy's breeches.

"Mistress Catherine? That is . . . I mean Lady Glenelg." She stumbled through an attempt at a curtsey.

Flinging herself out of the saddle, Catherine laughed and hugged the old woman, delighted to see a familiar face. "Is my cousin at home?" she asked.

"He's due back at any moment."

"And Lady Appleton? Is she still in residence at Appleton Manor?"

"Oh, yes, madam. She was here in Manchester

only two days ago on some business or other. She told Master Grimshaw she means to stay on at least another week. There is another gentlewoman living at Appleton Manor," the housekeeper added as she escorted Catherine and Wynda to the chamber they would share.

"Yes. Eleanor Lowell."

"Master Grimshaw says he's going to make her his wife."

Hiding her surprise at this news, Catherine wondered how Matthew's interest had affected Susanna's quest for information. And how much he had been told about Eleanor's past. And why, now that she thought of it, any woman would want to wed Matthew Grimshaw.

"Has she accepted his proposal?"

"Not yet, but he presses his suit at every opportunity." She lowered her voice. "I am not supposed to say so, for you know how Master Grimshaw dislikes gossip, but he stays there at Appleton Manor sometimes. He was even her guest at Yuletide. After so much time in close company, 'twould be wise of her to accept him."

Catherine had to agree. The last thing Eleanor Lowell needed was a second child born out of wedlock. She was about to say so when Wynda began to cough, a horrible hacking sound.

"I've just the thing for that," Matthew's housekeeper declared. She fetched a bright blue bottle and offered it to Catherine to inspect. "Master Grimshaw bought it from the apothecary for a catarrh. Powder of pearl and ivory, it is, and cloves, cinnamon, galingale, aloes, nutmeg, ginger, and camphor."

It sounded as unappealing as it was expensive, but then Catherine did much dislike anything that contained ginger. "Perhaps I should leave Wynda in your care, Judith, when I continue on to Appleton Manor in the morning."

A loud voice from the front of the house cut off Judith's reply. "What is all this?" Matthew Grimshaw demanded. "Who let these strangers into my house."

"No strangers, cousin!" Catherine called out. She flew down the stairs to greet him. "The Scots have invaded, but in friendship, I do assure you."

A bit stiffly, he returned her cousinly embrace. "This is unexpected," he said, stating the obvious. "And most inappropriate," he added when she stepped back and he saw her attire.

"But exceeding practical." She was not about to let him bully her into putting on petticoats, kirtle, and bodice. "I have come to help Susanna. I will dispatch a messenger to Appleton Manor at first light to tell her I am on my way and send a message to Denholm Hall, as well. I will reside there while my dear sister-by-marriage remains in Lancashire."

Matthew toyed with the strings that tied his ruff and scowled.

Into the silence came a horrible hacking sound as Wynda suffered another fit of coughing. "Only my maid," Catherine said before Matthew could scare the woman to death by storming up the stairs and demanding to know what was amiss. "We had to spend several nights in the open on our journey."

One, near Fiend's Fell, the highest point in the Pennines, where they'd camped out in a howling storm that began in blinding snow and ended with hailstones big as a man's fist, had been unfortunate. They'd gotten off the old Roman road called the Maiden Way and mistaken a sheep track for the path to the nearest village. Such things happened in winter. They'd huddled together for warmth and the next morning had found their way again, but Wynda had been coughing and sniffling ever since.

"You were foolish to travel in such weather." Matthew led her to his study and poured out goblets of wine for them both.

"Clashy and foundby, the locals called it." She'd always been fascinated by variations in regional speech. Clashy was stormy and foundby meant cold. Other days had been better, only packy, which according to their local guide was "when th' cannot see yon moor an' t' mists rollin' abart."

"What was your husband thinking to let you come all this way?"

Catherine straightened her shoulders and fixed him with a foundby stare. "My husband loves Susanna as much as I do."

Matthew opened his mouth and closed it again.

He seemed relieved when the door opened. "Good. Bring that here." He indicated a small table. A few minutes later, when Matthew had finished blustering at his housekeeper and been thus restored to even temper, Catherine and her cousin settled themselves in two heavily carved chairs and attacked a platter of cold meat and cheeses.

"I perceive you have been in correspondence with Lady Appleton," Matthew said.

"Yes. And Gilbert received several letters from Sir Walter."

Matthew abandoned the food to fold both hands over his slightly concave abdomen. The gesture drew Catherine's attention to the tense way he held himself. She waited, as Susanna had taught her, continuing to eat and letting the silence drag on. Eventually, he felt compelled to break it.

"This Pendennis . . . who is he?"

"An old friend of Robert's."

"Is that why he interests himself in this matter? To find out who killed Appleton?"

"Walter liked Robert, but he dotes on Susanna. He will not rest until he can prove her innocent by finding out who is guilty." Catherine refilled her goblet with a particularly fine Canary wine. She had not felt so warm or so mellow since she'd left Scotland. The traveling had been invigorating. She'd enjoyed the adventure. But she was not averse to wallowing in creature comforts when they were available.

Matthew was agitated about something, Catherine realized. As she watched, he ran one finger under his ruff and swallowed hard. "It seems to me she might have killed her husband," he said. "When one spouse is murdered, the constables look hard at the other."

"I'd sooner suspect Mistress Eleanor Lowell." Catherine meant to be provoking and watched Matthew's face as she spoke.

"Eleanor Lowell is a sweet and gentle lady. She'd not harm a fly."

"You know her well, then?"

"Aye, I do. And your sainted Lady Appleton had no right to accuse her."

"Eleanor never left home, then?" The sheer distance to London had always seemed to argue against Eleanor's guilt, just as it had against Annabel's.

"She's been no farther away from Appleton Manor than Manchester since I've known her. Her servants bore witness to that and I, too, could swear to it."

"In that case, why is Susanna still in Lancashire?"

"The weather kept her from leaving."

All this time? Aloud she said, "It must have been difficult for her to share a house with her husband's former mistress." In spite of Matthew's obvious attachment to the woman, Catherine was prepared to dislike both Eleanor and her daughter.

"Lady Appleton will soon be on the road again, searching elsewhere for her poisoner."

"Where?"

"I have no notion where. Or who. And in truth, I care not. I never liked your brother, Catherine. His death was no great tragedy." He launched into an account of how he had been forced to do Robert Appleton's bidding, and Susanna's, too, at the time Catherine went to live at Leigh Abbey. The story he told was not as she remembered it, but she let him prattle on, grumbling over old slights, until the wine and the warmth of the room had her falling asleep.

Into a hesitation in his monologue, Catherine yawned. A sheepish look on her face, she apologized, but she used the opportunity to escape. "I must be up early in the morning. Good night to you, cousin."

He caught her arm as she rose. "Why did you come all this way, Catherine?"

"Why to lend support to my sister-by-marriage."

"Take advice from one of your own family. Distance yourself from Lady Appleton."

"I thank you for your concern, Matthew, but I have already made my decision."

"You are still a child, Catherine. Innocent. Go back to your husband . . . unless you wish to journey to London and witness Lady Appleton's execution."

Infuriated, Catherine jerked free. "It will not come to that. Susanna Appleton is clever and determined. She will discover the truth."

She stormed out of the room before Matthew could infect her with his pessimism.

Chapter 28

Susanna recognized the banner the riders carried before she could make out the face of their leader. The bee and thistle crest of Lord Glenelg was a bright spot of color against the gray winter sky.

Her joy at seeing Catherine again was diminished, though only slightly, when she recognized Matthew Grimshaw riding beside her.

"Lady Glenelg is wearing breeches." Jennet sounded appalled.

"Indeed she is. Most sensible for such a long journey. And necessary, since she rides astride."

But Susanna understood Jennet's disapproval. Both wearing men's apparel and riding astride were unacceptable in a noblewoman. So was riding a stallion, which Vanguard most assuredly was. A true lady was expected to choose a gentler mount, a sweet-tempered mare or a plodding gelding.

Susanna greeted her sister-by-marriage with a warm hug while Eleanor hurried up to Matthew Grimshaw, Rosamond at her heels. From the way Catherine watched them, Susanna knew she had already heard of her cousin's romantic interest in Mistress Lowell.

"What do you think of Rosamond?" Susanna asked, adding, "She is your niece, Catherine," when she saw the flash of distaste on the younger woman's face.

They moved a little aside to leave the others more room to dismount.

Catherine sighed. "I suppose I pity her. I know how I felt when people mistook me for Robert's byblow. In a few years, when Rosamond has to face similar whispers and nudges, she will not have the advantage I did. The circumstances of my birth may have been irregular, but at least I was not born a bastard."

"Now, knave. Not next week." Grimshaw's voice, loud with annoyance, barked at Bernard Bates.

Ever stoic and silent, the Londoner did not trouble to correct the lawyer's mistaken impression that he was one of Susanna's grooms.

"Who is that man?" Catherine asked. "I do not remember him from Leigh Abbey."

"My guard."

Catherine's look of astonishment made Susanna smile. "Come inside and I will explain how he came to be in my employ." She imagined Catherine had questions about her brother's death, as well.

They sought the privacy of the chamber Susanna shared with Jennet. Within a short span of time, Susanna had given Catherine a full account of Robert's last hours.

"Could he have died of natural causes?" she asked. "What if he was ill before he entered that tavern?"

"Only the woman who was with him there can tell us if he was in poor health before he ate his last meal."

"Food gone bad," Catherine murmured, speculating, "or the wrong sort of mushroom in the meat pie."

"I considered that his death could have been an accident. It is still a possibility."

"But if that is so, how could they accuse you of—"

"The circumstances were suspicious. I was in the wrong place at the wrong time. And I thought it was poison myself. I still do." She managed a faint smile. "If ever a man lived to be murdered, it was Robert."

"You sound as if you want him to have been poisoned."

Susanna had long since faced an unpalatable truth. "If he was not, I have no hope at all of proving mine innocence."

Tears welled up in Catherine's eyes but before they could overflow, Walter's knock interrupted them. He entered the room at their invitation, closely followed by Jennet. She slammed the door in Bates's face and smirked in satisfaction when she heard a faint sound of pain from the other side, proof she'd succeeded in clipping the end of his nose.

"Well, Catherine?" Walter demanded. "Have you found proof that Annabel MacReynolds killed Robert?"

"Annabel had naught to do with his death." Catherine sounded fierce in her defense of the Scotswoman, surprising Susanna.

"You are certain?" Sir Walter's disappointment was almost palpable, revealing the direction his suspicions had taken.

"Yes."

"What is it, Walter?" Susanna asked. "Do you know something more about this woman than you've told me?"

He hesitated, his accustomed caution reasserting itself. Keeping secrets was, after all, his business.

"You were quick enough to tell Gilbert."

In the face of Catherine's taunt, Walter capitulated. "Annabel MacReynolds is an agent of the French queen mother, the Italian-born Catherine de' Medici," he added for Jennet's benefit. "A well-known expert on poisons."

Catherine glowered at him. "Even if that is true, it does not make her a murderer. How is what she's done different from what you do? What Robert did?"

"So. She cozened you, just as she did your brother."

"Not at all," Catherine insisted. "And it does seem to me that Robert took most unfair advantage of her."

"Did she tell you that?"

"No, but—"

"Mistress MacReynolds gained far more from their association than Robert did."

Walter sent an apologetic glance in Susanna's direction. She realized then that he'd hoped to keep her from learning some of the less palatable details of Robert's life.

"The first time Robert took Annabel to bed, it was because Catherine de' Medici sent her to him as a gift. Poor fool. He did not realize he was being lured into a trap. Indeed, some two years passed before the Italian woman gave orders to spring it. When Robert encountered Annabel again, at the Scots court, he thought it all his idea to make her his mistress. He never guessed that she offered him her body in order to have access to the information he was collecting for me."

"Have you proof?" Catherine demanded.

"Information reached France which could only have come from Annabel reading Robert's correspondence, including letters Susanna wrote to him from Madderly Castle. That means Annabel knew the code they devised, the Knox cipher, the same code used to lure Susanna to Westminster on the night Robert died."

Susanna had been listening with more interest than dismay, but this announcement took her aback. "You knew we used Master Knox's book?" Until this moment, she had believed only she and Robert had shared that secret.

When they all turned to look at her, she realized she had been foolish to think Robert would have kept anything just between the two of them. She'd confided in Jennet. Why suppose he'd not told Walter? And if Walter, why not inform his mistress? Perhaps all his mistresses wrote to him in codes!

"Susanna—"

"No, Walter. It can scarce matter now that Annabel and I were both privy to more than Robert's . . . affection."

"It may matter a great deal if the message you received to lure you to the Black Jack came from someone other than Robert."

"It did not come from Annabel." Hands on her hips, Catherine looked ready to slap Walter's face if he persisted in accusing the Scotswoman. "You are as wrong about her as Robert was. He saw only a pretty face and vapid expression and assumed Annabel lacked a mind of her own or any skill at dissembling. You admit she was better than any man at gathering intelligence, but you use that against her and assume she must also be capable of killing."

"She is clever," Walter argued. "She has deceived you into thinking she—"

"She swore she did not kill Robert, and I believe her." Catherine turned to Susanna. "And she has sent a message to you, Susanna. She said I was to tell you that Robert was no threat to anyone in France, that he was not important enough to be assassinated for political reasons."

"A fact he would no doubt find most distressing."

"Annabel did not have anything to do with Robert's murder."

"You like her," Susanna guessed.

"Yes, I do. She has become a friend."

"Then you will understand why I do not want to believe Eleanor might have killed Robert, either."

They shared a bittersweet smile. "Pity," Catherine said. "She seemed an ideal villainess to me."

"Madam?"

"Yes, Jennet."

"You must not be so quick to rule out Eleanor Lowell."

For a moment, Susanna closed her eyes, gathering the strength she'd need to once more deflect Jennet's wild speculations. She appreciated the other woman's loyalty but she knew what Jennet had been up to since the night they'd caught her searching Eleanor's chamber. As she expected, a quick glance at Jennet's hands revealed that her fingers were clenched tight around the talisman tied to her waist.

"Eleanor did not leave Lancashire," Susanna pointed out. "Therefore she could not have poisoned Robert."

That Jennet was sticking to her witchcraft theory was plain from the expression on her face. Since she knew already what Susanna thought of such nonsense, however, she did not speak of that aloud.

"She has lied to you, madam," she said instead. "You cannot deny that."

"Enough, Jennet." Walter's features were set in grim lines.

"I think the time has come to share all you know," Susanna told him.

"The man she insists is called Secole was no doubt Robert," he admitted, "but Eleanor had neither motive nor opportunity to kill him, and he left here over six months before his death."

"If Annabel did not kill him and Eleanor did not," Catherine asked, "then who did?"

Susanna had no answer for her.

Worse, she knew she no longer had any excuse to remain at Appleton Manor. She had welcomed the respite brought on by bad weather, but the roads were passable again now, and there were more questions to be asked, questions whose answers lay far to the south . . . in London.

Catherine stayed to sup. By mutual agreement, they did not speak of Robert's murder in the presence of the others. And when Catherine left Appleton Manor for her own house, taking her cousin with her, Susanna retired for the night.

She needed to think. To plan. She had put off facing what must be done for much too long.

As she climbed the stairs to her chamber, she realized she was rubbing her leg. The cold and damp had made it ache again.

Old injuries, she thought. Old memories. The past always seemed to impinge on the present.

How far into Robert's past, she wondered as Jennet untied the laces that held her sleeves to her bodice, would she have to search to find his murderer?

She had not ruled anyone out, in spite of her liking for Eleanor and Catherine's championship of Annabel. Her list of possible murderers included both of them. And Alys and her husband. And Constance. Susanna had believed her at the time of their meeting but on thinking over their conversation, she'd realized Constance could have been lying to her. What if she had seen Robert again after that day in the garden at Durham House? For all Susanna knew, they might have been lovers until the day he died.

She stepped out of her kirtle and petticoats. She hated having to suspect everyone, but it seemed that was the only way she was going to get out of this horrible situation alive.

Who else? The Lady Mary had cause to hate Robert.

Her expression grim, Susanna sat on the bed to remove her shoes. To be fair, she must also consider Walter a suspect. He might have killed Robert out of jealousy. It was a powerful motive, and he had wanted to marry her—until he'd met Eleanor. If he'd seen Robert as the only barrier separating them . . .

Clad only in the stockings and chemise in which she would sleep for warmth, Susanna slid beneath the covers. Next she would be suspecting Catherine!

The idea was absurd, but it reminded her that

Robert had once before been the target of a murderous rage. Her thoughts skipped back five years, to the time when Robert, and Susanna herself, and even Matthew Grimshaw, had borne some responsibility for three deaths, one of them a suicide. She returned to the present with a sickening jolt as a new possibility occurred to her.

"Jennet?"

"Yes, madam." She paused in the act of closing the bed hangings. She'd already rolled out the truckle bed for herself. One candle and the remains of the fire in the hearth cast eerie shadows throughout the chamber.

"What if it was not an accident that Robert was identified? What if that was meant to happen, and I was meant to be there?"

"But how could anyone know exactly where he'd die? You could be lured to the tavern, but you might have gone in another direction entirely when you left it."

"There is one explanation, something that crossed my mind when I was in Newgate. I dismissed it then as impossible. I told myself Robert would never—." She broke off as an involuntary shudder racked her body. "Poison could have taken a long time to kill him, and it would have been an agonizing death. His fall spared him that. What if he ascended the steps of the Eleanor Cross not because of any connection to Eleanor Lowell, but because he knew it was high enough to suit his purpose? What if he had been watching me? Knew where I was? What if he hired some woman to pretend to be me in the tavern? What if his life had lost all meaning for him, if he had lost all hope, but he wanted me to be blamed for his death because he blamed me for his downfall?"

"You think Sir Robert might have taken his own life in order to put the blame on you?"

Jennet's astonishment eased Susanna's fears, but she could not quite dismiss her suspicions. "Things might have been that bad for him. We have not been able to discover how he spent the last eighteen months of his life."

"Suicide is a terrible sin," Jennet whispered. In her agitation she clenched her fists on the edges of the bedcurtains.

"Aye."

"It does not seem the sort of thing Sir Robert would do, not even to avenge himself on you."

"If it is what happened, I may never be able to prove it."

Jennet was chewing on her lower lip, a sign of deep thought. "If Sir Robert devised this scheme and sent for you, then he expected you to be there with him when he took the poison. He'd have made sure you were in place to be blamed when he killed himself. There'd have been no need for another woman! Indeed, he'd never have risked being seen with anyone else if he wanted you to be blamed."

Susanna laughed aloud in relief and delight.

"You have the right of it. My heartfelt thanks, old friend."

Pleased with herself, Jennet pinched out the candle and drew the bedcurtains closed.

★ ★ ★

For once, Susanna slept without troubling dreams. But in the wee hours of the morning, she woke to the touch of a tiny hand on her shoulder.

Rosamond.

The child burrowed under the covers until she was nestled snug against Susanna. It seemed natural to slide one arm across the small hip.

Content, Rosamond cuddled closer, murmured, "Mama," and drifted into sleep.

Chapter 29

Rosamond was sleeping in Lady Appleton's bed.

Jennet scowled at the child then felt her features soften as she saw that her mistress held the small intruder in a comforting embrace.

Sometime during the night, Rosamond had left her own chamber, toddled down one flight of stairs and up another, and climbed into the bed. Not so surprising, Jennet supposed. The child had been accustomed to sleeping in this room with her nurse.

Nurse Bond. There had been a wasted trip. Ten miles each way to talk to a woman who had naught to say about Eleanor Lowell. And not a word about Master Secole, either. She claimed she'd had nothing to do with anyone but the maids and Rosamond.

Jennet would have admired the woman's loyalty if she'd been in Lady Appleton's service. As it was, she dearly wished Nurse Bond could have given them some sort of evidence to use against Eleanor.

And if wishes were horses, she thought, beggars might ride.

Rosamond appeared sweet when she was sleeping, but a few hours later the little girl put on a fearsome display of temper.

Hands over her ears, Lady Appleton stared at

Rosamond in wonder. "How can such howls come from a human throat?"

"Ignore her." Eleanor concentrated on her needlework, pretending to hear nothing out of the ordinary. "She'll quiet down all the quicker if you do not coddle her."

Jennet agreed, having had some experience of her own with cranky children, but when Rosamond tore off up the stairs toward her mother's bedchamber and Lady Appleton went after her, Jennet followed.

"Something has provoked this rage. Did I do something wrong?" Lady Appleton hovered near Rosamond, who had thrown herself on the floor and was beating it with her fists.

"You have done naught but indulge the child, madam, playing with her after you broke your fast." Jennet had watched, astonished, as her mistress flopped down on the ground and thrashed about to make a snow angel alongside Rosamond's.

"Rosamond," Lady Appleton pleaded, "what is the matter?"

"She's too young to explain anything complex," Jennet said. "And this tantrum may have been brought on by nothing at all. Children her age are often unreasonable."

"Such heats cannot be good for a child. If words will not calm her, then mayhap herbs— Stop that, Rosamond."

On her feet again, she tossed her mother's possessions onto the floor and began to jump up and down on them. Determined to bring the child under control, Lady Appleton caught her by the back of her bodice and lifted her clear off her feet. This sudden move so startled Rosamond that she stopped her racket to stare in disbelief at her captor.

Taking advantage of the momentary silence, Lady Appleton plunked Rosamond down on the edge of the bed, giving her a warning look. "No more of this nonsense, Rosamond. You are old enough to start learning how to behave like a young gentlewoman. Furthermore, you will put this room back to rights or you will do without your supper."

Jennet decided this would be a good time to leave, before she was pressed into service as a watchdog, but as she backed toward the door, her foot struck something. When she bent to pick it up, she discovered it was a book, one that was familiar to her. She began to smile. She had been right about Eleanor Lowell, after all.

"Madam," Jennet whispered, "There is something here you should see." She handed over a copy of John Knox's diatribe against women rulers.

For several minutes, Lady Appleton did not speak. Rosamond, over the worst of her fit of rage, had also lapsed into silence. Thumb in mouth, she lay curled in a small, pitiful-looking ball on the bed.

"Say nothing of this to anyone," Lady Appleton said at last.

"But, madam—"

"You will obey me, Jennet. Sir Walter loves Eleanor. If she loves him in return, she will tell him everything before it becomes necessary to force her to do so. She just needs a little more time."

"But we are leaving here soon."

"We can delay our departure a while longer."

Lips pursed in disapproval, Jennet watched her mistress tuck a blanket around Rosamond and listened to her murmur to the child. She was getting much too attached to the girl and taking a foolish risk on Rosamond's mother besides.

It was not that Jennet wanted to rush back to London but staying longer at Appleton Manor seemed to her to be a mistake, too. To her mind there was only one sensible course. At her first opportunity, a little later that same day, she walked to Denholm Hall.

"Lady Glenelg," Jennet whispered, looking over her shoulder to make sure the two of them were alone in the stable. "I have a plan."

Fishing a piece of dried apple out of a pocket in her cloak, Catherine Glenelg offered it to Vanguard. "To do what?"

"To save Lady Appleton from a horrible death. If she cannot find the real killer, she must not risk her life by returning to London."

"What do you have in mind?"

"Take her back to Scotland with you. Take all of us. We can live with you on your husband's estates. No one from England will trouble to come after her there."

"What an appalling fate! Would you condemn her to exile in that wretched and backward land?"

"I would save her life."

But Lady Glenelg shook her head, unconvinced. And to make matters worse, when Jennet left the stable, she ran full force into Bates, who was lurking near the door. He had overheard everything.

"If you make a run for the border," he said, in the longest sentence Jennet had ever heard him utter, "I will have to come after you and bring you back."

Chapter 30

The last day of February ended the shortest month of the year. Lady Mary Grey had always felt a certain kinship with February. On St. Valentine's Day, two weeks earlier, she had made her decision. Now she lay in her lover's arms in one of the chambers above the water gate at Whitehall, staring at the ornately embroidered canopy over their heads.

At last she understood why her sister Catherine had defied the queen in order to marry. This was bliss. All of it. 'Twould even be worth spending the rest of her life in prison to have just a little more of such pleasure and the contentment after.

"Did I hurt you?" The concerned whisper warmed her.

"Nay."

"I must seem overlarge to you."

"Too tall?" Laughing, she ran her fingers over her lover's sinewy chest, and lower, reveling in the discovery of textures so different from those of her own skin. "Everyone is, compared to me."

"That is not what I meant." He dipped his head to kiss the end of her nose. "And I think you are perfect."

He was wonderfully inspiring. She had never felt so alive, so clever, so full of ideas. Overlarge? Oh, no.

When she left him a few hours later to creep back into the room assigned to her in the palace, she found herself thinking about Lady Appleton. She had used that word, too—*overlarge*—though with quite a different meaning.

Lady Mary had not given Susanna Appleton a thought in weeks, but now it came to her that she might be able to assist her friend. Unless she had found his killer in her travels, Susanna would need help to escape the terrible dilemma created by Sir Robert Appleton's murder.

I will help her, Lady Mary decided, *if she will agree to do a special favor for me in return.*

Chapter 31

Appleton Manor
March 6, 1565

Lady Appleton announced the winner of the pancake toss and presented him with his prize, more pancakes. Unlike the plain ones used in the competition, these had been prepared from fine wheat flour, seasoned with cloves, mace, cinnamon, and nutmeg, and fried in sweet butter.

Seeing her mistress's open smile, Jennet was glad she had postponed their departure for London until after these festivities. She wished now that they never had to leave for the south. After all, Lancashire was almost as remote as Scotland. If they stayed here, there was a chance no one would bother to come after her. Bates, Jennet had realized, seemed to like Lady Appleton. And he'd shown himself to be open to bribery. Mayhap—

"Mabel tells me this is not the first time Shrove Tuesday games have been held at Appleton Manor," Lady Glenelg remarked as she came up beside Jennet. She, too, watched Lady Appleton.

"When Mark was steward here, we used them as a way to sweeten the neighbors." The residents of the nearest village, Gorbury, two miles distant, had been passing unfriendly when Jennet first met them, wary of the inhabitants of Appleton Manor, but they'd responded well to the offer of free food and lively games.

"I expect Eleanor had little to do with the villagers."

They exchanged a look. Neither shared Lady Appleton's trust in Eleanor. Rosamond's mother seemed happy to have Sir Walter's company and tolerated the rest of them but she stuck to her story. She had not seen Sir Robert Appleton since before Rosamond's birth. She had received only one letter from him.

"If friend Secole was Sir Robert, some old beldame might have recognized him from his boyhood."

"Have you asked among the villagers?"

Jennet nodded. "One or two remember catching sight of Secole during his stay here and allowed that he bore some slight resemblance to the Appletons." She sighed, dispirited. "At least one fellow said so only in hope of a reward. I cannot judge what the truth is."

Lady Glenelg started to make some comment but fell to coughing instead. The sound alarmed Jennet, but the noblewoman took the fit in stride, fishing a horehound drop out of the pocket hidden in a placket in her kirtle and popping it into her mouth. She sucked hard, wiped her streaming eyes, and blew her nose on the handkerchief she kept tucked in her sleeve. Like her maidservant before her, Lady Glenelg was afflicted with a catarrh.

"You should let Lady Appleton physic you," Jennet said.

"I have sampled her remedies." Lady Glenelg shuddered at the memory.

Jennet sympathized. She had been on the receiving end of some foul-tasting medicines herself. "A hot infusion of hyssop and horehound is not unpleasant to the taste."

"Susanna would have me to gargle at least once a day with a decoction of agrimony leaves mixed with honey in syrup of mulberries." Lady Glenelg made a horrible face.

"If she believes you are too ill to travel, she will remain here longer."

"Aye. There is that." Lady Glenelg looked thoughtful. "It is not a brilliant plan, Jennet, but I can think of nothing better."

She wandered off to watch the last event of the day, the cock-throwing, in which native-born Lancashire folk seemed to delight. Jennet felt sorry for the cock, which was tied by a long string to a post while the competitors took turns throwing cudgels at it. The dead bird went to the man who killed it.

The winner had just collected his prize when Jennet realized that a large party on horseback was approaching Appleton Manor. Puzzled, she shaded her eyes to watch as the clattered across the stone bridge. A woman led them, a woman riding sideways on her own horse as Lady Appleton did.

Bright winter sunlight glinted off brilliant red curls as the woman pushed back her hood. For a moment, Jennet wondered if it was the queen who'd come to Appleton Manor. Queen Elizabeth had such a saddle and that color hair.

"By all that's holy," Lady Glenelg whispered. "Annabel." More fleet of foot than Jennet, Lady Glenelg reached the newcomers first, embracing Annabel MacReynolds in welcome the moment she dismounted.

Outraged, Jennet skidded to a halt a short distance away and glowered at them when they began to whisper together. How could Lady Glenelg look so happy to see the woman now that she knew Annabel was naught but a spy for that Italian woman who ruled France as regent?

Jennet glanced around, searching for Lady Appleton. She was watching the display of affection with a speculative gleam in her eyes. She did not appear to be upset. Just the opposite. Peculiar as it seemed to Jennet, she looked pleased by this latest development.

"Madam?" Jennet ventured.

"Let us find out what our visitor wants," she suggested in a mild voice. "And no scowling, Jennet. I hoped, at the beginning of my quest, to speak face to face with Mistress MacReynolds. I am not unhappy to have been granted my wish."

"Be careful what you ask for, they do say." Grumbling, Jennet followed after her mistress.

"Welcome to Appleton Manor," Lady Appleton said.

"A charming place," the red-haired woman replied. "I apologize for arriving unannounced, but the matter seemed urgent." She gave Jennet a sharp look. "I suggest we go within, where we may speak privily."

"I keep few secrets from my companions," Lady Appleton told her.

"I must insist," Annabel said in her odd, accented English.

"Annabel," Lady Glenelg protested. "I—"

"What I have to say is for Lady Appleton's ears only."

That gentlewoman considered a moment, then agreed, but not before she'd sent Jennet a significant look.

Lady Glenelg did not like being excluded. Neither did Sir Walter. It did not seem to occur to either of them to take matters into their own hands.

To Jennet the proper course of action was obvious. She scurried into the house by the back way and had secreted herself behind the bed hangings well before Lady Appleton led her guest into the chamber. From that hiding place, Jennet could hear every word they said to each other and even see a bit through the gap where the folds of fabric did not quite meet.

Annabel took off her traveling cloak, revealing rich velvet beneath. The bodice had been cut low to show off her bosom but the effect was diminished somewhat by the canvas safeguard attached over the lower half of her kirtle to protect that garment from the filth of the roads. "No doubt you wonder at my coming here," Annabel began. "You have no reason to trust me and even less to accept my help."

"Mayhap I am not so narrowminded as you think. And I am not in a position, just now, to refuse any offer of aid."

"Indeed, your case is passing perilous. That is why I have been sent."

"Sent by whom?"

"Catherine de' Medici."

"Ah."

Lady Appleton did not sound surprised, but Jennet had to clap both hands over her mouth to prevent a gasp from escaping. The queen mother of France wanted to help Sir Robert's widow? Why should she?

"Why?" Lady Appleton asked.

"Queen Catherine does not explain herself to me. She gives orders and I obey."

A long silence suggested that Lady Appleton was considering that notion. Or trying to prompt Annabel to reveal more.

"Why?" she asked again. "Why do you do her bidding? You might be accused of treason were your association with the French queen to become known in Scotland."

Annabel laughed. "I perceive you are already aware of our association. Did Robert tell you?"

"Robert never knew." Jennet thought she heard a smile in Lady Appleton's voice. "As far as I can determine, he never guessed you were anything but what you seemed. Sir Walter Pendennis was not so easily deceived."

By the rustle of fabric, Jennet guessed Lady Appleton had crossed the room, mayhap to place a comforting hand on Annabel's arm. Her voice was full of sympathy.

"I accept that you do not know why you have been sent here to help me," Lady Appleton said, "but before I can give you my trust, I think you must explain yourself further. How did you come to be in the queen mother's service? I have some knowledge of information gatherers. Robert engaged in espionage in the hope of a title. Sir Walter is driven by his love for England."

A silvery laugh interrupted her. "Do not imagine my actions can be redeemed by noble motives, Lady Appleton. I wanted money. That is why I seduced your husband."

"Indeed?"

Jennet thought Lady Appleton sounded amused. How she could be anything but furious and hurt was beyond Jennet's ken.

"I warrant you were very young when you went to France with Queen Mary. At the time Queen Catherine ordered you to warm my husband's bed you could not have been more than eighteen."

Eighteen? Jennet frowned. At eighteen, many women were married and mothers, at least among the gentry and nobility. Lady Appleton herself had been wed at eighteen. Annabel's age scarce seemed any excuse.

"The excitement drew me, Lady Appleton."

"Ah. And the secrecy? The sense of getting away with something?"

"And of knowing things others did not."

"Most understandable. But to give your body to strangers, that seems—"

Again, Annabel laughed. "Do you accuse me of whoredom, madam?"

Jennet heard Lady Appleton's chuckle. "If I did so, it would not be an insult. One of the most trustworthy women I ever met once earned her living in the stews of Southwark."

Unable to resist seeing Annabel MacReynolds's reaction to that statement, Jennet leaned closer to the gap in the hangings. She did not realize how close the Scotswoman was standing until Annabel's lusty peal of laughter rang out right next to her ear. Startled, Jennet lost her balance and tumbled out from behind the bedcurtains.

To her chagrin, Annabel found that amusing, too.

Chapter 32

By the first Sunday in Lent, five days after Shrove Tuesday, Susanna could not justify remaining in Lancashire any longer. Catherine was on the mend, not that she'd been grievous sick to begin with. Eleanor had not changed her story and did not seem inclined to do so. As for Susanna's growing attachment to Rosamond— she had a course of action in mind, one that might kill two cocks with one cudgel.

That afternoon, following church, Susanna invited Eleanor to walk with her in the garden, where the first shy primroses had begun to poke their heads through the still-frosty ground.

"I must return to London," she told Rosamond's mother. "The twenty-second day of April is Easter Sunday. Seventeen days later, when the Easter Term begins, I am required to appear in court to answer charges that I did murder mine own husband."

Eleanor's eyes widened in shock. "I did not realize. Matthew said you were a suspect, but—"

"I took care that you should not know, Eleanor, but the truth is that I was always the most obvious suspect. I was taken into custody at the scene of Robert's death and held in Newgate. Bates travels with me as my guard, not my manservant."

Staring off at the distant horizon, Eleanor twisted her hands in her apron. "Then, if you return without having found the real killer, you could be found guilty and executed."

"I am aware of the danger, but I gave my word. I will not go back on it. Sir Walter's agents in London and Dover, and even in France, continue to ask questions. And if all else fails, there is still the possibility that I may, by virtue of calm reason, win my freedom by convincing judge and jury I am innocent."

With a sigh, Eleanor sank onto a stone bench. She stared at her hands, which were clasped so tight in her lap that the knuckles were white. "You are braver than I am, Susanna. Were I accused of murder, I would flee with all speed and never look back."

"But you are not accused. And you can help me, Eleanor." Susanna sat down beside her.

"How?" At last, Eleanor met her eyes and Susanna recognized the sincerity in the other woman's gaze.

"Come with me."

"To London? Oh, no. I—"

"Come with me and bring Rosamond. Your daughter's future may depend upon it."

"The child would be better off here in Lancashire."

"I must insist."

Eleanor's eyes narrowed. "This is not an invitation, then, but an order?" Bitterness tinged her words, and she stood to put a little distance between them.

"The journey will benefit you both. I wish to make provision for Robert's child. She must not suffer, no matter what becomes of me." Susanna debated with herself for a moment, then sweetened the bait. "Consider also that Sir Walter accompanies us. You know he is fond of you. Away from here, he might be inclined—"

"I have learned it is safest to avoid entanglements with men." Eleanor's face turned a mottled red.

Susanna refrained from comment. During all the time she had been able to observe them, neither Walter nor Matthew Grimshaw had shown any diminution in interest. If Eleanor did not encourage male admirers, neither did she do anything to deter them.

"Will you come with me?" she asked again.

"What choice have I? I will come. And I will bring Rosamond."

"Good. I will tell the others at supper."

★ ★ ★

Several hours later, Susanna cleared her throat to get everyone's attention. When the hall fell quiet, she spoke in a loud, clear voice. "I leave for London in two days."

"'Tis Scotland we should be heading for," Jennet muttered.

"I will accompany you to London," Catherine said.

Annabel spoke up next. "You are right to seek answers there. I will also go with you."

"What can you do?" Jennet demanded.

"Lady Appleton has many friends working on her behalf."

That evasive answer had Jennet looking skeptical and provoked Walter to a suspicious frown, but Susanna was inclined to give the Scotswoman the benefit of the doubt. Queen Catherine might have maneuvered Robert into taking Annabel as his mistress, but she had also sent a gift to Susanna all those years ago, the recipe for an antidote to certain poisons, an antidote that had soon after saved someone's life.

"I welcome your company," she told Annabel. Then she nodded in Eleanor's direction. "Eleanor and Rosamond will also accompany me."

When the meal resumed, Walter leaned close to whisper a question in Susanna's ear. "Do you mean to bring all your suspects together?"

Her only answer was the most enigmatic smile she could manage.

Chapter 33

Coventry
March 20, 1565

Eleanor glided toward him through the early evening mist. At four days past the full, the moon gave off enough light to reveal bright eyes and a tremulous smile. She was a tragic heroine in this, Walter thought. A victim. She needed him to rescue her.

He'd asked her to meet him in the coal yard next to the privy in back of the inn. It was not the most romantic of locations, but it had one advantage. They'd needed no excuse beyond the obvious to escape the others in their party.

That was no small consideration.

They had been traveling for eight days. Rain and melting snow had made the roads into quagmires. With such a large party, including as it did a young child, four gentlewomen, and two other women, they had on some days been fortunate to advance five miles.

Eleanor had ridden apillion behind him all those days, her arms wrapped tight around him, her chin resting against his back. He would have thought he was in heaven had it not been for all the troubles that awaited them at journey's end.

And he could have dispensed with Matthew

Grimshaw's company. When the Manchester lawyer had learned of Eleanor's plans, he'd insisted upon joining their party. He'd made some excuse about looking after Susanna's legal interests, but Walter knew the real reason he'd come along. Eleanor.

At every stop on the way south, Grimshaw had monopolized her company, preventing any private exchanges with Walter. Walter thought Grimshaw's constant presence made Eleanor uneasy, but she had not told him to go away. That fact had Walter doubting his own instincts, a rare occurrence.

He had tried to be content with hearing the sound of her light, musical laughter every day, with inhaling the scent of her sweet marjoram perfume. It clung to his clothes when the day's ride was done, tormenting his dreams. But now those painful pleasures were not enough. He could stand the uncertainty no longer.

She advanced a few steps closer and stopped.

"I should not have come," she whispered.

"Eleanor." He put everything he was feeling into that single word.

With a joyful little sound, she walked into his arms and let him enfold them both in his cloak. He stepped back into the shadows between the building and a small evergreen someone had planted in the yard, taking her with him.

She sighed against his chest. "I do not know why I am here, or why I agreed to go to London." Her voice was sad.

"Because Susanna asked you to." Walter tilted her face upward, using one finger to lift her chin. "She is a good woman, one who does not deserve to be executed for a crime she did not commit. I think you can help her even more than you have already, Eleanor. Will you? If not for Susanna's sake, will you do it for me?"

"Do you care for her so much?"

"As a friend." He'd come to realize during their weeks together at Appleton Manor that his feelings for Susanna had never run as deep as those he now had for Eleanor. "As a friend or a brother. Not as a lover."

Again Eleanor sighed, but this time he thought the sound expressed relief as well as sadness. "She never told me she'd been bound over for trial. In all the time she was at Appleton Manor, she did not mention that until the last day when she bade me make this journey with her."

What Susanna had hoped to gain by keeping Eleanor in the dark for so long had puzzled Walter at the time, but he had discovered years earlier that it was best to let her go her own way. In truth, Susanna had not needed him with her at Appleton Manor, though he was glad he had insisted upon accompanying her.

How else would he have met Eleanor?

"Ever since Susanna told me she might have to stand trial," Eleanor whispered, "I have been afraid—" She broke off, still reluctant to trust him, still fearful of saying too much. "Is Susanna innocent of Robert's murder? Are you certain of it?"

"I am certain."

"What I was concealing did not seem important, not at first."

Pain twisted in Walter's chest. He dreaded hearing her confession. He had learned long ago that appearances could be deceiving. No matter how much he wanted to believe Eleanor innocent, he had to remember that she could be lying. Everyone lied when circumstances demanded it. Even Susanna. And Walter himself twisted the truth more often than he told it.

"You know how hard it is for me to trust anyone," she continued. "I have had to learn to be careful."

"With Robert. But Robert is dead." He stroked his hands down her arms, soothing and caressing all at once. Was this to be the truth now? Or a new lie?

Eleanor's next words revealed that her thoughts ran in a similar vein. "Lady Appleton told me Robert was dead once before and that death turned out to be false."

"Eleanor, if you have information that will help us find his killer, you must share it with me."

Her face buried against his cloak, Eleanor wrapped her arms about his waist and began to sob. He let her cry, wondering whether the tears were genuine or yet another women's ploy. When they subsided, he had to strain to make out her muffled words.

"Robert was at Appleton Manor," Eleanor confessed. "He called himself John Secole. He forced me to shelter him."

Shifting his grip to her shoulders, Walter set her from him. He wanted to see her face but that proved impossible in the darkness of their hiding place. "Did he threaten you?"

"He . . . not in so many words. But he bade me keep his presence secret. I had to dismiss any servants who might recognize him."

"So no one knew he was there but you?" The quality of her sudden stillness gave him his answer. "Who?"

"Matthew," Eleanor admitted. "He found out by accident. Then Robert bullied him into swearing he'd remain silent, too. He reminded Matthew that the Appletons were his clients. Matthew told me that means he cannot, in good conscience, betray anything Robert told him."

Walter was unimpressed by Grimshaw's ethical stand and suspected he'd kept silent as much to protect Eleanor, and himself, as to appease Robert Appleton.

"Do you care for him?" Walter demanded.

"Robert? I—"

"Grimshaw."

Eleanor's brief hesitation was enough to stop his breath. "I did not even realize Matthew had begun to court me until Robert pointed it out. Robert was . . . amused."

And doubtless he'd let Grimshaw see his reaction. For a moment, Walter almost felt sorry for the lawyer.

"It was only after Robert had gone away again that Matthew began to talk about marrying me. I did not mean to encourage him but Appleton Manor can be a lonely place."

His grip on her shoulders tightened.

"I did not let him into my bed," Eleanor blurted.

"Robert?"

"Matthew! I mean neither. I mean, not since London. With Robert. Ohhhh. You are trying to confuse me!" She attempted to pull away from him but he would not release her.

"Shhh." Although he was not sure he believed her denial, he appreciated the sentiment behind the lie. She did not want him to think ill of her. That meant she cared. He tugged her close and bent his head, meaning to kiss her.

"I think Matthew believes I did kill Robert," she whispered when his lips were a scant inch from their target. "He must. He bribed my servants to swear that I never left Appleton Manor, and he invented that story of a visit of his own in order to support their claims."

So that was why her retainers had seemed so nervous. Distracted, Walter substituted another embrace for the kiss he'd intended. He'd seen enough of Grimshaw's behavior to know the man would have accompanied his bribes with threats.

Eleanor stirred in his arms. "Do you believe me innocent of Robert's murder?"

"Lack of trust is not much of a recommendation in a suitor." He did kiss her then, and she returned it with considerable fervor, but before matters could progress much further the slam of a door had them breaking apart in alarm.

A woman carrying a lantern scurried across the coal yard to the privy. Walter pulled Eleanor close once more, to wrap her in the concealing folds of his dark cloak.

"Jennet," he whispered.

"She does not like me," Eleanor whispered back.

"She is loyal to Susanna. She dislikes all of Robert's mistresses."

"Perhaps she killed him," Eleanor suggested, then fell silent.

They might be interrupted again at any moment, Walter realized. And they had been absent from the common room far too long. Bates and Fulke had been absorbed in one of their endless games of Put when they'd slipped away, but the others were bound to notice if they did not return soon.

"Eleanor, I beg you to trust me," he pleaded. "If you know more than you have told us about what Robert planned to do after he left Appleton Manor, you must confide in me now."

He felt her stiffen in his arms.

"Have faith in me. I'll not hold aught you say against you." His innards twisted at the thought she'd refuse.

Reluctance vibrating in every word, she at last began to speak. "Robert did not say much about the future, but he did tell me how he spent the months before he came to Lancashire."

"He had us convinced he'd drowned in the Solent."

He felt her nod, for her cheek once more rested against his chest. "His original plan was to live in Spain. That changed when his mission failed. He never said what it was or what went wrong."

Walter did not enlighten her. After a moment, she resumed her account.

"France, he said, would not have welcomed him, either, so he went to Jersey to regroup. There something unforeseen happened, and he lost all his money."

A similar fate had befallen Eleanor, Walter recalled. No doubt Robert's plight had aroused her sympathy.

"He sent word to me in advance of his arrival, as I have told you. He wrote that he would be using a false name, John Secole."

Walter waited for her to refer to the Knox cipher and the book Susanna had told him she'd found in Eleanor's chamber, but she said nothing about it.

Jennet, weaving slightly, left the privy and returned to the inn. He wondered if she'd been sick. He was feeling a bit queasy himself. Ignoring the growing discomfort in his belly, he continued his gentle interrogation of Eleanor.

"Did Robert write again after he left you?"

"No. Nor did I expect him to. I do not know where he meant to go, Walter. You must believe me. Oh, he'd talked of places in general terms. Of Muscovy and the Indies. Places where he said a clever man might make his fortune. But he was never specific. He did not confide in me, only warned me against telling anyone I'd seen him. He convinced me that Susanna would throw me out into the street if she learned I'd helped him."

"And you believed him?"

"I did not know what to believe. I still do not. Oh, she has said she'll provide for Rosamond, but—"

"Yes. Rosamond." A flare of jealousy seared him at the thought Robert might have wanted to take Eleanor and Rosamond with him. The girl was his only child, and Eleanor had given her to him. "Did Robert—?"

A muffled sound from Eleanor cut him off. It was somewhere between a snort and a laugh. "Robert did not take to fatherhood."

They did not speak for several minutes, content to hold each other in a quiet embrace. "What else can you tell me?" he asked at length. They had little time left if they were to return to the common room without arousing suspicion.

"What else should I know?"

The way she phrased the question made him frown. There was a great deal more he could ask. Had she loved Robert? Did she still seek to protect him? Instead he posed a less crucial question.

"Did he shave his head and beard before or after he left Lancashire?"

She pulled away from him in surprise. "Robert was bald?"

"Aye."

"He died that way?"

The same thought struck them both. Robert had been passing proud of his thick, wavy head of hair. And he'd tended the beard, which had been grown in imitation of Lord Robin, the earl of Leicester, with inordinate care.

Walter tried to fight off a wave of inappropriate mirth but it was no use. Eleanor did not even make the attempt to stay her laughter. A moment later, Walter joined her.

Tears streamed down her face by the time they subsided. Walter's ribs ached. She had not loved Robert. Knowing that, he could hope that she might yet come to love him.

Going their separate ways, they returned to the common room, only to discover that they'd had no need to worry about being missed. Fully half their party had been struck down, apparently by tainted meat, and within the hour Walter, too, was groaning and casting up his accounts.

Their departure was delayed by a day while everyone recovered. The only bright spot was that Eleanor did not fall ill. Working together, she and Susanna and the few others who remained unaffected, nursed the stricken members of their entourage back to health.

Chapter 34

Catherine smelled London before they reached it. A miasma compounded from the stench of tannery and soap factory, sewer and slaughterhouse eddied out into the countryside to give the traveler fair warning of what lay ahead.

Following Aldersgate Street into the city from the northwest, their party of twenty adults and one child arrived on the second day of April, a Monday, having spent Mid-Lent Sunday in Islington. Ten of their number were outriders, the six who had come to Appleton Manor with Annabel and Catherine's escort of four.

Catherine had visited London before, but she had never lived within the city walls. There was something about the place, she decided, sprawling and crowded and noisy as it was, that infused new energy into blood and bone. She sat up straighter in her saddle, straining to see everything at once.

Even the reactions of her traveling companions interested her. Eleanor seemed uneasy, Walter preoccupied. Matthew, as always, was surly. Annabel affected boredom, no doubt convinced that after Paris, no other city could compare. Though she fussed and carried on when she grew overtired, Rosamond, who rode with Susanna, shared Catherine's interest in seeing new things.

And Jennet? Jennet's irritation predominated over other emotions, as it had for most of the journey south. She'd complained bitterly the whole way, until Catherine was ready to suggest leaving her behind at some convenient inn.

She meant well, Catherine reminded herself. Jennet was as concerned about Susanna as Catherine was. That bond kept them tolerant of each other even if they did not agree about how to proceed. Kidnap Susanna? Spirit her away to Scotland? Even as a last, desperate measure to save her life, Catherine could not see any merit in the idea. She would not wish life in Dunfallandy on her worst enemy.

Thinking of that place reminded her of yet another unpleasant fact. Gilbert's mother resided in London. Catherine supposed she would have to call upon her but she did not look forward to the visit. The elderly Scotswoman would want to know why Catherine had deserted her son. And why there were as yet no bairns in Gilbert's nursery.

Up ahead, Susanna reined in her mare. "There is no need for all of us to go to Silver Street."

That was where, according to one of Walter's intelligence gatherers, Robert had kept a room during the last months of his life. The search for it had taken three men more than two months of asking questions all over London and Westminster about a bald man who'd not been seen since the first week in January. At length, their perseverance had paid off and word of their success had reached Walter on the way south.

It must have been the saving grace of the last few weeks for him, Catherine thought. At Coventry, he'd been more ill than anyone else from eating bad meat, and then, just north of Islington, he'd been the only one injured when brigands tried to rob them. His arm was still in a sling.

Catherine shivered, remembering the attack. Such incidents were not uncommon. Travelers were often easy prey. But these fellows had been bold indeed to attack so large a party. Annabel's men had driven them off but not before one had shot Walter with an arrow.

Before going on, Susanna dispatched Annabel and those same henchmen to find an inn large enough to accommodate everyone.

"Accompany them," Catherine ordered her escort.

"And you, Fulke," Susanna added. "You go, too, and when the rooms are bespoken, return to tell us where we will lodge."

Jennet, perforce, went with him, but Susanna did not send Eleanor away.

Walter led the smaller party to the corner of Silver and Mugwell Streets. "This is an area largely inhabited by clothmakers," he remarked. "The house we seek belongs to a French-born tiremaker who specializes in headdresses and periwigs." Robert had hidden in plain sight, counting on his shaved head and beardlessness to be sufficient disguise.

They entered a small enclave created by the north-west angle of the city wall and reined in before a brick house with twin gables. The ground floor was a shop. Robert's room was in the garret.

"Did your lodger have many visitors?" Susanna asked the tiremaker's wife.

The woman wanted no trouble in her adopted country, and Walter handed her a hefty purse to further encourage her cooperation. She assured them that if there had been any, they had taken care not to be seen. She also revealed that the bald man, who'd given his name as John Secole, had paid her well, and in advance, to assure his privacy.

"Do you recognize any among us?" Susanna asked. Their party was still large enough to block the narrow street in front of the shop.

The woman squinted at them—Catherine, Walter, Matthew, Bates, and Eleanor, to whom Susanna had passed Rosamond when they dismounted. She hesitated, then shook her graying head. "Non."

"You are certain?" Susanna pointed to Eleanor. "Not that gentlewoman?"

Both Walter and Matthew started to protest but subsided when the Frenchwoman insisted she'd never seen Eleanor before.

The tiny chamber Robert had occupied was squeezed in under one of the gables. There was barely room to move once Susanna, Catherine, and Walter crowded in.

Walter retreated in order to let Eleanor enter. "I will go and inquire about Robert's horse and leave you three to search."

"What about Matthew?" Eleanor asked. They could hear the lawyer on the stairs.

"He can go wait with Bates."

Poor Bates, Catherine thought. He did not look happy to be back in London. She could only suppose it was because he had become fond of the woman he'd been assigned to guard. Susanna had been unfailingly courteous to him. And she paid him well, besides.

In a battered chest, they found several rolled charts. "Routes to Muscovy," Susanna murmured. She glanced at Catherine. "Your brother was in the duke of Northumberland's household at the time the first expedition was sent there."

She said no more, but Catherine could almost hear her mind working. It flew like a spindle in the hands of an expert spinster.

By the time Fulke appeared, Walter had claimed Robert's horse, a poor specimen compared to Vanguard, and Susanna had turned the Silver Street lodgings upside down and inside out. They carried away with them all of the murdered man's possessions.

A pitiful few, Catherine thought, for a man who'd loved to acquire things. There were no letters from Eleanor or anyone else and only one book, a new copy of John Knox's *The First Blast of the Trumpet Against the Monstrous Regiment of Women* with some of the pages still uncut.

Following Fulke, they left the city through Aldgate on the main road heading east. "No other place was large enough to accommodate so many," he said as he led them through the outer gateway of an inn just beyond the city wall.

The Crowne was larger than it appeared from the street. At the front it extended less than fifty feet, but it was more than three times that long and had been constructed around not one but two yards. The first was surrounded by the main buildings of the inn. Through a second gateway with stories over it lay a stableyard with haylofts. Catherine smiled. Vanguard would be well taken care of.

Their party required all twelve chambers. Their hostess, a widow who introduced herself as Johanne Turnbull, showed them first into the parlor, a wainscotted room comfortably furnished with settles and chairs. An attached gallery looked down into the courtyard. Most pleasing, Catherine decided. But something about the place was not right. Widow Turnbull seemed passing nervous, and Eleanor had lost every bit of the color in her face.

A few minutes later, when Fulke had been dispatched to Leigh Abbey with messages and Susanna had closeted herself with Jennet and Walter to show them the charts she had found, Catherine gave Wynda charge of the child and took Eleanor aside.

"You have been here before. Widow Turnbull recognizes you."

"This is where Robert and I were accustomed to meet." She gave a mirthless little laugh. "Rosamond was conceived here."

Catherine uttered a mild curse. "Did Fulke know this?"

"Certes, he did."

But Fulke had not been in charge of the group assigned to find lodgings. Annabel had. Catherine did not like what she was thinking about her friend's motives, but she knew that Annabel, like Jennet, still thought Eleanor had more cause than anyone else to want Robert dead. With him gone, she'd have expected to stay on as the lady of Appleton Manor and, through Rosamond, might have hoped to one day lay claim to other Appleton holdings. Was staying here a deliberate attempt to put pressure on Eleanor? Catherine shook her head. If it was, Annabel had ignored the fact that Susanna, too, might feel uncomfortable if someone told her the place's significance. Best to keep her in the dark.

"There is no need for Susanna to know," Catherine told Eleanor. Susanna's feelings must be spared. "Instruct Widow Turnbull that she must pretend she has never met you before. Or Fulke. While you deal with her, I will go down to the stables. The ostler is sure to have recognized Vanguard but no doubt a bribe will persuade him to hold his tongue."

"Walter knows about this place." Eleanor said.

"You need not worry about him. He'd never do anything to cause Susanna pain."

But as Catherine watched Eleanor walk away, she wondered. A master of espionage he might be, yet when it came to women, Walter's feelings were as transparent as a clear stream. Susanna had fascinated him for years but he was in love with Eleanor. If the only way to save one woman was to sacrifice the other, Catherine was no longer certain what Sir Walter Pendennis would choose to do.

Chapter 35

Jennet's husband, Mark, arrived at the Crowne on Passion Sunday, bringing their children with him and accompanied by Lionel, Fulke, and Jennet's sister-by-marriage, who had been looking after the three young Jaffreys in Jennet's absence.

Lady Appleton, who had sent Fulke to Leigh Abbey merely to inform Mark that they were now in London, needed only one quick glance at the little group to realize that Jennet had sent a message of her own. "In my chamber," she ordered. "Now."

"Do you think she is angry?" Mark asked.

Jennet did not bother to answer.

The inn's rooms were large and well furnished, with hardwood floors and plaster walls. Lady Appleton's chamber contained a bed, a chair, a window seat and a table set out with green, lead-glazed earthenware mugs and an earthenware jug filled with the best ale. Lady Appleton did not offer her steward a drink. She waved Mark and Jennet in, closed the door, and stood with her back against it.

"Well, Mark?"

"Madam?"

"Why have you brought your children to London?"

"Mistress Rosamond needs other little ones to play with," Jennet suggested, in the faint hope that Lady Appleton had not guessed their true intent—to gather the family together in preparation to flee the country.

"Indeed, she does," Lady Appleton agreed, "but I had planned to send her to Leigh Abbey, not import playmates for her."

This was news to Jennet. She frowned, unsure how to respond.

"Rosamond is my heir," Lady Appleton informed Mark.

Jennet made a sound of protest, but Lady Appleton did not give her time to speak.

"I have lawyers working to assure her right to inherit even if I am executed for killing her father. Matters will, however, be much simpler if I can avoid that fate. In either case, her mother and I have agreed that Rosamond should live at Leigh Abbey."

Mark looked worried.

"Are there problems?" Lady Appleton asked.

"No more than there were when you left."

"Ah. People believe I am guilty."

"They would not be so certain of it if Alys Putney had kept her mouth shut. She and her husband have gone out of their way to spread rumors. They even claim you have done other murders, madam, using poisons from that book you wrote."

Lady Appleton closed her eyes as if she fought

257

a wave of pain. Jennet knew what she was thinking. Lady Appleton had never poisoned anyone. She'd written her cautionary herbal in an attempt to save lives, but other less scrupulous people had realized that they could find recipes for death within its pages. For that, Jennet's mistress held herself accountable.

"Go on," Lady Appleton said to Mark. "What else do the Putneys say?"

"They talk of making a special trip to London to attend your trial and witness your execution. Alys seems to relish that prospect in particular."

"How delightful." Lady Appleton sounded more amused than annoyed. "You give me greater incentive, Mark, to discover the identity of the real murderer. I am loath to provide so much entertainment for my husband's former mistress. But, tell me, what other news from Leigh Abbey?"

"Jennet's cow is thriving." Mark grinned.

Jennet did not see the humor in his remark, but she shared his relief at being able to turn the conversation away from the coming trial.

"Excellent," Lady Appleton declared. "And the other livestock?"

Mark made his report. It evolved into a discussion of spring planting and from there the talk moved on to the subject of the increased cost of fish in Lent. Jennet stopped listening. Instead, she brooded.

Little had been accomplished since their arrival in London. They'd found nothing helpful in Sir

Robert's lodgings. Questioning residents of that area of London had yielded no useful information. Even a meeting with Nicholas Baldwin had been futile.

Leigh Abbey's nearest neighbor was a merchant of the staple, as his father had been. His primary business was the export of wool, but he also owned several ships. In his younger days, he had gone as a stipendiary to Muscovy and traveled much in exotic lands. After finding the maps Sir Robert had left behind, Lady Appleton had hoped Master Baldwin might help her trace Sir Robert's movements in the days before his death.

"Jennet?"

Recalled to the present, Jennet started and stared. Lady Appleton's brows lifted. "Woolgathering? Making more plans to assure my well-being?"

The sarcastic question pushed Jennet into impulsive speech. "You cannot expect us to allow you to forfeit your life."

"You must not act rashly," Lady Appleton warned.

"We must act as we see fit. Legal or illegal, it matters not when—"

"Jennet! I cannot allow this." She put one hand on Jennet's shoulder, the other on Mark's forearm. "Think, my dear friends. If you try to rescue me and fail, you will yourselves be put on trial. You have children to think of, your own and Rosamond. Take them to Leigh Abbey. Stay there. If the worst happens and the Crown seizes all I own, I have Catherine's promise that she will look out for you."

Tears stained Jennet's cheeks. It would not come to that. She'd not allow it, no matter what Lady Appleton said.

When Mark left for Leigh Abbey the next morning, he took the children, but Jennet stayed at her mistress's side.

Chapter 36

"Come, Bates. We've places to go. People to see."

"The stews again?" There was a hopeful note in his voice.

In the three weeks they'd been back in London, Bates had ceased to be either surprised or shocked by the breadth of Susanna's acquaintance. She'd twice visited the Sign of the Smock, the brothel in Southwark where she'd left her horse on the day she'd gone to Westminster to meet Robert.

Vincent Cheyne, who owned the place now, had access to the underworld of London, where rumors flew and secrets proliferated. Just as Walter had investigated the possibility that some foreign power had wanted Robert dead, Vincent was trying to verify that no one connected to the brothels, past or present, had taken a hand in the murder.

"Not today, Bates," she told her guard. "Our destination this time is Whitehall."

An hour later, she was private with the Lady Mary in the same room over the water gate where they had met before. Once again she'd come in response to a letter from the noblewoman.

"I intend to ask the queen to pardon you if you are found guilty," the Lady Mary said.

"I appreciate your kindness, my lady," Susanna

replied, "but the queen may not be inclined to grant a pardon. The earl of Leicester has her ear, and he believes me guilty."

"The earl cannot compete with the one thing which it is in my power to trade for this favor. I mean to tell my cousin that I will give up my claim to the throne, renounce it forever, if she will let you go free."

Susanna struggled to hide her surprise and fought, too, with the oppressive sense of impending doom that had of late become her frequent companion. After all this time, they were no closer to finding proof of her innocence than they had been at the beginning.

"I pray it does not come to that, my lady," she said when she had control of her emotions, "and that there will be no need for you to make such a sacrifice."

"It is no great sacrifice," the Lady Mary assured her, "though Queen Elizabeth will never believe that. I have always longed to disentangle myself from the intrigues of the court. I have no desire to rule this land and little hope, in truth, of surviving my cousin to do so. The royal blood in my veins does naught but threaten my happiness."

"Your . . . happiness?"

"Aye." She lowered her voice, though there was no one in the room with them to overhear what she said. "Once I am no longer in line for the succession, I will be able to marry the man I love."

Susanna felt her face lose its color. When the

Lady Mary's sister, the Lady Catherine, had found herself to be with child, she had confided in Lady St.Loe, and even though that gentlewoman had promptly betrayed her trust, she'd ended up spending an uncomfortable stretch in the Tower of London, imprisoned for the misfortune of knowing what she should not. The Lady Mary had just placed Susanna in the selfsame untenable position.

"Your pardon, my lady, but there is a flaw in your logic."

"What flaw?" It was plain to Susanna that she had not given the Lady Mary the response she had hoped for.

"Any child you bear in wedlock will have a claim to the throne. The queen will not grant you permission to marry for that reason and if you elope, as your sister did, you will doubtless share her fate—separated from your husband and imprisoned for the rest of your life."

"I thought you were my friend!" the Lady Mary shouted. The Tudor blood in her veins became readily apparent when she lost her temper. "I expected you to be happy for me!"

"Friends must be honest with one another," Susanna said in a quiet voice.

"Here's honesty, then! If you do not agree to help me to marry, in secret if need be, I will not lift a finger to prevent your execution."

Stifling a sigh, Susanna sketched a curtsey. She owed the Lady Mary a great deal. "I will do all I can for you, no matter the outcome of the trial, but I beg you, my lady, for your own sake, be discreet."

Mollified, the Lady Mary gave a regal nod, told her she would hold her to her promise, and dismissed her.

The quickest way back to the Crowne from Westminster was by water. As she boarded a wherry for the short journey, Susanna caught herself wishing she and Bates had come on horseback. Her stomach lurched in response to every bob of the small boat.

Susanna frowned and considered her symptoms. Could there be another cause? No, she supposed not. She knew this particular feeling all too well. And yet, ever since that incident at Coventry, she had found herself watching her companions closely, noting every morsel each of them ate, alert for any sign of a reaction. A worrying possibility nagged at her—had someone added poison to their food? She did not like to think that her quest for Robert's killer had placed her friends in jeopardy.

As the unsettled feeling grew stronger, Susanna was obliged to abandon her deliberations and fix her gaze on the near shore. If she stared at it and willed herself to ignore the physical discomfort she could combat the sense of panic that accompanied it. She knew now that she was not ill. This was only an unfortunate reaction to being afloat on the Thames.

It galled her that the condition seemed to be growing more acute. If she did not remember to dose herself with ginger or peppermint, and that on top of the ginger root already contained in her daily tonic, she could scarce abide the sight of open water. In the course of the last year, what had once been a simple case of *mal de mer* on choppy seas had grown into something much more pervasive.

Susanna's relief was near overwhelming when the wherry set them ashore just west of London bridge. It was high tide, the boatman said, and he did not wish to risk shooting the arches. Susanna applauded his caution. Stronger stomachs than hers had been overset during such fast and dangerous rides beneath the bridge.

"We are hard by Master Baldwin's place of business," she told Bates after she had surveyed the immediate area. When she'd last been here, it had been in Walter's company. It occurred to her now, somewhat belatedly, that if Baldwin knew Walter was an intelligence gatherer, he might have been loath to share information. But if she returned alone . . .

Billingsgate harbor was the largest inlet east of London Bridge and was located convenient to the Customs House. All manner of wares were unloaded onto its wharves. From the old parish church of St. Botolph, which had been secularized and was now let out as chambers and apartments, she had no difficulty spotting the large stone building that housed Baldwin's business. A cavernous warehouse occupied the entire ground floor. On the upper level were a hall, kitchen, and parlor.

When she and Bates gave their names and were shown into the latter, Susanna expected to find Nick Baldwin waiting. Instead, she faced a formidable female some two decades her senior. From certain similarities about the eyes and chin, Susanna concluded this was Baldwin's mother. His father, she recalled, had died shortly before the younger Baldwin's return to England from a long sojourn in Muscovy and Persia.

Susanna's hostess did not seem pleased to have visitors. She folded plump, beringed hands over her stomacher and regarded both Susanna and Bates with distaste. The hands, too, gave away her identity. Like her son, she had short, thick fingers.

Susanna was unsure what to say. With a sense of mild surprise, she realized that although she'd come to ask Baldwin specific questions, she'd also counted on using him as a sounding board. Her old friends were blindly loyal to her. Those under suspicion had their own agendas. She longed to discuss what little she had found out with someone who was not directly involved in the investigation.

"I am Winifred Baldwin," the woman said, breaking the uncomfortable silence. "Nick is my son."

"Forgive my intrusion, Mistress Baldwin. I am Susanna Appleton. I came in the hope that your son might have uncovered information concerning my late husband's plans to journey to Muscovy."

Mistress Baldwin's nostrils flared. "Muscovy? Cursed place!"

Susanna had noticed the contents of the small parlor when she first entered it. Now her gaze slipped unbidden to the proof that, however much she might dislike her son's interest in trade with the east, she enjoyed its benefits. Every table was covered with Turkey carpet. A chased-silver timepiece sat on the one nearest the hearth. Another held a delicate green glass vase containing an arrangement of dried flowers. Even Mistress Baldwin herself displayed the advantages of trade with exotic ports. She wore an underdress of silk, doubtless from Persia, and a gown trimmed with lettice fur from Muscovy. Her hands were adorned with a small fortune in opals.

"Cursed it may be," said a deep voice from the doorway, "but always profitable." Baldwin nodded to Susanna as he crossed the room to kiss his mother's leathery cheek.

"Your father never saw the need to travel farther than Calais," she grumbled.

"Calais no longer belongs to England," he reminded her.

"Antwerp, then."

An apprentice had followed Baldwin into the room, his dark fustian and plain linen a marked contrast to his master's flame-colored satin doublet. Baldwin's surcoat and cap were plain black wool, but his shirt was of lawn and elaborately embroidered.

"Lady Appleton and I have business to discuss in the counting house," he told his mother.

She sputtered a protest, but he whisked Susanna and Bates from the room. The apprentice remained behind to assure their privacy.

A few minutes later, Bates had been relegated to the street outside the warehouse, and Susanna was alone with Baldwin in the small, cluttered room from which he ran his business. "I have been unable to find anyone who dealt with Sir Robert," he told her. "I am sorry."

Baldwin motioned for her to take the chair pulled up to his writing table. In neat order atop it were a leather-bound ledger stitched with crisscross vellum and buckled with leather straps, two slender pewter inkwells, an assortment of quills, a box of sand to sprinkle over the wet ink of his letters, and his seal and signet ring.

Susanna felt too restless to sit. She shook her head and went to the small chamber's only window. It looked east along the river.

"Have you found out any more about your husband's plans to go to Muscovy?"

Susanna turned her back on the window. Baldwin stood beside a carved wooden shelf that held several standing boxes made of spruce and pinewood and hasped with steel. She presumed they contained papers he had filed. Tucked in beneath the shelf was a round moneybox. A pomander ball hung down next to it, scenting the air with cloves.

"Sir Walter continues to ask questions," Susanna said. "Answers are rare."

Baldwin's intent gaze discomfited her. She evaded it by pretending an interest in the narrow laths that ran around the paneled walls. They served, she saw, as letter racks.

"I have found nothing to indicate he did intend to journey to Muscovy. Only one annual journey is possible by the northern route England controls. Ships leave London in May and return between August and October."

Susanna considered this. "Then either Robert laid his plans well in advance, or he had some other scheme in mind." It would have been dangerous to wait around London that long after she brought him the gold. On the other hand, he had paid for his lodgings in Silver Street through Easter.

"He might have intended to purchase his own ship. The Muscovy Company is supposed to control all trade between England and Russia, but in practice free agents trade in Narva, on the Baltic. Even merchants who are part of the Muscovy Company sometimes engage in private trade."

He slanted a smile in her direction and reminded her that he had himself made such an expedition to Persia, without official backing. He had acquired considerable wealth as a result. For a little while, Susanna permitted herself to talk of such pleasant things as spices and silk and exotic locales, but in the end, she had to return to her present dilemma.

He made a most excellent sounding board, even if talking to him did not lead her to any new conclusions. "Did Robert ever speak to you of your travels?" she asked when she had gone to stand by the window again. She saw that a large ship had anchored in mid river while they'd talked. A second was maneuvering away from the Customs House. "I do not doubt what you said when I came here in Sir Walter's company, but perhaps there is more you are willing to say outside his hearing?"

"You know Sir Robert and I spoke of my travels on one occasion. We met in my house in Kent a short time before he left on his mission to Spain."

That had been the same trip that had taken him away from England and prevented him from knowing of it when Eleanor gave birth to Rosamond. Susanna also remembered that the meeting between the two men had not been an amicable encounter. Baldwin had taken an instant dislike to his new neighbor. When Susanna had first met him a few days later, the animosity had initially spilled over onto her.

"I thought perhaps you had seen him again," she said softly, "or had some word of him."

"I'd have told you, even in Sir Walter's presence." He came up beside her. "I could have you on a ship in an hour and it would take you any-where you chose."

Susanna could not help herself. She started to laugh. There were tears streaming down her cheeks by the time she had control of herself again. Baldwin looked alternately alarmed and confused by her reaction. When she explained the reason for her outburst, he stared at her with somber eyes.

"You put overmuch faith in the law. Perhaps your friends, all of us, have the right of it."

Perhaps they did, but Susanna could not allow herself to think that way. She would be plunged into the depths of despair if she let herself dwell on the horrifying possibilities.

"Say rather that I trust in mine own abilities and the common sense of a jury." She was deter-mined to sound optimistic. "There's time yet."

To her surprise, he took her hands in his. "I hope you are right, Susanna. I find I want very much to keep you in my life."

He said no more, to her relief, and shifted his grip to her elbow to guide her outside to the wait-ing Bernard Bates. It was nearly dusk, for she had spent far longer than she'd intended in Nick Baldwin's company.

With a final wave, he vanished back into the warehouse.

Susanna started walking. The oyster shells beneath her feet gave way to cobblestones. She followed no particular route as she considered what to do next and paid little attention to her surroundings. She had only a vague awareness of many tenements and a proliferation of narrow alleys, dark as the inside of a coal mine, that ran between the close-set buildings.

The attack came without warning. Bates, struck down by a blow to the head from behind, had no chance to defend her. Susanna was roughly seized and dragged into an opening no wider than a doorway. Before she could draw breath to scream, a dirty hand clapped over her mouth.

The upper stories of buildings on either side jutted out, narrowing the alley still further and preventing anyone above her from seeing what was happening. Susanna kicked out, her wooden heel connecting with her captor's shin, but her only reward was a clout to the head. Ears ringing, she fought dizziness as he shoved the fabric of her own hood over her face to cut off her air.

What must have been a shout, perhaps even a bellow of rage, reached Susanna only as a dull grunt. She was perilous near unconsciousness when a second pair of strong hands seized her and pulled her backwards. Bates had recovered, she thought, as she tumbled to the hard, filthy ground and rolled over twice before she could stop herself. By the time she'd thrown back her hood and struggled to a sitting position, the battle was over.

A man stood over his fallen opponent, his breathing ragged and his chest heaving. Not

Bates. Baldwin. As if he felt her eyes upon him, he turned to stare at her.

"Are you hurt?" he asked.

"No." She got her feet under her and rose. "Are you?"

Instead of answering, he knelt by the attacker for a moment. "I hit him too hard," he said.

Approaching with caution, she was near enough when Baldwin flexed his fist to see that his knuckles were flecked with blood. "You are hurt. Let me see."

But he shook his head and evaded her touch. "I hit him too hard," he said again. "He is dead."

"You saved my life."

"Thank my mother," he said in a grim voice. "She's the one who was watching for your departure from her window and saw that you were followed when you left the warehouse."

The implications hit Susanna all at once. She swayed. If the wall of a house had not been there to support her, she might well have fallen.

"Someone just tried to kill me," she whispered.

And it might not have been the first time.

Chapter 37

"Marry me, Eleanor."

Slowly her eyes opened. The passion that had been there moments before faded away, replaced by sudden alarm. Then that, too, vanished. She sat up in Walter's bed, brought her knees to her chest, wrapped her arms around them, and began to sob.

"Eleanor, I did not mean . . . I—I—" He broke off, bereft of words, and before he could regroup there came a knocking too loud and insistent to ignore.

"Stay here, love," he told her as he struggled into hose and shirt, doublet and ruff. "A moment!" he shouted in the direction of the outer room. He'd given his manservant the day off shortly after Eleanor arrived at his door.

Her sobbing subsided into muffled sniffles. Walter was loath to leave her this way. Memories of an unfortunate incident in his youth haunted him.

"Promise me you will not do anything foolish." He fixed her with a hard stare. A grim note entered his voice. "Swear it, Eleanor."

Wiping the tears from her face, she took the clothing he passed through the bed curtains and gave him a watery but reassuring smile. "I swear."

The outer room contained signs he'd had a visitor but none that would give away her identity.

Walter closed the door to his bedchamber, tugged a final time at his doublet to make sure it hung straight, and answered the insistent hammering, which had now resumed with less force but just as much urgency.

Susanna nearly fell into his lodgings. Bernard Bates, eyes glassy and a huge lump rising on his forehead, followed after.

"What in God's name—?"

"Someone tried to kill me, Walter."

"Are you hurt?"

She shook her head. "Master Baldwin came to my rescue."

"The attacker?"

"Dead."

"Did you recognize him?"

"No. He was a vagabond by his clothing. But strong." Her hand drifted to her lips. If he looked closely, he could just make out the imprint of a man's fingers in the soft flesh around her mouth.

A table by the window held a large brown earthenware flask of ale, but both Bates and Susanna looked as if they could do with something more potent. Walter unearthed a bottle of aqua vitae from a cupboard and poured out three portions.

"Sit," he ordered. Susanna moved restlessly about the room.

"I cannot be still."

He thrust the cup into her hand and steered her toward the Glastonbury chair. "Sit," he repeated. "Drink this down."

"Which of us is the healer?" she demanded as reluctant amusement made one corner of her mouth quirk upward.

She sat. She drank. She made a face at the fiery taste of the liquid but she obeyed his command. If he had not been so troubled by what had happened to Susanna, Walter would have appreciated the remarkableness of having compelled two strong-minded women to do his bidding in the space of a few minutes.

With careful questioning, he soon had the details of the attack and had heard, although without specifics, of Susanna's visit to the Lady Mary. She did not think she had been followed from Whitehall, but she could not be sure. Bates had not noticed anything, either. He'd been hit from behind and fallen forward. The lump on his forehead from a hard landing had a twin behind his right ear.

"It might have been a random act of violence," Walter suggested. "A thief after your purse."

"He tried to smother me, Walter, not pick my pocket."

"A pity he is dead and cannot be questioned."

"Yes."

"This Baldwin . . . had he any enmity with Robert?"

"Not sufficient to want to kill him. And he had no reason to harm me. Or to frighten and then rescue me, either, if that is what you are thinking."

"I do not know what to think," Walter admitted,

not about what had befallen Susanna nor about what had passed between himself and Eleanor.

"There's more," Susanna said.

"More?"

"What if the robbers north of Islington were paid to attack us? I could as easily have been struck by their arrows as you. If someone is willing to pay to have others kill, then it is even possible the woman with Robert was hired, paid, and given poison to put in his food. Paid to kiss him, too."

"She might have done that of her own accord. Susanna, this seems far-fetched." Absently, he rubbed his arm where the healing arrow wound still felt sore to the touch. "Footpads, on the road or in London, are always a hazard to honest folk."

"And the tainted meat at Coventry?"

"You cannot think—"

"I do not know what to think!" Hands in the air, she gave him a look filled with frustration." Nor do I know who to suspect. It could be any one of them." A rueful smile flashed and was gone. "At least this seems to confirm that I've been on the right track. I had begun to wonder if concentrating on former mistresses was a mistake. But if Robert was killed by some foreign mercenary, or by an old enemy we knew nothing about, then no one would be bothering about me now."

"Unless these are random incidents with no connection to each other or to your investigation." Walter picked up his cup of aqua vitae and drank deeply. "But assuming you are correct, is it not significant that there were no problems until after Annabel joined us?"

"There were none until we started for London. None until I insisted Eleanor and Rosamond accompany me here."

"She could have been struck by that arrow," he reminded her. His body had shielded Eleanor during the attack.

Susanna said nothing.

Walter's experiences working for the queen's government had taught him to be suspicious of everyone but a few hours earlier, when Eleanor had surprised him by arriving unannounced and unescorted at his lodgings, he'd not looked for ulterior motives. She'd said she needed his help, that Matthew Grimshaw was making her life a misery. One thing had led to another, in what had appeared to Walter to be a natural manner. After keeping careful distance from him since that night in Coventry, save for sharing his horse, she'd given herself to him at last, even told him that she loved him.

It had not occurred to him till now that Eleanor might have come to him to distract him, to keep him away from Susanna. In the course of his day, as had been his habit since their return to London, he'd have gone to the Crowne. He'd have been there when Susanna left to meet with the Lady Mary, and he'd have insisted upon accompanying her. If she'd had a two-man escort, she'd not have been so vulnerable to attack. The attempt might not have been made at all.

But he had not been with Susanna, and someone had tried to kill her.

Someone had hired the fellow. That seemed certain. London was not so infected with crime that a woman with an escort was in danger of attack. Not in the ordinary way of things.

One question nagged at him above all others. Had Eleanor arranged today's events? If so, she might have put something in the food at Coventry. She could have hired vagabonds to ambush their party. And if she had done all those things, it could only have been because she had killed Robert.

With sudden bitterness, Walter remembered that Eleanor had claimed Matthew Grimshaw, in a fit of jealous pique, had threatened her, told her that if she did not return with him to Lancashire at once and marry him, he would swear she had been gone from Appleton Manor at Yuletide. A lie, she'd vowed. But would it have been? What if her story about Grimshaw was the lie, told to rouse his jealousy as well as his protective instincts?

Walter knew her servants had been bribed. She'd told him so herself. According to her earlier story, Grimshaw had bribed them to back up his story that he'd been with her when Robert died and could thus swear she'd never left Appleton Manor, a fabrication designed to bolster Eleanor's claim of innocence. Grimshaw, she'd told Walter, had insisted she'd need a gentleman's word to verify her whereabouts and had been willing to perjure himself to help her. Eleanor claimed she'd needed no such saving, but if her servants would lie for Grimshaw's gold, they'd have lied for Eleanor's.

What if she had come to London to be with Robert, her old lover? What if they had fallen out?

Eleanor had cried, and Walter had comforted her. They'd ended up in bed together, pleasuring each other in the most splendid ways imaginable. All a fraud? He wanted to believe in her, but if he was wrong, his error in judgment could cost Susanna her life.

He would have to ask more questions, he decided. Discover if anyone had seen a woman and a child near Robert's lodgings in Silver Street. Or at the Crowne. Or a woman without a baby, he supposed, since Eleanor had seemed willing enough to send the child off to Kent with Susanna's steward.

"Round and round," he muttered. Who was telling the truth? Who was lying? And what had Susanna done to acquire such a relentless enemy?

"Walter, you are behaving in a most strange manner." Susanna's sharp voice broke in on his thoughts.

"I apologize, my dear."

Susanna seemed calm now, her old self. Her gaze, fixed on him, was too sharp for his liking. "Why would anyone want me dead before the trial? We have made so little progress in proving my innocence that most people would conclude my fate sealed. Why attempt to save the executioner the trouble of doing his job?"

"Perhaps someone has reason to fear what might be revealed at your trial."

Susanna sighed and swallowed the last of the aqua vitae, grimacing at the taste. "This attack on me today, at least, must be connected to Robert's murder."

Walter answered her with a reluctant nod. He would not condemn Eleanor out of hand. There were other possibilities. He glanced at Susanna's guard. The fellow had a way of fading into the background. People forgot he was there.

"What did you see, Bates?"

"Stars." He rubbed the lump on his head.

"No one lurking in the shadows?"

"Only the villain who attacked us and him too late."

"Bates did his best." Susanna sighed. "And now, you must agree, we can limit our suspects to those traveling with us."

"And to Alys Putney and her husband." A glimmer of hope raised Walter's spirits. Putney could have hired someone to dispose of Susanna. "According to the most recent report from my agents there, both Putney and his wife were absent from Dover on the third day of January."

"But why would Robert be so friendly with Alys? She makes no attempt to hide her contempt for him."

"To convince her husband to arrange passage out of the country?" Resting one hip against the table and staring off into space, Walter warmed to a theory that had no connection to Eleanor. "Putney is more than a simple innkeeper, Susanna. He's a known smuggler." Walter's men had confirmed that fact in recent months, though they had not proof enough to arrest him.

With irrefutable logic, Susanna dismantled Walter's case. "If Putney wanted Robert dead, why would he resort to poison? It would have been far simpler to provide him with the ship he wanted and then dispose of him at sea. As for the attack on me, what profit in that for Putney or his wife? I am told they look forward to seeing me burn."

"Perhaps that is only what they want people to think. A clever—"

"Putney? Clever?" At Walter's wince, Susanna left the chair to lay a comforting hand on his arm.

"We must consider every one of Robert's former mistresses a suspect," she said, "no matter how painful it is. I have come to like Eleanor, too. Indeed, she would make you an admirable wife."

He choked on the swallow of aqua vitae he'd just taken. "Susanna—"

"No, say nothing. I do but offer my opinion." She hesitated. "'Twas kind of you both to try to spare my feelings about the inn."

"You knew—?"

"That Eleanor was accustomed to meet Robert

there? That Rosamond was conceived in one of the Crowne's chambers?" Her smile was faint and tinged with sadness."That small mystery, at least, I was capable of solving. No doubt you paid our hostess well, but she has no skill at hiding her reactions. I saw at once that she recognized Eleanor. Then there was Fulke's behavior. Deception does not suit him. He looked guilty every time he saw me and even lost some of his enjoyment in trying to beat Bates at cards."

"Staying at the Crowne was not Eleanor's doing."

"I never thought it was. Annabel selected the inn. Fulke admitted she'd asked him where Robert stayed in the old days. Once she had out of him its connection to Eleanor, she deliberately chose the Crowne."

Walter wondered why. The most obvious reason was to pressure Eleanor into revealing what little she knew of Robert's activities as an intelligence gatherer from the days before Rosamond's birth. "For all her charm and sense of humor," he said aloud, "we would be wise to remember that Annabel MacReynolds is in the pay of France."

"And yet she has seemed content to do no more than keep Catherine company these last few weeks in London."

"Seemed," Walter agreed. "She has found time to visit the Scots ambassador and stop at the French embassy."

"Oh, most suspicious!" Her eyes twinkled. They

both knew it would have been more unusual if Annabel had not done so.

"I will find out more. We have time yet before the quarter sessions begin."

"Less than a fortnight." She left him to wander the room. He'd never seen her less able to remain still.

"Robert's killer has made a mistake," he said in a soft voice. "Indeed, we may be able to use the fact that you were attacked as evidence that you did not poison your husband, that you have made whoever did . . . nervous."

"A tenuous argument at best." Walter did not think he'd ever heard Susanna sound so discouraged.

"You are tired. You have been through an ordeal. And it grows late. I will send for an armed escort to take you back to the Crowne."

"Back to where a murderer may also lodge."

"Bates will be more watchful now. And he will explain the situation to Fulke, who will help him." He gave the guard a meaningful look. "It would be best, however, not to tell anyone else what happened this evening. Whoever paid your attacker may make a foolish mistake in an attempt to discover why and how he failed to kill you."

"And there is no sense in frightening the others." She nodded. "Agreed."

★ ★ ★

When Susanna and Bates had gone, Walter had to face the fear that had been gnawing at him all

284

the while they'd been with him. If Eleanor had tried and failed to bring about Susanna's death, there was a possibility she might have taken her own life rather than face his questions.

Once before he had been the cause of a woman's death. Her image simmered in his mind's eye, a tall lass with a porcelain pallor, colt-like features, and red-gold hair. A maidservant in his father's house. She had been Walter's first woman. And his brother's. One of them had gotten her with child. She'd died trying to rid herself of the babe. Whether the suicide had been intentional or not, it had been regarded as such by the church. She had been buried at the crossroads instead of in the churchyard, a stake driven through her heart to prevent her from coming back to haunt the living.

With trepidation that bordered on dread, Walter entered his bedchamber. He'd heard not a whisper of sound from the other side of the door in all the time Susanna had been in the outer room. At first, he'd convinced himself that was good. He'd not wanted Susanna to learn of Eleanor's presence.

Now he feared the worst. How distraught had Eleanor been? His heart gave a painful lurch when he parted the bed hangings and saw her lying so still.

Asleep, he realized after an agonizing moment. Only asleep. The sleep of the innocent?

He let the curtains fall back into place. He loved her. He loved Eleanor, and he might lose her.

The most logical argument Susanna could present in court to prove herself innocent would point the finger of suspicion at Eleanor.

Unless he himself confessed.

The idea shocked Walter at first but the more he thought about it, the more sense it made. He had it in his power to save both Susanna and Eleanor. All he had to do was stand up in court and swear he had murdered Robert Appleton.

The reason? There was fine irony. He could say, with truth, that all those weeks ago he'd wanted Robert dead so that Susanna would marry him. Had he but known Robert was still alive to be killed, that motive might indeed have been sufficient to tempt him to murder.

Chapter 38

The Crowne Inn
May 4, 1565

Susanna looked up in surprise when Catherine burst into the inn's parlor.

"Annabel is gone," she cried.

"What do you mean *gone*?" Walter demanded.

A glance around proved she was the only one missing. Bates and Fulke suspended one of their endless games of Put to stare at Catherine. Jennet continued to mend a sleeve by the light from the window, but she was alert and listening. Walter had been passing the time at chess, playing against Matthew Grimshaw, while Susanna and Eleanor talked together in a quiet corner.

Over the last week, Susanna had attempted to teach Rosamond's mother all she knew about managing an estate. The trial was only days away, and the prospect of acquittal grew ever more remote. Susanna had learned nothing new about Robert's murder since the attack on her in Billingsgate. She had even begun to wonder if the two crimes were connected.

"My guess is that Annabel is halfway to Dover by now," Catherine said. "The weather has been fair and dry since May Day. She'll make good time." Her voice broke under her distress. "I was so sure Annabel was sincere when she said she wanted to help, but she left without a word and took her escort and all her possessions with her."

Matthew Grimshaw gave a crow of triumph. "Check," he said. And then, "There's your poisoner, I warrant. Flight from justice is proof of guilt."

Susanna saw his eyes dart to Eleanor in hope of praise for this clever deduction. When Eleanor did not notice, Grimshaw's face took on an expression of longing so pained that Susanna almost pitied him. He had to know that Eleanor favored Walter Pendennis. Everyone else did.

"There's a chance yet to catch her," Walter said. "A woman traveling with an escort of six brawny Scots should be easy to spot." He left the room to arrange to send men after them.

"She's guilty," Grimshaw repeated. "Mark my words, she poisoned Sir Robert."

"Difficult to prove if she eludes Sir Walter's men." Given the threatening expression on the intelligence gatherer's face, Susanna almost hoped Annabel did manage to cross the Narrow Seas ahead her pursuers.

"There might be another reason to go to France." Catherine brightened. "Perhaps she has gone to ask Queen Catherine to intervene on Susanna's behalf."

"What influence does a Frenchwoman, even a queen, have in England?" Grimshaw scoffed. "Running away proves her guilt, I say. Clear and simple."

Catherine turned on her cousin. "Why don't you just go back to Lancashire. No one wants you here. You'll be no help whatsoever when it comes to defending Susanna."

"Defend her? But no lawyer can do that. Did you not realize? This is a criminal trial. Those accused of murder are not permitted any legal representation. And although the accused may call witnesses, they are not sworn. The prosecution case is, by definition, assumed to be unanswerable."

"What nonsense!" Catherine's protest was echoed by Jennet but Walter, who had returned to the room in time to hear Grimshaw's words, said nothing.

Grimshaw shrugged. "Such is the law. Ask Sir Walter if you do not believe me. He is no lawyer, but he is familiar with trials. He will confirm what I say."

Susanna sent a considering look in Walter's direction, noted how uncomfortable he looked, and suggested that it was time the two of them spoke in private. A short while later, in her bed-chamber, Susanna steeled herself to hear the whole truth.

"How will my trial proceed?" she asked. "Spare me no detail."

Walter took the window seat. Susanna sat on the bed. Jennet, who had slipped into the room uninvited, remained by the door, quiet as a mouse but listening intently to every word.

"About a half dozen persons are tried at a time," he told them, after he reminded her that her case had already been presented to a grand jury. The presentment had become an indictment when it had been written down in the prescribed Latin form. "A jury is impanelled only after enough prisoners have been arraigned. The sheriff has jurymen in attendance and they are called into court one by one. As each juror steps forward, his name is marked with a dot by the clerk. A prisoner has the right to challenge up to a total of twenty of these jurors without giving any reason for the challenge."

He stopped speaking and looked thoughtful.

"If every prisoner exercised this right, it would delay the trial. If they took their challenges in turns, it would become near impossible to try any one. A panel of 132 would be needed to exhaust all the challenges of only six offenders."

"What purpose would delay serve?" Susanna asked. "And why, if this method is so effective, is it not done by all prisoners all the time?"

"Few try this means to delay the trial because they have no one to advise them it might work. Grimshaw was correct to say you are allowed no counsel. You will be told you have nothing to lose and everything to gain from telling your story yourself."

"And if I attempt this challenge?"

"The justices could deal with it by giving you a separate jury."

She thought that sounded sensible, but from the look on Walter's face deduced it was a bad idea. "Am I permitted to ask questions of the witnesses against me?"

"Aye."

"Good. I have given some thought to that fellow Higgins from the Black Jack. Is it possible that, faced with several women, all hooded, he might admit he could not be sure he saw me that night?"

Jennet, who had stood silent till now, startled Walter when she spoke up. "You could force them to be present. Alys and Eleanor and, can you but capture her, Annabel."

"Even if they all agree to cooperate," Walter said, "Higgins will not be inclined to help. A Crown witness can be punished if he gives evidence that leads to the acquittal of a prisoner."

Jennet protested the unfairness of such a policy but Susanna said nothing. Perhaps, she thought, she should have inquired into trial procedures at an earlier date. Then another thought struck her. "I am permitted witnesses, am I not?" Grimshaw had said so, but he had little experience with this sort of law. Most of his business in Manchester dealt with wills and land disputes.

"Aye. Since Queen Mary's time, those who can be brought in to speak in favor of the accused are heard, though no law requires this. But although such witnesses are exhorted to stand in fear of God and tell the truth, they are not sworn, as Crown witnesses are, and this makes all they say suspect."

"I had thought to bring Vincent Cheyne in, to swear to the time I left my horse with him."

"Even if he noted the time, those in the Black Jack did not." Walter looked pained. "Besides, once Cheyne's ownership of the Sign of the Smock is revealed, the jurors will assume he is a 'knight of the post,' a hired perjurer."

"I feel the need for one! All you say makes it clear I am found guilty before my trial has even begun."

"It is the general belief in law that the Crown does not make mistakes." He hesitated, then added, "That is why it is rare for a case to take long to hear. Most are dispensed within a few minutes, a few hours at most."

"I might be found not guilty," Susanna argued.

"That is devoutly to be hoped, for acquittal is final and cannot be questioned by the Crown. But jurors are wary of letting accused persons go free. They risk finding themselves in difficulty if they go against the prosecution."

"Trial by ordeal might be simpler," Susanna said with a wry smile. "An old way, and full of superstition, but mayhap fairer than the present system."

"You would be proven innocent," Jennet said staunchly.

Susanna drew in a deep breath. "What about the neck verse?" she asked. "I can read. Will that save my head from the noose?"

"Benefit of clergy does not apply in your case for a number of reasons, the most obvious that you are a woman. Unless you can prove you were once a nun, literacy will not save you. There is a chance a case may be extended if the jury cannot agree, or if a juror is taken ill, but either event is rare."

"Go on. Tell me the rest. What will happen after I am proven guilty." She no longer said *if*.

"The law does not require proof of guilt to convict an accused felon, only the appearance of it. And once a conviction is handed down, even the fairest judge has no choice in the sentence he gives."

"There is no appeal?"

"There are one or two things left to do." Walter's lack of enthusiasm for trying them was all too evident. "You may ask for *allocutus*, in other words plead for arrest of judgment before sentence is given." He frowned. "This provides an opportunity to allege anything that might prevent the court from ordering your execution. The most common ploys are for the accused to claim insanity. Or, in the case of a woman, that she is with child. The latter condition delays carrying out the sentence until she is delivered."

"You could lie," Jennet suggested.

They both turned to look at her. "An immaculate conception," Susanna murmured. "Doubtful."

"She would be . . . examined." Walter cleared his throat, ill at ease with the turn their discussion

293

had taken. "And there is another drawback."

"Only one?" The sarcasm slipped in before Susanna could stop it, but Walter's serious mein did not alter.

"If the plea for arrest of judgment is denied, the judge passes sentence at once instead of waiting until the end of the term."

Susanna felt her throat close for an instant as she comprehended the significance of this. Short as it might be, that little time between conviction and sentencing might mean the difference between life and death. "With opportunity to prepare before judgment is given, we might discover some way to challenge the verdict."

"Or escape," Jennet mumbled. Susanna ignored her.

"The court of the Queen's Bench has the authority to reverse the judgment of a lower court for an error in the records. A mistake in the wording of the charge, which is in Latin, might be enough, which is one reason prisoners, in particular the better educated ones, are not permitted to see the written indictments."

Susanna acknowledged this with a small, rueful smile. If it were that simple, no one would reach Tyburn.

"There is also something called a special verdict but in that case legal doubts must arise before conviction. Jurors refuse to render a verdict and submit the question of guilt to the court. The trial judge, together with other judges, decides the case in an informal, private meeting." At Susanna's hopeful look, he shook his head. "It is rare for this to happen. A better possibility is what is called a reserved case. The prisoner is reprieved until the next assizes while judges review the case. If they think the conviction is wrong, they recommend a pardon."

This mention of a pardon reminded Susanna that the Lady Mary had promised to ask for one on her behalf. Did she dare count on the queen's mercy? Her Majesty did not know Robert had been a traitor to the Crown. And she was fond of the earl of Leicester, who had been quick to blame Susanna for his old friend's death.

Susanna considered the Lady Mary's motives. Had she acquired a suitor? Or was that story a lie to cover her involvement in Robert's death? Robert had tried to extort money from her. What if she had talked of a pardon only to assuage her own guilt? When it came to making good on her promise, she might decide her own safety demanded Susanna die for the crime.

There was no need to ask what would happen if she was sentenced to death and not pardoned. The keeper of Newgate's bloodthirsty wife had been happy to provide those details.

A shudder racked Susanna's frame. The emotional defenses she had constructed so carefully over the last months began to crumble. When she felt tears welling up at the backs of her eyes, she sent both Jennet and Walter away.

As soon as they left, she threw herself flat on the soft featherbed and lay there staring up at the ceiler. She did not see it.

Opening her mind, she let in the full horror of what might lie ahead. She heard a call for silence, saw a judge assume the square cap all judges put on before they pronounced judgment. For petty treason the words were uncompromising and blunt: "Thou shalt go to the place of execution, and there thou shalt be burnt with fire till thou be dead."

Her hands went to her mouth to keep her from screaming out in terror and denial as she visualized every dreadful detail of death by fire. She was drawn to the gallows in a dead cart, sitting on her own casket. A symbolic rope was put round her neck and then she was fastened to a stake by an iron chain which encircled her body. Faggots were laid. The sheriff ordered the fire lit. It took, she had been told, three hours to reduce a living person to ashes.

Tears streamed unchecked down Susanna's cheeks. But she had faced it now, the worst that could happen to her. An odd sort of calm enveloped her.

"I can always bribe the executioner to strangle me," she muttered as she wiped the moisture from her face.

She had never understood the term *gallows' humor* until that moment. Although it brought no comfort, she did notice a diminution of her panic.

Her mind began to function in a rational manner. As she had remarked to someone when she was first accused, the threat of imminent death did force one to focus on what was essential.

She had a few days left in which to reconsider everything she had seen and heard these last months. She must sift through each detail, no matter how insignificant it seemed. Somewhere there was a clue she had missed. This time she must find it.

And if she could not?

Well, Susanna decided, finding more amusement than she'd expected in the defiant thought, she would face her execution with dignity . . . and shake the truth out of Robert when she met him again in the hereafter.

With that idea in her mind, she drifted into exhausted sleep and dreamed that she and Robert had agreed to work together once more, this time with none of the acrimony that had always existed between them in life. They left the heavenly realm to return to earth and haunt Robert's murderer.

Although Susanna could not quite make out that person's identity, her slumbering form relaxed. Her lips curved into the shadow of a smile.

Chapter 39

Sessions House, Old Bailey Street
May 9, 1565

The simple, unadorned building containing the Justice Hall where Lady Appleton would be tried was surrounded by secluded, enclosed gardens.

"Sir Walter tells me they were added for the comfort and amusement of the justices," Lady Appleton said as she and Jennet paused a moment before going in.

Fulke and Bates stood a little apart, having escorted the two women through London at Lady Appleton's request. She had insisted upon walking all the way from the Crowne, saying it might be her last chance to experience the joyous bustle and confusion of that great city.

Jennet looked into the garden with little enthusiasm. Then her gaze shifted to the steep hill running down toward Fleet Ditch and Holborn Bridge. She sighed. It was too late now to convince her mistress to run.

As soon as Lady Appleton entered the hall, she surrendered herself to the sheriff. Even though she had returned of her own volition, she was shackled and turned over to a gaoler, as if she were the worst sort of felon.

Jennet's protests were cut short just before she

was herself arrested. Sir Walter seized her firmly by the arm and escorted her behind the wooden barrier he called the bar of the court. It was situated below the judges' bench and opposite a long green-baize table. Lady Appleton remained at the back with the gaoler and the other prisoners the sheriff had delivered to court from Newgate.

"Stand here," Sir Walter ordered, "and be silent."

The rest of their party had already arrived and made places for themselves in the midst of counsels, attorneys, and observers from the general population.

Jennet's heart pounded in her ears and she wanted to scream with frustration, but she forced herself to be calm. She had to think. Had to plan. Had to look for escape routes.

Notice everything. That was what Lady Appleton always advised. Jennet took a deep breath and looked around her.

Noise and confusion greater than anything they'd encountered on the walk through London abounded in this cramped space. The smell of humanity packed too close together added to the bad feeling Jennet had about this place. Her fingers went to the sprig of celandine she'd pinned at her waist. Wearing that plant to court was supposed to win favor from judge and jury. To work properly, it should have been Lady Appleton who wore the herb on her person but she had refused, just as she had rejected Jennet's alternate suggestion that she carry gillyflowers.

Jennet's gaze fell on Alys Putney, dressed very fine for an innkeeper's wife and clinging to her husband's arm. When she caught Jennet staring at her, she sneered. She was gloating, the stupid sow! Jennet's fists clenched at her sides. No matter the outcome of this trial, she vowed, she would find a way to make Alys sorry for that.

The next person Jennet recognized was Master Baldwin, just entering the sessions house in company with a woman older than he was. His mother? She got a sour look on her face when she realized her son was watching Lady Appleton, an expression of despair in his eyes. Jennet blinked. Master Baldwin cared about her, as a man cared for a woman. She sighed. His feelings signified nothing if he had not discovered a way to set Lady Appleton free.

A sudden stirring in the crowd warned Jennet that the judges were about to come into the court. Fanfare and solemn procession marked their progress to the raised bench. Jennet's eyes widened at the display of brilliant colors. The judges were in robes which varied in hue from scarlet to violet, and the serjeants-at-law were even more brilliantly attired in parti-colored robes, blue on one side and green on the other. The junior counsels and clerks blended into the woodwork in comparison to their superiors.

As soon as the judges and their entourage were seated, the voice of a crier filled the hall. Jennet tugged on Sir Walter's sleeve. "What is he saying.

I cannot understand a word of it."

"No one does. The language of law is a doggerel mixture of Latin, Norman French, and English." His words were clipped, his tone cold, though Jennet noticed he had moved closer to Eleanor Lowell, who stood on the other side of him. As Jennet watched them out of the corner of her eye, Sir Walter took Eleanor's hand.

Jennet fidgeted throughout the preliminary business conducted by the court. She wished she had someone to hold her hand and offer her comfort. Mark was still at Leigh Abbey.

"Susanna Appleton," the clerk called out in a remarkable nasal voice. "Come to the bar."

Sir Walter went stiff as a pikestaff, his free hand clenching and unclenching convulsively. Lady Appleton, her face pale as a winding sheet, came and stood where the clerk indicated.

"The jurors and our lady the queen do present that Susanna Appleton of Leigh Abbey in the county of Kent, widow of Sir Robert Appleton, knight, on three January . . ."

Jennet blocked out the rest of the damning words. Lies. All lies. But they had not found Sir Robert's real murderer and thus had no way to halt these proceedings.

A brief silence in the courtroom jerked Jennet's attention back to the clerk, a short man with a heavy pelt of hair, an aggressive set to his shoulders, and an air of self-importance about him. He had finished reading the indictment. "How sayest thou, Susanna Appleton?" he asked. "Art thou guilty of this felony, as it is laid in the indictment whereof thou standest indicted, or not guilty?"

"Not guilty." Lady Appleton's clear, steady voice carried to every corner of the courtroom. The clerk was not impressed. "Culprit, how wilt thou be tried?"

"By God and the country."

"God send thee a good deliverance." With a chilling absence of outward emotion, the clerk scribbled a few words on the indictment papers.

Lady Appleton's irons and shackles were removed, and she was permitted to sit and allowed pen and paper. It would have been a blessing, Jennet thought, if they might start the trial right then. Instead, the clerk arraigned another prisoner on the next indictment and then another, continuing on until there were sufficient for a jury to try.

Jury selection did not take much time. Although all the accused were informed that they might challenge any of the jurors, none did. Each unchallenged juror was sworn with the same words: "You shall well and truly try and true deliverance make between our sovereign lady the queen and the prisoners at the bar whom you shall have in charge, and a true verdict give according to your evidence. So help you God." As each took the oath, the clerk marked down his name. When twelve men had been so marked, he issued another command. "*Countez.*"

The crier, the man possessed of that wonderfully resonant voice, counted the jurors as the clerk once again read over their names. Once they had heard their charge, they were told to stand to the right of the clerk's table, behind the accused. They heard two cases, each in less than ten minutes, before they came to Lady Appleton.

"Look upon the prisoner, you that be sworn," the clerk commanded, "and hearken to her cause. You shall understand that she is here indicted."

He continued speaking for some minutes, again reciting the indictment against Lady Appleton and adding that she had entered the plea of not guilty. The jurors were then charged to inquire whether she was guilty or not, and the trial commenced. The deposition the examining justice had taken was read out first. Then the Crown's witnesses entered the court.

Jennet leaned forward as Ned Higgins, owner of the Black Jack Tavern, swore the evidence he gave was the truth, the whole truth, and nothing but the truth. She felt relief when he said he'd not seen Lady Appleton put poison in her husband's meal, but it was clear he thought her guilty.

So did the crowner who'd examined the body and the constable who had questioned those in the crowd around the Eleanor Cross.

"A man told you he saw the accused with the deceased at the Black Jack?" the trial judge, a burly man with a bulbous nose, asked the constable.

"Aye."

"What man?"

"I know not, m'lord. 'E did not stay to be questioned further, but 'e swore 'twas true, right enough. Said 'e knew 'er by the way she walked and the color of 'er 'air."

There could not have been much to see of either, Jennet thought, in the dimness of the tavern or in the darkness of the evening outside. She glanced at the jurors but could not tell what they thought of the evidence. They listened with every indication of interest, intrigued, no doubt, by the novelty of trying a gentlewoman.

A woman testified next, saying she'd been in the crowd around the Eleanor Cross and heard Lady Appleton claim her husband had been poisoned.

"She admitted her guilt?" The queen's counsel pounced on that tidbit.

The woman looked confused and repeated what she'd already said. Jennet breathed a sigh of relief, but the emotion was short lived. Far more damaging testimony came next, in the form of a deposition given by the earl of Leicester.

Sir Walter's face went taut and even Lady Appleton's control slipped for an instant during the reading of this document. Leicester's words left their hearer with the impression that if Lady Appleton knew poison had been used, it must follow that she had been the one to administer it.

"But it was the fall and a blow to the head that actually killed Sir Robert," Jennet protested in a whisper.

"That is irrelevant." Sir Walter did not look at her as he answered. His gaze had fixed on the man making his way toward them around the periphery of the hall—one of his agents.

Jennet's hopes rose again when the fellow delivered a note to Sir Walter, only to be dashed once more by his reaction to its contents.

Sir Walter read the missive, then crumpled it in one hand, and used the other to massage his temples.

Chapter 40

Tension gripped Walter Pendennis. He knew now what the Scotswoman had intended when she fled. Catherine had been right about her. But Annabel's efforts on Susanna's behalf might have unforeseen consequences.

The queen was already disinclined to be lenient with Susanna Appleton. The crime with which she was charged was called "petty treason" because a husband was considered to be the head of the household in the same way a monarch was the head of a country. To the queen's way of thinking, if she allowed petty treason then she encouraged high treason. That Catherine de'Medici was willing to offer Susanna sanctuary in France, proposing exile instead of execution, would only irritate Elizabeth Tudor. The queen of England did not respond well to anything she perceived as interference in the governing of her realm. In particular, she did not like being dictated to by the French.

He could save Susanna by claiming he'd killed Robert, Walter thought. He glanced at Eleanor. He would do so if Susanna cast suspicions her way. He looked back at Susanna. She was so brave. So fierce. He still loved her, but not as a man loved the woman he wanted to marry, not enough to sacrifice his own hope of happiness for her sake.

Susanna began to tell her story in a clear, even voice, revealing that she'd been summoned to London by a letter from the husband she'd been told was dead. As she related the events of the evening of January 3, she made eye contact with each juror in turn. At intervals, she also sent a piercing glance in the direction of the spectators.

Why, Walter wondered, had she insisted he make sure everyone attend her trial? There had been no difficulty arranging it. Her friends came to support her. Her enemies wanted to see her suffer.

Walter surveyed the familiar faces closest at hand. Jennet chewed industriously on her lower lip, unaware that she'd made it bleed. Eleanor looked nervous, but that was only to be expected. She was worried about Susanna. They had become friends. And she knew how much he cared for the other woman.

Next to Eleanor was Catherine, who appeared close to tears. Beyond her stood Matthew Grimshaw, wearing the second new hat he'd acquired since coming to London. The fellow's wardrobe had undergone considerable change, an obvious attempt to compete with Walter's finery. The floppy brim of this fashionable bonnet shaded his face, making it difficult for Walter to make out his expression. He could see only Grimshaw's lips, which were compressed into a thin line as he listened to Susanna's testimony, and his beardless chin.

Walter's gaze skipped over Fulke and Bates to find the Lady Mary, her face hidden by a visor but her height making her instantly recognizable to any who'd met her. The tall man with her was also easy to identify by height—Thomas Keyes, keeper of Whitehall's water gate. Some said he was the tallest man in the kingdom.

Near them stood Constance Crane, a sour expression on her face. If Walter had not called upon her in person and insisted, he doubted she'd have come. Susanna had asked that she be present, he'd told her. Constance had protested that Lady Northampton could not be left alone. Walter had threatened to discuss the matter with Lady Northampton himself. To shield her dying mistress, Constance had given in.

Walter's gaze went next to Nicholas Baldwin and the woman at his side. His mother, Walter assumed. She hung on every word with avid interest, her eyes glittering, her lips pursed as tightly as Matthew Grimshaw's. It was so apparent to Walter that she did not like Susanna that he began to wonder if there might be another explanation for the attack on her in Billingsgate. A woman whose only son took an interest in someone she deemed unsuitable could be driven to desperate measures. It was passing convenient that the villain was dead and unable to tell anyone who had hired him.

Walter shifted his attention to Leonard Putney on that thought. If anyone had the means to recruit ruffians, it was the Dover innkeeper. A sneer curled Putney's lip as he listened to Susanna's version of events. He was enjoying the prospect of witnessing her ruin. Next to him, Alys wore an expression that could only be called smug. It grew more so when the queen's counsel interrupted Susanna with a question.

"Is it not true, Lady Appleton, that the herbal you wrote is naught but a guidebook for murderers?"

For just a moment, a flash of guilt showed in Susanna's eyes. It must have been evident to the jurors that she was aware it had been used in just that way. Walter knew she had not written it with that purpose in mind, but they did not, and he feared they were already biased against her. They were ordinary men who had not much insight into the ways of the gentry and were further cursed with a deep-seated mistrust of educated women.

"That was not its intent," Susanna explained. "It is called 'a cautionary herbal.' It was written in the hope of preventing accidental deaths by poison. Because I had studied a number of poisonous herbs, however, I recognized certain signs that indicated my husband had ingested aconite." She enumerated them for the jury. "I never said I poisoned him, for I did not."

Susanna called no witnesses. She made no accusations against any other person. Instead, she made a plea for common sense.

Walter despaired until, as she referred to the sort of wild speculation that went on in a crowd drawn to the grim spectacle of a man's death, he saw a change come over her face.

Chapter 41

Susanna knew who had killed Robert.

A tiny inconsistency she'd overlooked explained everything. Robert's death. The timing of the attack in Billingsgate.

She drew in a steadying breath.

Be calm, she ordered herself as the judge began to charge the jury.

She glanced at the crowd of spectators. At least her notoriety had served one purpose. No one had been inclined to leave the hall. They would stay until a verdict had been rendered, even the witnesses for the Crown.

"Good men, ye of the inquest," the judge intoned, "ye have heard what these men say against the prisoner. Ye have also heard what the prisoner can say for herself. Have an eye to your oath and to your duty, and do that which God shall put in your minds to the discharge of your consciences."

Speak now? Wait? Susanna knew she had a little time yet and she needed to think. It was not enough to know who had killed Robert. She had to be able to prove it.

The jurors would not decide her case until all the trials assigned to them were over, and they retired to consider them all together. Nine more accused felons waited to have their cases heard.

Best to take that long to plan, Susanna decided. She had pen and paper. Ignoring the activity around her, she listed the alternatives Walter had explained to her that day at the Crowne.

Appeal to the Queen's Bench.

Reserved case.

Request for pardon.

Arrest of judgment.

The workings of the law were convoluted and disliked allowing for the possibility that an accused felon might be innocent. Susanna decided that her best chance to bring Robert's killer to justice would come when the jury handed down its verdict. At that point, while everyone was still in the courtroom, she would ask for an arrest of judgment.

Panic threatened for a moment as she contemplated the risk involved. If she was wrong, she'd have done naught but hasten her own death. The judge could pronounce judgment at once, and she would be taken without delay to Tyburn.

But if she waited, she would lose the element of surprise. That, Susanna was convinced, was the one advantage she had. Accused without warning, the killer was sure to betray some sign of guilt. A confession was too much to hope for, but few people had complete control their reactions.

When the last case had been heard, a scant half hour after Susanna's, the jurors retired, given into the custody of a jury bailiff. They would not be gone long. They were kept without fire or refreshment until they reached their decisions.

They were back in ten minutes.

"What say you? Is she guilty or not guilty?" asked the clerk when it was Susanna's turn to hear the verdict.

"Guilty," the foreman announced.

Although she had expected this, for a moment Susanna felt numb with shock. She scarcely heard the words as the clerk asked the jury to say what property the convict had, so that it could be seized. The convict. Her.

The usual reply was "none to our knowledge," but everyone knew Susanna was a wealthy gentlewoman. Her holdings were duly listed, a considerable number, though fewer than there had been when Robert died. She had managed to transfer ownership of a good many properties to Rosamond.

Then, in rapid succession, the verdicts in the other trials were delivered. Susanna's moment was almost upon her. She readied herself to speak, sending a brief prayer heavenward. For one weak moment, she wished she'd heeded Jennet and carried a nosegay of gillyflowers. They were said to be a preventative against untimely death on the scaffold.

"Well then," the clerk said to the jurors in the oddly-phrased manner proscribed by law, "you say that Susanna Appleton is guilty of the felony in manner and form as she stands indicted. So say you all?"

None dissented and she stood convicted. The gaoler came forward to escort her to Newgate until the end of the law term, but before he could grasp her arm, Susanna stepped closer to the bench and raised her voice.

"I ask for the *allocutus.*"

Spectators gasped. The judge looked startled and stared down his oversized nose at her with eyes narrowed. He frowned, but he waved the gaoler away.

"Let the prisoner be brought forward." He nodded at her. "You have something to allege that may prevent the court from giving judgment?"

"Yes.

The entire courtroom seemed to hold its breath.

The judge's words were formal, as dictated by law and custom. "You do remember that before this time you have been indicted for a felony, upon your indictment you have been arraigned and have pleaded not guilty and for your trial have put yourself upon God and the country, which country hath found you guilty. Now, what can you say for yourself why, according to the law, you should not have judgment to suffer death? What sayest you, Susanna Appleton?"

He expected her to claim she was with child, or suffering from lunacy.

Leaning closer to the judge and speaking low, so that only he could hear her words, she made her request. "Let the constable who questioned those in the crowd at the Eleanor Cross look upon the spectators here today. There is one among them whose words cast suspicion upon me, one who would only have been in Westminster that day for one purpose—to bring about my husband's death."

The judge hesitated, then apparently decided to humor her. He sent a gaoler to fetch the man in question. Whispers and murmurs broke out all around them as the judge gave quiet instructions to the constable from Charing.

Aware of the consequences if his actions caused a person indicted by the Crown to be set free, the constable stared at each face in turn, strangers as well as those Susanna knew. The Lady Mary, mindful of the queen's disapproval should she learn of her connection to Susanna, hid herself behind her giant of an escort and went unnoticed by the constable but everyone else came under his scrutiny. Putney and Alys. Constance. Grimshaw and Catherine. Eleanor and Walter. He hesitated when he came to Jennet, then shifted back, squinting to examine one person's countenance more closely.

"Why, 'tis 'im, your lordship!" His voice went up an octave from sheer excitement. "'Tis the very fellow wot told me 'e saw 'er and the victim together at the Black Jack."

He pointed to Matthew Grimshaw.

Annoyance tightened Grimshaw's mouth. "You are mistaken my good man. I was in Lancashire when Sir Robert was murdered. Tell him, Eleanor."

Eleanor stared at him in slowly dawning horror and pressed herself closer to Walter Pendennis. "That is why you bribed my servants. Not to prove I was there, but so they would swear you were."

"Nonsense."

Susanna had hoped an accusation would bring out Grimshaw's tendency to grovel before those more powerful than he. Instead it had provoked the other side of his nature. He fell back on his instinct to bully and threaten.

Without stopping to think of the consequences and moving as fast as her bulky skirts would allow, Susanna rushed across the courtroom. It was not enough to accuse Grimshaw of Robert's murder. No one had seen the poison administered. Grimshaw was too tall to have passed for a woman in any event. Simply placing him near the Eleanor Cross proved little. But if she could make him angry enough, he might yet blurt out the truth.

"Was Sir Walter to be your next victim?" she demanded. "You will not get your hands on Appleton lands if you cannot persuade Eleanor to marry you."

She hoped Walter and Eleanor would forgive her for making their relationship public, but only by taunting Grimshaw in this way could she hope to make him lose his temper.

"You'd have done better to claim you were insane, Lady Appleton," Grimshaw told her.

"Confinement in Bedlam is the only way you'll escape burning."

"Robert would have said you belonged there. There is a strain of madness in the family." She shot an apologetic look at Catherine, who shared the same bloodline. "And all because you think yourselves ill treated by the Appleton family. What did Robert do to you, Grimshaw, aside from coming back from the dead?"

His small, dark eyes bored into hers, burning with hatred, erasing any doubt Susanna might have had about her conclusions. Grimshaw had been the one responsible for Robert's death and he'd plotted to have her accused of the crime.

"You did not expect me to have the freedom to journey to Lancashire, did you Grimshaw? That put the entire scheme in jeopardy. And then you were obliged to accompany me back to London, much against your better judgment, because if you did not you would be certain to lose Eleanor. She is the key to all this. Marry her and you get control of Rosamond's inheritance, your final revenge on the Appletons."

In an unconscious gesture of nervousness, Grimshaw's hand lifted to his ruff, as if it needed loosening. His gaunt face was livid.

Pressing her advantage, Susanna kept at him. "You hired someone to kill me, Grimshaw. He did not succeed." She took a chance that he did not know the man had been killed in the attempt. "Like the good constable here, he can identify you."

317

With a roar of rage, Grimshaw rushed the wooden barrier and flung himself at Susanna. His hands closed around her throat.

She fought back, kicking and scratching, but he was strong. Together they fell to the floor, rolling into the green baize table where the clerks sat. Papers scattered. Stools tumbled over. Susanna heard cries of alarm and outrage and then, just as her vision began to blur, she was free. Grimshaw flew into the air and backward as someone pulled him away from her.

Dazed, she sat up, aided by a strong grip on her shoulders. Walter. Nick Baldwin knelt in front of her, concern in his dark eyes. A short distance away, Grimshaw was held tight by Bates, Fulke, and the constable from Charing.

For a moment, Susanna found it difficult to get her breath. Her heart was racing and her ribs felt bruised. One hand went to her throat, where she knew she must bear the marks of Grimshaw's fingers. Her ruff had deflected some of the force, but anger had given him added strength. Another minute and he'd have succeeded in strangling the life out of her.

Pandemonium reigned all around them as Baldwin helped her to her feet. Quaking, she turned to look for one man who had the power to decide both her future and Grimshaw's.

Walter had already accosted him.

While Susanna watched from a little distance, the judge listened to Walter's exhortations, his face impassive. As the whispered conference continued, he fingered the white lapels of his miniver-lined crimson robe, then scratched his head beneath the white taffeta coif and the black velvet skullcap worn on top of it. At length the two men seemed to come to an agreement.

Walter left the judge's side to approach Susanna, his face set in an expression of grim satisfaction. "We have permission to remove to the garden." He extricated her from Baldwin's protective grasp, collected a dazed-looking Eleanor, and led both women out of the Justice Hall.

A sense of peace descended upon Susanna the moment they entered the realm of plants. An impenetrable outer hedge of privet kept the rest of the world at bay. Inside that enclosure, brick walls with flowers blooming among them divided the space into smaller plots. Walter chose a wide walk planted with wild thyme and bordered by a low-growing hedge of lavender. As it had been designed to do, the ground underfoot gave off a pleasing aroma as they trod on it.

A few minutes later, the two women were seated in a recess in one of the walls. Walter remained standing. "I gave the judge a brief account of our efforts to find Robert's murderer," he said, "and explained the exchange he witnessed in his courtroom between Grimshaw and Eleanor."

"Matthew killed Robert." It was not a question, but Eleanor sounded as if she still had difficulty accepting the lawyer's guilt.

Susanna could not blame her. She had herself been exceeding slow to realize what must have happened. "I was so certain one of Robert's mistresses must have killed him," she admitted, "that I did not stop to consider Grimshaw a suspect. But as you said in court, Eleanor, he lied to protect himself, not you."

"I do not understand any of this. Why? Why did he kill Robert?"

"Grimshaw wanted Appleton Manor. As my man of law in Lancashire, he knew I intended to provide for my husband's child. By marrying you, Eleanor, he'd hoped to gain control of her estate. Then Robert turned up, alive. Being Robert, he moved in, took over, and doubtless just to be difficult, gave Grimshaw reason to think he might take Eleanor and Rosamond with him when he fled the country."

This last was speculation, but it made sense to Susanna, knowing Robert as well as she had. She studied Eleanor, sitting with hands folded in her lap and eyes downcast. In spite of her liking for the woman, she did not for a moment believe that Eleanor had kept Robert at a distance during his stay at Appleton Manor.

Walter propped one foot on the edge of the stone bench and touched Susanna's shoulder. "If you did not suspect Master Grimshaw before, what happened during the trial to make you believe he'd been in London?"

"It was when I referred to the wild speculations

spreading through the crowd gathered around the Eleanor Cross. I remembered the constable's testimony. He said a man had told him he saw me with Robert at the Black Jack. I was never in the alehouse with my husband. There was no reason for anyone to make such a claim unless he sought to cast suspicion on me."

"And the attack in Billingsgate?"

"You told me Grimshaw threatened Eleanor in an attempt to coerce her into returning to Lancashire with him. The attack followed immediately after. Grimshaw must have been behind it. Perhaps he was afraid that someone in attendance at the trial would recognize him."

"That also explains the wide-brimmed hat he bought." For a moment, amusement broke the grimness of Walter's features. They hardened again as he spoke to Eleanor. "How did Grimshaw know Robert was in London?"

"I do not know. I did not know Robert was here or that Matthew was."

"No? No letters?" He glanced at Susanna. "No Knox cipher?"

Her bewilderment plain, Eleanor sought Walter's eyes. What she found there seemed to confuse her further.

"A book was found in your chamber at Appleton Manor," he said in a gentle but implacable voice. "Written by Master Knox."

Still puzzled, she nodded and shifted her gaze to Susanna. "I know the one. Robert brought it with him. I found it after he'd left. I suppose he did not think it important enough to take with him."

"There was another copy found in his room in Silver Street," Walter told her. "Robert must have purchased it in order to write that last message to Susanna. He used it to compose letters in code."

"But how did Matthew know where to find Robert? How did he know Robert was to meet Susanna at the Black Jack?"

Susanna stared at the pattern of the bricks in the wall, asking herself the same question. Roses grew to one side of her, honeysuckle to the other. She scarce noticed. A knot formed in her stomach and her palms began to sweat.

"He can now be charged with attempting to murder me but even if Grimshaw was in London, it does not of necessity follow that he hired a woman to kill Robert. Indeed, having been here, it seems reasonable that he would wish to hide that fact in order that he not be suspected of any wrongdoing."

And unless she could prove otherwise, Susanna's life remained forfeit. She had been convicted of murder. Although she had provoked Grimshaw into attacking her, he had not confessed to conspiring to poison Robert.

A glance toward the entrance to the garden showed her Bates, waiting half concealed by a cluster of clipped cypress, cedar, and box. He was still guarding her, still ready to take her into custody once more.

"Eleanor," Susanna begged, "is there nothing more you can tell us?"

Avoiding both Walter's eyes and Susanna's gaze, Eleanor began to speak in a low, shaky voice. "Matthew was furious when he discovered Robert's presence at Appleton Manor. He was sure Robert had committed some crime. What else could explain the false story of his death? But before Matthew could move against him, Robert found a way to insure his silence. I do not know what threat he used, but of a sudden Matthew changed. He became most anxious to do Robert's bidding and cautioned me to do the same."

"No doubt it had to do with what happened at Appleton Manor five years ago," Susanna told her. She did not intend to be more specific than that.

They'd all have been hurt by the scandal back then, if Robert had made certain family secrets public. He'd ensured Grimshaw's silence by threatening him with the loss of his commission as a justice of the peace. The lawyer would have been hounded out of Manchester, too, if the whole truth had come out. At the time, it had seemed a mutually beneficial arrangement, but she could see, with the clarity of hindsight, that letting Robert dictate to him must have rankled with Grimshaw. His resentment had grown stronger with the passage of time, and when Robert became a rival for Eleanor's favors, he'd sealed his own doom.

"Matthew and Robert were often closeted

together," Eleanor said. "Making plans, Robert told me. But neither of them ever told me what it was they were plotting." She dared a glance at Walter.

With intent watchfulness, he stared silently back. He must be wondering what else she had kept secret, Susanna thought. In her earlier confession to him, Eleanor had neglected to mention that Grimshaw and Robert had been up to something together. An unintentional oversight? Perhaps. Or perhaps Eleanor had more to hide than they imagined. Susanna was not sure she wanted to know. Eleanor had not been behind Robert's death. Of that much she was now certain.

"So Grimshaw might have known the Knox cipher," she mused aloud.

Eleanor nodded.

"Grimshaw had no reason to be fond of the Appletons. If he has been nursing old grievances all these years, Robert's high-handed behavior must have been the final straw."

"He was angry," Eleanor admitted. "He took care not to let Robert see it, but he could scarce contain his temper the whole time Robert was at Appleton Manor."

"It may be that Robert ordered Grimshaw to meet him in London," Walter speculated.

"Whatever the reason for the trip, he'd have had no difficulty explaining a long absence from Manchester. His housekeeper assumed he was at Appleton Manor." She'd told Catherine so.

"But who was the cloaked woman?" Walter's abrupt question was directed at Eleanor. His thoughts had apparently followed a course similar to Susanna's but led him to a different conclusion. If the servants had lied about Grimshaw's presence at Appleton Manor, they might also have lied about Eleanor being there.

Sad-eyed, Eleanor gave him a reproachful look. "I did not go with Matthew to London, Walter."

"Easy enough to hire a woman off the street and instruct her to take a message to Robert and to put a powder Grimshaw provided into his food or drink. London has no shortage of people desperate enough to do anything for a few coins and a warm wool cloak. And aconite is passing simple to obtain. He could have extracted enough to do the job from a cake of rat poison." Susanna stood and began to pace in the enclosed garden as she struggled to work out the remaining details. Grimshaw had come to London and met Robert, by chance or design. Perhaps he'd intercepted and decoded Robert's letter. Perhaps Robert had shown it to him and told him what he had planned. The specifics did not matter, Susanna decided. It was obvious that Grimshaw had known where she would meet Robert and had sent someone, cloaked and hooded to resemble her, to the Black Jack. Had Grimshaw been watching for her, perhaps intending to delay her arrival until his accomplice had left the tavern? In the event, there had been no need. She'd been late. Had he followed Robert to Charing? It seemed likely. And there, by sheer luck, he'd been given a second chance to implicate her in Robert's death.

A circuit of the garden brought Susanna back to the bench. She was not surprised to find Walter seated beside Eleanor, her hands clasped in his. She came to a halt in front of them and waited until she had their full attention.

"Grimshaw must have expected Robert's death to be written down an accident. By rights, the body should not have been identified, but on the chance that it might be, he arranged matters so that I could be blamed. Thus the woman in the black cloak. He must have been pleased to see me taken into custody. With Robert dead and me convicted of the crime, Rosamond stood to inherit. Oh, there would have been legal difficulties but none that could not be dealt with through a few judicious bribes. All he had to do was convince Eleanor to marry him."

Walter nodded slowly. "Everything you have said is sensible. And I have no doubt we can force a confession out of Grimshaw."

Susanna did not ask what means he would use. She did not want to know.

"With that, the judge will have no choice but to accept your motion for arrest of judgment. No sentence will be passed upon you."

"Your gloomy expression keeps me from rejoicing. What is it, Walter?"

"You have been convicted of a crime. The law requires that you return to prison and remain in custody until you can obtain a pardon."

★ ★ ★

Susanna spent two more nights in her previous lodgings in Newgate before Walter brought her that pardon. The document was unconditional and had been sealed with the Great Seal on the authority of the Privy Council.

"Was it necessary to seek the Lady Mary's assistance?" Susanna asked.

Walter shook his head. "She bade me tell you that you have no further obligation to her."

"I cannot explain that," she told him. She had no desire to spend more time in prison.

And yet, she could not help but worry about the younger woman. She feared the Lady Mary would not long be deterred from having her heart's desire. She would elope. She would be found out. And she would be imprisoned, losing the precious freedom she now enjoyed. Susanna wondered if it would do any good to try to reason with her, to tell her just how dreadful being locked away could be, even for a short time.

She doubted it.

"Grimshaw's confession was sufficient to convince everyone of your innocence," Walter told her. "He will be tried at the next quarter sessions. The verdict is not in doubt."

Nor was his fate. He'd be hanged for his crime. "Did he explain what drove him to kill Robert?"

"Robert brought it on himself. He ordered Grimshaw to London. Treated him like a servant. And then, apparently unable to resist baiting the man, he made one ill-advised remark too many about Eleanor. He told Grimshaw that he meant to send for her when he was safely settled in Muscovy. That was enough to push Grimshaw over the edge."

"And the man who attacked me in Billingsgate? Did Grimshaw hire him?"

"Aye. As he hired the woman, a pretty one, to distract Robert in the tavern and put the poison into his food. Grimshaw was behind the tainted meat at Coventry and the robbers at Islington, too, but those incidents were staged to do me harm, not you."

Jealousy again, Susanna thought. "But why try to kill me when it must have seemed certain I'd be convicted and executed?"

"Timing. Once you made Rosamond your heir, it was better to have you die in full possession of your estates."

Susanna felt herself blanch. That reasoning had never even crossed her mind. With an effort, she rallied, vowing not to dwell on what could not be changed. "Am I free to go home now?"

"Yes. As soon as you have settled your account." Walter held up what turned out to be the clerk's bill, but instead of handing it to her, he read the items aloud, his nasal whine a near perfect imitation of the pompous fellow who had written the list.

"Two shillings to be indicted. Thirteen shillings and fourpence to be charged with a felony. Two shillings for pleading not guilty. Five shillings and fourpence to discharge the recognizance under which you were released before your trial. And finally, four shillings and fourpence to be acquitted of a criminal offense."

Susanna could not help herself. Giddy with relief that her long ordeal was finally over, she began to laugh.

When she had control of herself once more, she paid the clerk with two gold sovereigns and did not ask for change.

Chapter 42

Three weeks later

From the window of her study at Leigh Abbey, Susanna stared out at the fields. Summer was upon them. Crops flourished, as did the cow Jennet had purchased so many months ago.

Two letters lay open on her writing table.

The first was from Walter, sent from the Low Countries. Immediately following their marriage, he and Eleanor had embarked from Gravesend on the first leg of a journey that would take them to the court of the king of Poland, where Walter was to take up his new duties as England's ambassador.

The second missive had come from Catherine. She was back in Scotland, although Susanna did not believe she would long remain there. If Catherine had her way, she and Gilbert would soon return. There were, after all, many good reasons why a representative of Scotland might live year-round in England.

Susanna put both letters into a casket for safekeeping. She had just returned it to its proper place atop her work table when she heard the door open.

"Mama?" a small voice inquired. The little person it belonged to peeped around the jamb.

"Come in, Rosamond."

Susanna had tried to teach the girl to distinguish between *mama* and *stepmama* but Rosamond, ever since she'd first heard Susanna refer to herself as her stepmama, persisted in shortening the word.

References to *papa* had for a time created similar confusion. The child listened to and understood more than any of the adults in her life had imagined. It appeared she'd started to call Walter *papa* long before Eleanor accepted his proposal of marriage, not because Eleanor had suggested the idea to her but because Rosamond had overheard the speculations of Eleanor's maidservants.

"Would you like to keep me company today?" It was, Susanna decided, time she gave thought to Rosamond's education. "We might look at plants, and I will tell you their names. Or I could show you how to form letters."

Rosamond stared up at her with Robert's eyes.

She was perhaps too young yet for reading or writing. Susanna knew she had much to learn about children. Still, the little girl was clever and those who had experience with two-year-olds seemed to feel she was passing well spoken for her age.

Perhaps," she mused, "I will teach you how to add."

She picked up an inkpot, a sheet of paper, and a quill.

"This is one," she said, putting the inkpot back on her writing table. "This is two." She placed the quill beside it. "And if you add this . . ." she handed Rosamond the paper ". . . that will make three."

The little girl poked at the inkpot with one chubby finger. "One," she said. "Two." She touched the quill, then put the paper on top of it. "Three."

"An excellent beginning, Rosamond."

Susanna smiled at the child in pride that mingled with relief. She felt certain now that she had made the right decision when she had convinced Eleanor and Walter to leave Rosamond with her.

"Add more?" Rosamond asked.

"Yes," Susanna agreed. "Add more. I have always found the ability to add things up correctly a most useful skill."

Two Historical Notes

In August, 1565, the Lady Mary Grey eloped with Thomas Keyes. He was 6'6" tall, a widower with several children. At court he was a gentleman porter who served as keeper of the queen's water gate. The queen found out about the marriage almost immediately and ordered Keyes imprisoned in the Fleet. The Lady Mary was sent away from London. She was kept close in a series of large country houses until some two years after Keyes died in 1571. Although she was still heiress presumptive, the Lady Mary was afterward allowed to do as she pleased. She bought a house in Aldersgate Street, London, and lived there with Keyes's children until her death on April 20, 1578.

Susanna's bill for court costs totalled twenty-seven shillings. She paid with two gold sovereigns, worth twenty shillings each. In terms of modern values, the bill amounted to about $540 in legal fees. Susanna's euphoric state ("giddy with relief that her long ordeal was finally over") had her leaving a very generous tip—she gave the clerk approximately $800. The clerk would have had no qualms about accepting it. Bribes were an accepted way of doing business in the middle of the sixteenth century.

About the Author

Kathy Lynn Emerson lives in rural Maine with her husband and several cats. She is the author of the Face Down Mystery Series, set in Elizabethan England, and the Diana Spaulding Mysteries, which take place in 1888 America. Kathy is the Agatha Award-winning author of *How To Write Killer Historical Mysteries: The Art and Adventure of Sleuthing Through the Past*. Readers are invited to contact her via her web site at www.KathyLynnEmerson.com.

We hope you have enjoyed this Large Print book. Other Delphi Books titles are available at your library, through your favorite bookstore, or directly from us via our website or by calling (800) 431-1579.

For information about titles, please visit our Web site at: www.DelphiBooks.us

To share your comments, please write:

Delphi Books
P.O. Box 6435
Lee's Summit, MO 64064
US

Printed in the United States
221368BV00001B/19/P